A GUN BEHIND YOU . . .

Cody flung himself out of the saddle as Parker twisted around and threw a couple of shots at him. He landed rolling and came up in a crouching run, heading for a thicket of mesquite trees that'd give him at least a little cover.

Cody bellied down among the scrubby mesquites as Parker dragged Leigh behind the rocks. "Might as well give it up, Parker!" the Ranger called. "You're not going anywhere!"

Parker didn't show himself, but his shouted reply carried clearly to Cody's ears. "Well, this girl's goin' to hell if you don't clear out and let me ride away!"

Suddenly movement at the top of the shallow cliff behind Parker's hiding place caught Cody's eye. He looked up to see a figure rising unsteadily into view—

Barry Whittingham.

Whittingham raised his gun. . . .

Cody's Law Series

Ask your bookseller for the books you have missed

CODY'S LAW
Book 6

||||||||||||||||||||||||||||||||||||||||||||||||||||||||||||||||||||||||||||||||||||||||

RENEGADE
TRAIL

||||||||||||||||||||||||||||||||||||||||||||||||||||||||||||||||||||||||||||||||||||||||

Matthew S. Hart

 Producers of **The Holts, The Patriots,**
and **The Frontier Trilogy: Westward!**

Book Creations Inc., Canaan, NY • *Lyle Kenyon Engel, Founder*

BANTAM BOOKS
NEW YORK • TORONTO • LONDON • SYDNEY • AUCKLAND

RENEGADE TRAIL

A Bantam Domain Book / published by arrangement with
Book Creations, Inc.

Bantam edition / August 1992

Produced by Book Creations, Inc.
Lyle Kenyon Engel, Founder

DOMAIN and the portrayal of a boxed "d" are trademarks of Bantam Books,
a division of Bantam Doubleday Dell Publishing Group, Inc.

ISBN 0-553-29768-6

Published simultaneously in the United States and Canada

Bantam Books are published by Bantam Books, a division of Bantam Doubleday Dell
Publishing Group, Inc. Its trademark, consisting of the words "Bantam Books"
and the portrayal of a rooster, is Registered in U.S. Patent and Trademark
Office and in other countries. Marca Registrada. Bantam Books, 666 Fifth Avenue,
New York, New York 10103.

PRINTED IN THE UNITED STATES OF AMERICA

RAD 0 9 8 7 6 5 4 3 2 1

CHAPTER

‖‖‖‖‖‖‖‖‖‖‖‖‖‖‖‖‖‖‖‖‖‖ **1** ‖‖‖‖‖‖‖‖‖‖‖‖‖‖‖‖‖‖‖‖‖

There were days, Cody thought, when it was good to be alive, and you knew from the time you got up in the morning that everything was going to be just fine.

Then there were days like today.

His hat clamped on tight, his brown eyes squinted against the midmorning sun, and his thick, dark mustache tugged down by a frown, the big Texas Ranger urged the rangy lineback dun beneath him on to greater speed, and as he leaned forward in the saddle, he slid the Winchester '73 from the sheath strapped under his right thigh. Guiding the dun with his knees, he worked the rifle's lever and jacked a shell into the chamber.

The horse was damn ugly standing still, but its ground-eating pace right now was a thing of beauty. Its deceptively easy stride carried Cody down a long, gentle slope toward the flatland, where the San Antonio-to-El Paso stage road ran. Bucketing along that trail—and kicking up a huge cloud of dust with its hurried passage—was a Concord coach being pulled by a six-horse hitch. The stagecoach swayed and bounced on its thick leather thoroughbraces as the driver shouted curses and flailed at the backs of the horses with his whip. On the box beside the driver the guard was twisted around, firing his revolver back at the group of riders pursuing the coach.

Cody's keen senses had immediately taken in the entire scene when he'd topped the rise a few moments earlier. Not that there was a hell of a lot else out here to see or hear. To his right was the shallow, slow-moving Rio

Grande, and beyond the river in Mexico were foothills rising into a low range of mountains. To the left was nothing but semiarid Texas prairie for as far as the eye could see. The stagecoach and the bandits chasing it easily stood out against the landscape, and the harsh crash and boom of gunfire shattered the hot stillness.

There was no doubt in Cody's mind that the men chasing the coach were outlaws. A holdup was the only reason for nearly a dozen riders to be racing after a stagecoach, firing their pistols as they rode. It didn't take a lot of experience as a lawman to recognize such a thing. As soon as Cody had realized what was going on, he'd heeled the dun out of its easy lope and into a gallop.

A saddle was the worst place in the world for shooting accurately, but Cody didn't really care if he hit anything. He triggered a couple of shots toward the outlaws, hoping that having somebody else take cards in this hand would spook the gang and they'd clear out.

The riders hesitated. They were close enough now that Cody could see they had their bandannas pulled up over their faces to form crude masks. The stagecoach came on toward him as he angled toward the trail.

His day hadn't started out nearly so vigorously, Cody thought, grumbling to himself. He had left El Paso early that morning while the air still held a hint of coolness. The dun was well rested, and so was Cody. So well rested, in fact, that he had even decided when looking in his hotel room mirror that morning that for a change he actually looked no older than the early thirties that he was, despite the craggy face that a life lived mostly in the saddle had given him. After riding out of the border city, he had meandered along the river instead of the road, content to take his time on the way back to Del Rio. It had looked like it was going to be a quiet, easy ride, which sure didn't bother the Ranger any. Then he'd heard shooting, seen a haze of dust rising in the air ahead of him and to the left, and sent the dun up the rise to see what was happening.

Now he knew.

Cody pumped a couple more rounds at the bandits, making them falter even more. Chasing a stagecoach was one thing;

going up against a man with a Winchester who clearly knew how to use it was another. The owlhoots had him outnumbered, all right, but they might not want to pay the price he'd extract from them before going down himself.

The outlaws hauled back on their reins, slowing their horses. They were going to turn and run—Cody sensed that with every instinct in his body. And then a goodsized rock at the edge of the stage road ruined everything.

The stage veered toward the shallow ditch at the left of the road. The driver recovered and jerked the team back toward the center of the trail, but not before the rear wheel clipped a rock that had apparently been thrown up when the ditch was dug. The wheel was jolted up, and with a crack that was audible even over the shooting and the pounding of hooves, the rear axle of the coach broke. The left wheel spun completely off, and that corner of the vehicle hit the ground, dragging a deep furrow in the hardpacked earth of the road for a few feet before the coach slewed around and started to tip over. The tongue snapped as the coach rolled, but the horses were still attached to it by their harness, and they were pulled down, too. A huge cloud of dust blossomed around the wreckage, hiding the coach and team for several seconds.

Cody cursed. The outlaws, who'd been on the verge of breaking off their attack, let out whoops of glee as they saw the stagecoach crash. It'd be easy pickings now, good reason to stay and dispose of the intruder. After all, ten-to-one odds were enough for just about anybody. Putting the spurs to their horses, the highwaymen surged forward again.

Cody yanked the dun to a stop. He couldn't settle for scaring off the desperadoes any longer; his shooting had to be more accurate now. Bringing the Winchester to his shoulder, he laid his cheek on the smooth wooden stock and settled the blade of the front sight on the breast pocket of one of the lead riders. A squeeze of the trigger made the rifle buck against Cody's shoulder as it cracked.

"Damn!" he exclaimed as he peered through the dust. The outlaw hadn't gone down, so the bullet had missed.

Wheeling the dun toward the coach, Cody kicked it into

a run again. The wrecked stagecoach was the only cover around here—and he was going to need some.

There wasn't much wind today, not enough to shred the dust and carry it off. It had to float away by itself, and that'd take some time. Cody plunged into the cloud, jerking the dun to a halt as he tried to locate the coach. His eyes smarted from the dust. After a second he saw the bulk of the overturned vehicle and swung down hurriedly from the saddle. A swat on the dun's rump sent it leaping away. The horse would run off out of range of the fighting, Cody knew, then turn and wait for him.

The big Ranger sprinted toward the stagecoach, hearing bullets whine through the haze around him. Realizing that if the driver or the guard had survived the crash they might think he was one of the outlaws and take a shot at him, he bellowed, "Ranger coming in! Texas Ranger!" Once he got close enough, they'd be able to see the badge on his vest, the already-famous silver star set within a silver circle, and they'd know he was telling the truth.

Muzzle flashes winked from behind the coach as Cody skirted the vehicle. The shots weren't directed at him, so he knew the defenders must have heard and understood him. He dropped into a crouch behind the wreckage, poked the barrel of his rifle over the coach, and fired three shots as fast as he could work the lever, aiming toward where the outlaws had been. The dust was beginning to thin out now, and he thought he could see shadowy forms on horseback.

A glance to his right showed Cody that three men were fighting along with him. One he recognized as the driver, so the other two must have been passengers in the stage, for the guard was lying on the ground, conscious but grimacing in pain from a leg that was bent at a strange, severe angle. Cody thought he glimpsed the whiteness of bone poking out through a rip in the man's pants.

"Anybody hurt inside the coach?" Cody asked.

The driver shook his head. "We was mighty lucky," he said. "These two gents were the only passengers. Matt there's the only one got hurt, and his leg's busted bad."

Cody dropped to a knee beside the injured guard. "I can

see that." He put a hand on the man's shoulder. "Hang on, friend. We'll drive those bandidos off, then see about fixing up that leg of yours."

"Give the . . . sonsabitches . . . a couple of slugs for me," the guard grated through clenched teeth.

Cody flashed him a grim smile, then stood up again and lifted the Winchester. He saw movement out of the corner of his eye to the left, wheeled in that direction, and held off on the trigger just long enough to recognize that one of the outlaws was swooping in close to the coach. The Ranger's rifle barked wickedly.

With a screech of pain the figure on horseback plunged from the saddle and landed in a limp heap on the ground. The couple of riders right behind him threw on the brakes, spun their horses, and went back in the other direction in a hurry.

"Good shootin', Ranger!" one of the passengers exclaimed.

The dust had cleared enough now for Cody to see that the remaining outlaws had pulled back and regrouped. He didn't try to fool himself into thinking they were going to pull out just because they had lost one man. If anything, that'd just make them more determined. The odds were all on their side, especially since, from the looks of things, the Ranger had the only Winchester. The other three men were using handguns.

"They'll be coming again in a minute," Cody cautioned. "Better get some fresh cartridges in your guns while you've got the chance."

He followed his own advice, taking shells from the loops on the left side of his gun belt and sliding them into the rifle's loading gate until the magazine was full again. Then he stooped and picked up the empty casings that had been ejected from the Winchester and put them in his pocket. Might as well be optimistic and assume that he'd have a chance to reload them when he got back to Del Rio, he thought.

Turning to his companions, he asked, "Why are those boys so determined? No offense, gents, but from the looks of you, they wouldn't make that big of a haul."

The two passengers were both middle-aged men in well-worn range clothes. One of them grinned and said, "Ordinarily you'd be right. We ride for the Seven-X spread out close to El Paso, and our boss sent us to San Antone to pick up some money at his bank. He's goin' to use the cash to pay off a fella he's buyin' some new breedin' stock from."

"How much cash?"

"Twenty-two thousand dollars."

Cody let out a low whistle and nodded toward the outlaws. "I reckon that bunch got wind of the deal?"

"Must have, though I don't see how they did."

"Your boss ought to use a bank in El Paso," Cody said dryly. "That'd be closer."

"That's what we been tellin' him, but Elmer's been bankin' in San Antone for a long time, and he's a stubborn ol' feller."

Cody understood the situation better now. That much money was an irresistible lure for lawless men. The ranch hands carrying it were probably longtime employees of the owner of the 7X, men who could be trusted not only with money, but also with the life of a friend. But it was always possible for things to go wrong—as they obviously had in this case.

"Here they come again!" the stage driver yelled.

Cody looked up to see the outlaws galloping toward them. The desperadoes weren't bunched up now. They were spreading out, veering to the sides. Cody grimaced. The outlaws were being smart. Instead of attacking head on, they were going to circle the wreckage and try to catch the defenders in a cross fire. Worse yet, they had pouched their sixes and brought out their long guns—which meant they were going to carry out the attack beyond pistol range.

"Keep your heads down," Cody warned his companions. "This is going to be bad."

Chances were they were all going to die.

Cody brought his Winchester to his shoulder again, set on bringing down a few of them. But before he could settle on a target and squeeze the trigger, one of the outlaws rolled from his saddle and thumped to the ground. A split second later Cody heard the far-distant sound of a shot.

Somebody else, somewhere else, had taken a hand.

But he couldn't wonder about that now. With bullets thudding into the coach beside him, Cody took aim and pulled the trigger. The blast of the rifle was rewarded by another outlaw knocked off his horse.

The driver and the two passengers had gone to ground to present smaller targets. Cody followed their example, dropping to one knee as he shifted his aim. He took a deep breath to steady himself and touched off another shot. One of the outlaws swayed in the saddle, hit but not knocked down. Still, the wounded man swung his horse away from the fight, and that was almost as good.

Cody heard more gunfire, saw another man drop. The odds were getting cut in a hurry now. The Ranger glanced to the east, squinting through the shifting clouds of dust, and saw another rider approaching. The newcomer sent his horse dashing forward several yards as he levered his rifle. He then jerked the animal to a halt, raised himself in his stirrups, aimed, and fired again.

The Ranger kept up his own shooting, emptying half of the Winchester's magazine in a matter of minutes. The line of outlaws was ragged now, holes being shot in it from both directions. They had lost four men—maybe more; it was hard to tell—and they hadn't done a lick of damage since the coach had crashed.

Twenty-two grand just wasn't enough when you were caught in a cross fire between two men who could shave a gnat's whiskers at a hundred yards. Yelling curses, the survivors of the gang whirled their horses toward the south and the Rio Grande. All they wanted now was to get the border river between them and the two riflemen taking such a heavy toll on their band.

Cody was more than willing to let them go.

He stood up and watched the fleeing bandits for a moment. The driver and the two passengers got to their feet, too, and brushed alkali dust from their clothes. Cody switched his attention to the man who had saved them by pitching in when he did. The stranger was cantering toward them

now, still holding his rifle ready across his chest in case
the outlaws decided to make one last try at the job.

There was something familiar about the man, and Cody
suddenly realized he wasn't a stranger after all. As the newcomer rode closer, Cody recognized the young man wearing
a flat-crowned brown hat, a buckskin shirt, whipcord pants,
and boot-topped moccasins. He had a thatch of blond hair
that hung almost to his shoulders and a ready grin that
split his lean face. A badge was pinned to his buckskin
shirt, not identical to the one Cody wore but shaped in the
same pattern; Rangers usually made their own badges, so
there were always subtle differences. Like Cody, he was
a member of Ranger Company C, headquartered far down
the Rio Grande at Del Rio, and though he claimed to be
twenty, Cody suspected the youngster was actually closer
to eighteen.

"Howdy, Cody," Seth called as he reined in. "Looks like
I came along just in time."

"I'd say so," Cody agreed, tucking his rifle under his left
arm. "No offense, Seth—but what the hell are you doing
here?"

Seth Williams kept grinning as he slid his rifle back
into the saddle boot and then swung down from his horse.
"Well, that's a fine way to greet a fella who just saved your
bacon," he groused good-naturedly. "Not even a 'Thanks,
Seth. We'd'a been buzzard bait without you.'"

One of the passengers spoke up. "I'll say it. Thanks,
young fella."

"You're welcome, mister. Just doing my duty as a Ranger."

"And you still haven't told me what you're doing here,"
Cody reminded him. "It's a long way to Del Rio."

Seth frowned. "Didn't you get Cap'n Vickery's wire?"

Cody leaned his rifle against the overturned coach and
knelt beside the injured guard, who was only half conscious
now from loss of blood and the shock of his broken leg.
While the driver went to cut loose the struggling horses
in his team and find out how badly they were hurt, Cody
examined the guard's leg, saying to Seth as he did so, "I
don't know anything about a wire. I haven't even been in

touch with headquarters since I got back to El Paso from Mexico. If the cap'n sent me a telegram, it must've gotten lost somewhere along the way."

Hunkering on the other side of the guard, Seth nodded. "Yeah, could be. How'd that job in Mexico wind up?"

"All right," the older Ranger grunted. Seth didn't need to know all the details; Cody would put them in his report to Captain Vickery when he got back to headquarters. "We've got to get this leg set. Find me something to use for a splint."

Seth and the two ranch hands from the 7X took on that chore. Out here in this largely treeless country, finding a piece of wood of a suitable length and thickness for a splint wasn't always easy. Seth solved the problem by bringing Cody a couple of pieces of the broken axle from the stagecoach.

"Wish I had some whiskey for you, friend," Cody said to the guard, not knowing if the man heard him or not. "This is going to hurt."

He had cut away the man's pant leg, exposing the gruesome injury. There was no way to get the pieces of bone back together without causing more damage to the tissue around them, but that couldn't be helped. Taking a deep breath, Cody grasped the man's leg and forced the bone sections back into place. The guard screamed in agony and tried to come up off the ground, but Seth and the two cowhands held him fast.

With the bone more or less back in place, Cody tied the splints in place and then bound up the wound with strips torn from the guard's shirt. The big Ranger had done all he could, but the man still needed a lot of medical attention as soon as possible.

Seth looked up. "Somebody comin'," he said.

Cody lifted his own gaze to the trail and saw a buckboard rattling and bouncing along it from the east, being drawn by a pair of old mules. At the reins was a swarthy, stocky man in the white cotton pants, faded serape, and broad-brimmed sombrero of a Mexican farmer. Beside him on the seat was a middle-aged woman wearing a dark dress and a shawl over her head—the farmer's wife, no doubt. Half a dozen children rode in the back of the wagon.

Cody stood up and raised a hand, gesturing for the peon to stop. The man hauled back on the reins and brought the mules to a halt. His dark face was impassive as he surveyed the wreckage of the stagecoach in the road. There was room for him to drive around it, but apparently for the moment he was content to see what Cody wanted. The youngsters clustered at the front of the wagon bed, peering curiously over the shoulders of their parents.

"Howdy, folks," Cody said. "We've had some trouble here. Hope you can give us a hand."

The woman spoke in a low voice to her husband, the liquid Spanish coming fast and furious. The man nodded, then said to Cody, "What is it you require of us, señor?"

"Got a man hurt here," Cody replied, pointing to the guard, who had passed out. "We need to get him on to El Paso so that a doctor can take a look at him."

"I see his leg is broken," the farmer said. He glanced nervously at the bodies of the fallen outlaws, sprawled motionlessly on the ground some fifty yards away. "Those men, they are responsible?"

"They're bandits," Cody told him, nodding. "They tried to rob the stagecoach. My friend, here, and I are Texas Rangers, and we were lucky enough to run off the rest of them."

"*Sí*, lucky."

The stagecoach driver stepped up beside Cody and said impatiently, "Look here, Pancho, are you goin' to sit there and jaw all day? You know what the Ranger's tellin' you. We need your wagon."

"I was getting around to asking, not telling," Cody pointed out in a quiet voice. Only someone who knew him well would've heard the anger in it.

"We don't have time to waste on a bunch of long-winded talk," snapped the driver. "Matt's hurt, and I intend to get him to town as soon as those Mexes climb down from that wagon."

Cody bit back his own curt response. The man was worried about his partner, and the Ranger couldn't blame him for that. But Cody didn't intend to stand by and watch the Mexican family being taken advantage of, either.

Digging in the pocket of his denim pants, Cody brought out a ten-dollar gold piece and flipped it to the farmer, who caught it deftly in midair. "We'd like to rent your wagon, señor, and hire your services as driver, too. Reckon there's room in the back for this injured man and the other folks, too?"

The man nodded eagerly, his eyes shining as he looked at the coin clutched in his callused hand. Likely it was more money than he'd seen in one place for quite a while. *"Sí,"* he said. "We go to visit my sister in El Paso del Norte, but as you can see, we have little in the way of belongings. Plenty of room in back."

The stage driver grumbled a little, but apparently even he could see that he had no right to commandeer the wagon and strand the farmer and his family out here in the middle of nowhere. They were damned lucky, in fact, that the buckboard had come along when it did. The injured man couldn't ride a horse, so they'd have been stuck out here in the hot sun all day while Cody and Seth rode back to El Paso and brought help. Of course, if the two Rangers hadn't happened along from opposite directions when they did, the occupants of the stagecoach probably wouldn't have survived the outlaw attack.

While the driver, the two cowhands, and the farmer were carefully loading the guard into the buckboard, Cody turned to Seth and asked, "Now, what was this about some telegram Cap'n Vickery sent me?"

Seth grinned. "The old mossback's got a job for us."

"Us?" repeated Cody. "And you wouldn't talk about the cap'n like that if he was here."

"Damn right I wouldn't! He'd skin me alive." Then Seth's expression became more serious. "Anyway, I was on my way to meet you. We're supposed to join up and take a little detour into the Davis Mountains. Orders are to meet a fella at Fort Davis and take care of a small chore up there before headin' back to Del Rio."

Cody frowned and rubbed his jaw in consternation. Riding all the way up to the army post in the Davis Mountains of West Texas was hardly a "little detour." It'd mean several days of hard traveling. Whatever the assignment was, it had to be serious.

"Maybe we'd better ride back into El Paso so that I can wire the cap'n and get all the details," he said.

"No need to do that," Seth said quickly. "I can fill you in, Cody." He waved at the group of people clustered around the buckboard. "These folks don't need our help anymore. That bunch of owlhoots won't be back. And if you backtrack all the way to El Paso, that'll just delay things that much more. Better just to head on to Fort Davis."

Cody waited for Seth's protests to end, then asked, "Are you sure you know what this is all about?"

The young Ranger nodded emphatically. "Alan and I were there when the cap'n was talkin' about it with Lieutenant Whitcomb. We even got a look at the letter from the sheriff at Fort Davis, askin' for the Rangers to give him a hand. I can tell you all about it."

"All right, fair enough," Cody decided. "Besides, I've seen enough of El Paso to last me for a while. We'll head north as soon as these people are on their way."

"What about those dead outlaws?"

Cody just shrugged, and that was answer enough. It was too hot to be wasting sweat digging graves for owlhoots. The coyotes would take care of them.

Even with the injured guard stretched out in the back of the buckboard, there was room for the two worn carpetbags of the 7X cowhands. They took the bags from the stagecoach boot and piled them in the wagon while the driver retrieved the mail pouch from the box. That was all they had. The three men then piled into the wagon bed with the Mexican youngsters while the farmer took his seat again and picked up the reins. As loaded down as it was, the buckboard wouldn't make very good time going into El Paso, but it sure beat nothing.

Cody whistled for his dun, which was still standing about a hundred yards away, watching the goings-on. The horse came to the Ranger at a trot and stopped right in front of him, nuzzling the hand Cody held out. He patted the dun's nose, then stepped up into the saddle. Edging the horse over beside the wagon as Seth mounted up, Cody said to the stage driver, "You treat these folks right. Remember, they're the ones helping you."

The man nodded sheepishly. "I know, Ranger. Reckon I got a little worked up earlier 'cause I was worried about Matt. Won't happen again."

"Figured as much." Cody lifted a finger to the brim of his hat and nodded to the woman. "*Buenos días, señora.* And *gracias* to you and your husband."

The two Rangers sat, hands crossed on their saddle horns, and watched as the buckboard pulled away. They stayed there until it had dwindled to a speck in the heat and dust, and then Cody turned the dun's head toward the northeast.

"Let's go," he said. "You can tell me all about it on the way."

CHAPTER

▐▌▌▌▌▌▌▌▌▌▌▌▌▌▌▌▌▌▌▌▌▌ 2 ▐▌▌▌▌▌▌▌▌▌▌▌▌▌▌▌▌▌▌▌▌

Samuel Clayton Woodbine Cody was his full name, but time and preference had whittled it down considerably. To a few people, most notably his mother and sisters, he was Sam. A certain redheaded French lady back in Del Rio called him Samuel. To just about everybody else he was Cody, and that was the way he liked it.

Even on horseback it was easy to see he was a big man, tall and broad-shouldered. His outfit was that of a typical range rider: worn black boots, denim pants, a light blue, bib-front cotton shirt that time and the sun had faded almost to white, a dark-brown vest, and a high-crowned, wide-brimmed, cream-colored Stetson that had seen better days, though it still performed admirably when it came to shading his head from sun or rain. A cartridge belt of black leather circled his lean waist, and riding in its holster was a walnut-butted Colt .45 single-action Army revolver. On his left hip was a sheathed bowie knife, a razor-sharp, heavy-bladed weapon that had been forged in Louisiana by James Black nearly half a century earlier.

Silver spurs were strapped onto Cody's boots, a legacy from his father, Adam Cody, one of the original Texas Rangers. Along with those spurs, Sam Cody had inherited his father's skill with weapons and horses and men. It was only natural that he'd ride with the Rangers, though for a time in his younger years it had appeared that he might wind up on the other side of the law.

Cody had never regretted the choice he had made.

Now, as he rode northeast toward the Davis Mountains

with Seth Williams, he asked the younger man, "What's this job you were talking about?"

"Well, I told you the cap'n got a wire from the sheriff at Fort Davis, the settlement there close by the Army post. Fella's name is Randine or somethin' like that. He said there's a gang of outlaws raisin' hell thereabouts, and he needs the Rangers' help in roundin' them up."

Cody grunted. It wasn't unusual for the Rangers to get a call for help from a local star packer, and nine times out of ten the trouble was what Seth had just described: a bunch of owlhoots either too big or too shifty for the sheriff to deal with.

"Surprised the cap'n's sending two of us," Cody commented. "One man ought to be enough."

"Well, there's a little more to it than that. . . ."

Cody shot a sharp glance over at Seth. He should've figured as much, he thought. "What is it?"

"Vickery said to tell you the leader of the gang is Barry Whittingham."

That revelation made Cody sit up straighter in the saddle. His mouth tightened into a grim line as his eyes narrowed in surprise.

"The way the cap'n said it, I figured that name had to mean somethin' to you," Seth said. "I can see now it does. Who is this Whittingham fella, Cody?"

The older Ranger's thoughts went back several years, and in his mind's eye he saw a slim, blond man with a neatly trimmed mustache, a man who, despite his gentlemanly background, could ride a horse and handle a gun just fine. A man who, for a while, had been Cody's colleague.

"He used to be a Ranger," he said.

"And now he's an outlaw?" Seth sounded as if he couldn't believe such a thing was possible.

Cody shrugged. "According to what you just told me, he is. I reckon we'll have to talk to that sheriff to get all the details."

Seth let out a low whistle. "A Ranger gone bad! Hard to figure. Did you know this Whittingham fella very well? I reckon he was part of the company before my time."

"That's right," Cody said. "Like me, he joined up right

after the carpetbaggers were booted out of Texas and the Rangers formed up again. We rode together over in the Frio River country; then we were both assigned to Company C in Del Rio. I reckon Cap'n Vickery remembers him, and he knew I would, too."

"Then you and Whittingham were friends?"

"I knew him," Cody said as he kept the dun at an easy trot that gobbled up the miles. "And I reckon we were friendly enough, even though we weren't special *amigos* or anything like that. Whittingham never saved my life that I know of, and I don't reckon I ever saved his. But we got along all right, even if he was an Englishman."

"An Englishman!" repeated Seth. "I swear, Cody, gettin' a story out of you's like pourin' molasses in a blue norther."

Cody chuckled. "All right. Whittingham was the second son of a noble family over there in England. You know what primogeniture means?"

"Primo . . . what?"

"It's a fancy way of saying that if you're an Englishman and you're the second son, you don't inherit anything. Any title your pa's got and all of his holdings go to your older brother when your pa dies."

"That don't hardly seem fair."

"To our way of thinking, I reckon it's not," Cody said. "But those English folks see things different. That's the way they've been doing it for hundreds of years, and they don't ever get in an all-fired hurry to change anything. Anyway, Barry didn't stand to inherit anything, and he didn't much like it. He didn't like the idea of winding up as a remittance man, either."

"That's another one you're goin' to have to explain." Seth shook his head. "I didn't know those Englishers were such peculiar folks. I figured they were about like us, except for the fact they talk funnier'n Yankees even."

Cody grinned and said, "Barry had an accent, all right, but not much of one. He'd been over here in the States for quite a while before he drifted to Texas. Anyway, he told me that sometimes the parents over in England will send their second sons to India or America or some other place far away, and then send them money—a remittance—to stay there where they won't be an embarrassment to the family. Out of sight, out of mind, I reckon you could say."

"Sounds like a damn foolish way of doing things, if you ask me."

"Nobody did, son." Cody paused, then resumed his story. "Whittingham came over to this country on his own, didn't even tell his family where he was going. He was just naturally fiddlefooted, and he wound up in Texas about the time the Rangers got started again. Fighting outlaws and Indians sounded like a grand adventure to him, or so he told me later, so he joined up. Found out, though, within a few months that it wasn't as exciting as he'd thought it'd be. He drew his pay and resigned, and Major Jones didn't argue with him. The major said we didn't need anybody in the Frontier Battalion who didn't want to be there." Cody shook his head slowly. "That day in San Antonio was the last time I ever saw Barry Whittingham."

"You think he might be leadin' a bunch of outlaws?"

"No way of knowing just yet," Cody said. "I reckon it's possible. There was something about him. . . . When he talked, folks usually listened. He was smart, and he was a good fighting man." The Ranger shrugged, then went on, "I reckon he could have gotten a gang together. He'd be sharp enough and tough enough to keep a bunch of owlhoots in line. Yep, it could just be true."

"Never thought I'd be sent out to bring in a fella who used to be a Ranger," Seth said gloomily.

"Neither did I."

They rode along in silence for a while, and gradually Seth's mood brightened. By nightfall, when the two Rangers had found a small creek to camp by, the youngster had regained his usual exuberance.

There were still a few bands of hostile Indians in this part of the country, but they were few enough in number that Cody decided it would be all right to have a campfire. Pooling their supplies, the twosome fried some bacon, heated a pot of beans, and cooked some cornbread. Washed down with hot, strong Arbuckle's coffee, the food made an excellent meal, and Seth gave a moan of contentment from an overfull stomach as he leaned back against a small boulder.

"You know, Cody," he said, "I've been thinkin'."

Across the fire, Cody looked up sharply. Seth thinking was not always a good sign.

The younger man went on, "I know how you like to go in by yourself on a job like some sort of lone wolf and work undercover. But you can't do that on this assignment, can you? I mean, Whittingham knows you, knows you're a Ranger."

"I reckon that's right," Cody said slowly.

"But he doesn't know me! I joined the Rangers after he'd left. *I* can handle all the undercover stuff this time!"

"Don't know if we'll need to do that."

Seth leaned forward eagerly. "But think about it! If I take my badge off and we don't ride in together, I can pretend I'm just a driftin' cowhand. Sometimes folks'll talk a lot more freely to an hombre like that than they will to a lawman, even a Ranger."

The boy had a point—damn it. Cody sighed. "We'll see," he promised.

"Better make up your mind before we get to Fort Davis, or it won't do any good. Myself, I think it's a right fine idea."

"I said we'll see."

Seth subsided. "Sure, Cody. But think about it."

That was exactly what Cody did, staring up sleeplessly at the brilliant stars in the Texas sky long after Seth had dropped off and started snoring nearly loud enough to rattle the mesquite beans. Seth's idea was a good one, and the youngster did have a little experience at working undercover. He and Cody had teamed up on a similar job a few months earlier, in fact. Anyway, despite the exuberance and recklessness that sometimes got Seth into trouble, he was a good Ranger, and running risks was part of the job. They would proceed as Seth had suggested, Cody decided.

The decision made, Cody went right to sleep.

In the morning, after Seth had let out a whoop of joy, they ate breakfast, mounted up, and rode on toward Fort

Davis to pick up the trail of the renegade former Ranger.
And Cody hoped he wasn't making one hell of a mistake.

Two and a half days later, in the middle of the afternoon,
Cody rode into the settlement called Fort Davis, half a mile
from the actual military post. The Ranger was alone. Seth
would ride in by himself later in the day so that it'd look
like there was no connection between the two of them. They
had parted company while still several miles out of town,
eliminating the possibility of anyone just happening to spot
them approaching.

The Davis Mountains were sort of the tail end of the
Rockies, and while they weren't nearly as tall and majestic
as some of the ranges Cody had seen farther north, they
were still plenty rugged. The town and the fort sat in a small
basin in the foothills, the mountains themselves rising to the
north and west. On an afternoon like this the sunshine was
warm, but Cody knew how the temperature would plunge
at night due to the elevation.

The higher reaches of the mountains were covered with
pines, while the valleys lower down were lined with cotton-
wood, oak, cedar, and juniper trees. Clear, cold creeks
trickled through those valleys and watered pastures lush
with grass and wildflowers. Looming over everything were
the craggy slopes of Sawtooth Mountain, Baldy Peak, Black
Mountain, and all the other mountains in this range. It was
pretty country, good country, and Fort Davis was a nice
little town, serving both the military post and the numerous
ranches in the area. If an outlaw gang was raising hell
around here, Cody'd be more than happy to try to put a
stop to it.

The Ranger rode down the main street of the settlement,
past saloons, general stores, livery stables, a saddlemaker,
and a blacksmith shop, then the Limpia Hotel, the town's
biggest and fanciest building. Just past the hotel was a small
stone building with a plank sign over its door, proclaiming
it the office of the sheriff of Presidio County, Texas. Cody
brought the dun to a stop, dismounted, and flipped the reins
over the hitch rail in front of the office.

The Ranger was wearing his badge, and the sight of it caused the man sitting behind a desk to sit up and take notice when Cody stepped into the office. "You the sheriff?" Cody asked him.

The man replaced the pen he had been using in its inkwell and stood up. He was stocky, slightly below medium height, with dark hair and a short beard shot through with gray. His belly hadn't quite turned into a paunch—yet. Despite his unimpressive appearance, as he came out from behind the desk he moved with a graceful ease that told Cody he could handle himself in a fight. A five-pointed sheriff's badge was pinned to his cowhide vest, and he wore a Colt with the butt tipped forward.

"Philo Randine," the lawman said, extending a hand to Cody. "I don't have to ask who you are, mister. Or, rather, what you are." He nodded toward the Ranger badge.

"Name's Cody. Glad to meet you, Sheriff. My cap'n said you were having some trouble up here."

Randine let go of Cody's hand and laughed harshly, humorlessly. "You could say that. There's a gang of outlaws making life miserable around here for a lot of folks, me included." The sheriff frowned slightly. "I was hoping a whole troop of Rangers would show up, to tell you the truth."

"One's usually enough. Hope you're not too disappointed."

Randine waved off the comment. "I'm thankful for any help I can get, let me tell you. Have a seat, Cody."

There was a ladder-back chair by the wall of the small office. Cody picked it up, reversed it, and straddled it as he sat down in front of the sheriff's desk. He cuffed his hat to the back of his head and said, "I'm told the leader of this gang is a man called Barry Whittingham."

"That's right." Randine sank back in his own chair.

"Are you sure about that?"

"Sure as I can be. You see, Whittingham worked around here for a brief time as a cowhand before he went bad. He rode for the Rafter Nine outfit, and that was the first place he robbed. Got the crew's payroll one day when the ranch manager was bringing it out from town. The manager identified Whittingham positively. So have several other people since then. It's him, all right."

Cody shook his head grimly, furrows appearing in his cheeks above the full mustache.

Randine squinted at him. "You don't believe me?"

"Oh, I believe you all right, Sheriff. I was just hoping there was some room for a mistake to have been made. You see, Whittingham used to be a Ranger. Fact is, I rode with him for a while."

"And they sent *you* to bring him in?" Randine snapped, suspicion appearing in his eyes.

Cody's jaw tightened in anger. "I never let personal considerations interfere with my job, Sheriff," he said curtly. "I'll bring in Whittingham, just like I'd bring in any other desperado."

Randine grimaced. "Sorry," he said, obviously knowing that he had stepped over the line. "I guess I'm just a little touchy. This business has got folks thinking maybe they need to vote for somebody else come election time."

The sheriff's comment didn't surprise Cody. Like a lot of men in his position, Randine was as much politician as lawman, though Cody had a feeling the man was competent enough at his job. "Tell me what Whittingham's been up to," he said.

"Well, I told you he got the Rafter Nine payroll. Pulled that job by himself, but it wasn't long before he got himself a gang. There's plenty of hardcases drifting through this part of the country. For a while they raided ranches, drove off stock, that sort of thing. Then they started hitting stagecoaches."

That made Cody think back several days to the stage holdup he and Seth had foiled down by the Rio Grande. It was too much to hope that the gang they had routed there might have been Whittingham's bunch; that would be stretching coincidence too far. But outlaws had been known to range a long way in their depredations, so he asked, "Have they been seen in the last few days?"

"As a matter of fact, they widelooped a bunch of cattle just two days ago. Ran 'em up toward the New Mexico line. I rode after them with a posse, but they gave us the slip."

Cody nodded. A raid up here two days earlier made it certain that Whittingham and his gang hadn't been down on the Rio. He said, "Didn't mean to jump ahead. Go on, Sheriff."

"Sure. Not much else to tell, anyway. Whittingham got braver, even came into town a couple of times to hit the bank and some of the stores. That's when Frank Parker showed up."

"Frank Parker?" Cody echoed with a frown. The name was familiar.

"That's right. Used to ride with the Vaughn gang back in central Texas. He was in on the Lampassas raid. I've got dodgers on him. . . ."

Cody shook his head as the sheriff reached for one of the drawers in the desk. "No need to dig through them, Sheriff. I remember him now. He's been on the wrong side of the law for a long time. Never headed up his own gang, but he's ridden with some of the worst of 'em."

"That's Parker, all right," Randine confirmed, nodding. "From what the witnesses tell us, he's the second in command of Whittingham's bunch. If anything, they've gotten more bloodthirsty since Parker's joined up. Whittingham's first few jobs, nobody got hurt. Since then, though, they've gunned down quite a few folks."

The bad taste in Cody's mouth was getting worse. He felt a desire growing in him to put a stop to Whittingham's vicious crimes any way that he could, and if that meant putting a bullet in the man, then former Ranger or not, so be it.

Randine folded his hands over his stomach and went on, "You need to go see the commanding officer at the fort, too. When he found out I sent for the Rangers, he wanted to see whoever showed up. He's also looking for Whittingham, since the gang held up a couple of Army supply trains. Could be he'll be more help than I can be. He's got a bunch of soldiers who can lend a hand, while I've just got a handful of deputies to cover damn near half of West Texas."

Cody nodded, well aware of how difficult it was to enforce the law in these far-flung West Texas counties with a limited amount of money and manpower. Randine's suggestion that he work with the Army was a good one.

"What's the commander's name?"

"Major Vance Monroe," Randine replied. "I don't know a lot about him; he hasn't been here long. But I reckon he'll cooperate with you. He's as anxious to see Whittingham behind bars or at the end of a rope as I am."

"I'll pay a call on him," Cody said. "You haven't been able to get a line on where Whittingham's hiding out?"

Randine barked a laugh again. "You ever spent much time in the Davis Mountains, Cody?"

"Some," the Ranger said with a shrug.

"Then you know there's more hiding places in those canyons and gullies than just about anywhere in the state. And there's enough rocky ground that anybody who knows what he's doing can avoid leaving many tracks." Randine shook his head. "I've spent more days than I like to think about poking around up there, and I haven't found a damn thing. Whittingham's slippery, mighty slippery. You're going to need some luck to catch him."

Cody didn't doubt that for a second.

The military post that was named after former Secretary of War—and later President of the Confederacy—Jefferson Davis sprawled out across a good-sized compound northeast of the settlement. Like most of the other forts across the Southwest, Fort Davis was open, lacking stockade walls. A long row of offices, officers' quarters, and barracks for the enlisted men was fronted by a large parade ground. Behind the buildings a rugged bluff rose sharply toward the blue sky. A troop of cavalry was drilling smartly on the parade ground as Cody rode up to the fort.

He wasn't surprised to see the dark faces of the troopers. Most of the men stationed at Fort Davis were black, "buffalo soldiers" as the Indians called them. Many were former slaves, freed by the War Between the States, and they had proven to be excellent soldiers. Cody rode past them, lifting a hand in greeting to the sergeant who was putting the men through their paces, and guided the dun to the hitchrack in front of the regimental commander's office.

After tying up the horse, Cody went inside and said to the orderly on duty at the desk, "I'd like to see Major Monroe. Name's Cody. I'm a Texas Ranger."

"Yes, sir," the young corporal said crisply. "Is the major expecting you?"

"Well, I don't have an appointment, if that's what you mean, son. But Sheriff Randine said the major wanted to see me as soon as I got here."

"Yes, sir. I'll tell the major you're here."

Cody didn't have to cool his heels for long. The orderly was back in less than a minute, and he ushered Cody through a door into the commander's office.

Major Vance Monroe was on his feet. He came out from behind his desk, smiled, and thrust out his hand. "Mr. Cody!" he said eagerly. "I'm glad to meet you, sir. I've heard a great deal about the Texas Rangers."

Cody pegged Monroe as an easterner from his accent. The major was young, probably still in his mid-twenties. He was slender, with thick dark hair worn a bit longer than most military men. Clean shaven, his features were lean and rather austere, though he wore a friendly smile at the moment. His uniform was crisply pressed and spotless—an accomplishment not to be taken lightly in the dusty reaches of West Texas.

"Sheriff Randine suggested that I talk to you, Major. He said you were looking for Barry Whittingham and the gang riding with him. That's why I'm here."

Monroe nodded. "Yes, I understood that Randine had summoned some aid from the Rangers. That's why I told him I wanted to see whoever responded to his plea. It's very important that we understand each other."

"Yes, sir, that's my thinking exactly." Cody took the chair that the major waved him into, then went on, "I'm glad you're willing to give me a hand. This is big country around here."

Major Monroe was settling back into his own chair. He looked up quickly and frowned at Cody's statement. "Give you a hand? No, I'm afraid there's been some misunderstanding, Mr. Cody."

It was Cody's turn to frown. "How's that?"

"The reason I asked Randine to send any Rangers to see me was so that I could make it clear to them that the Army will not place itself under the jurisdiction of, and neither will it assist in, any sort of civilian agency's investigation."

Cody's eyes narrowed in surprise. "You're saying you won't cooperate with me?"

"I'm saying that while I won't hinder any of your own efforts, Mr. Cody, I'm not going to place myself or my men at your beck and call, either. We're searching for this outlaw Whittingham on our own, and we intend to continue doing so."

For a moment Cody didn't say anything as he digested the major's acerbic comments. Monroe was smiling again, but there was no warmth in his pale-gray eyes.

"Reckon you're one of those by-the-book officers," Cody finally said. He suppressed the urge to spit on the floor as he spoke.

"Going by the book, as you call it, Mr. Cody, has served the United States Army quite well for a long time. I intend to continue that tradition, no matter what sort of god-forsaken pesthole I'm stationed at."

Now the officer's true feelings were coming out, Cody thought. Monroe resented being put in charge of such an isolated post. That, and his attitude concerning rules and regulations, meant he'd be a hard man to deal with.

Cody felt beholden to give it a try, though. He said, "Look, Major, we want the same thing: to put a stop to Whittingham's hell-raising around here. No reason that we can't work together to accomplish that."

"Other than the fact that Army regulations make no provision for such a thing. Believe me, Mr. Cody, if they did, I'd be the first one to cooperate with you to the fullest extent." Monroe leaned back in his chair and spread his hands. "But as it is, I have no choice but to refuse any request you may have been about to make for Army assistance."

Cody bit back the angry retort that sprang to his lips.

Cussing out this stiff-necked young officer wouldn't accomplish anything. Instead, he stood up and said, "Well, you've made your position clear enough, Major. Reckon I'll be going."

"Just a moment, please, Mr. Cody," Monroe said sharply. "Just as I am unable to assist you in your investigation, I must insist that you not interfere in ours. To that end I've decided to assign one of my noncommissioned officers to you to serve as a liaison."

"You mean a watchdog," Cody snapped.

Monroe shrugged. "Call it what you will." He stood and called out, "Corporal Deakins!"

The orderly appeared in the door of the office. "Yes, Major?"

"Summon Sergeant Gresham."

"Yes, sir!" Corporal Deakins vanished again. The boy was fast on his feet, Cody had to give him that.

The Ranger kept a tight rein on his temper—but his brain was moving rapidly. When Monroe had first said that he was going to assign a man to Cody, the big Texan had been tempted to tell the major to forget it. He had decided to hold off on that reaction, though. Since Monroe obviously wasn't going to cooperate, going along with this notion of having a liaison between the Ranger and the Army might be the closest Cody would come to getting some help. It would all depend on how reasonable this Sergeant Gresham was.

A few minutes later the black noncom whom Cody had seen drilling the troops on the parade ground knocked on the open door of the office. "You wanted to see me, Major?" he asked in a deep voice.

"Come in, Sergeant." Monroe returned the salute the sergeant gave him, then said, "Sergeant Gresham, this is Mr. Cody. Mr. Cody is a Texas Ranger."

"I can see that, sir." Gresham's gaze touched on the badge pinned to Cody's vest, then lifted and met the Ranger's eyes squarely. "Pleased to meet you, Mr. Cody. I'm Rufe Gresham."

Cody took the sergeant's hand, knowing that Gresham's grip would be firm. He wasn't disappointed. "Howdy, Sergeant."

"Mr. Cody is here to search for that outlaw who's been plaguing the district, Sergeant. I'm appointing you to serve as the liaison between his efforts and ours. Mr. Cody, you'll report all of your activities to Sergeant Gresham so that he can pass them along to me, just to make sure you're not infringing on anything in which the Army has jurisdiction."

Cody knew without asking that any reporting being done would be one way. The major wasn't about to give up any information he or his troops uncovered. Still, all Cody wanted to do now was get out of here and get on with his job, so he nodded. Better to save some time than argue.

"That's all, Sergeant." Monroe sat down again, and from his demeanor it was plain he had dismissed both Cody and Gresham from his thoughts as well as his office.

Gresham inclined his head toward the door. Cody nodded again and went out, trailed by the sergeant.

When they were outside the headquarters building, Gresham said in a low voice, "I'm impressed, Mr. Cody."

"Why's that?"

"I've seen enough of you Texans to know that what you really wanted to do was knock the major on his skinny little ass."

Cody had to chuckle. "I reckon you're right, Sergeant."

They had come to a stop beside Cody's dun. Gresham looked the animal over, then commented, "Good horse. Bet he could run all day if he had to."

"He can," Cody confirmed. "And he has, several times. Saved my hide more than once, too. You've got a good eye for horseflesh, Sergeant."

"I was raised up in Kentucky. Horseflesh is something we got plenty of."

Cody felt an instinctive liking for the noncom, who was older, in his forties probably, with a strong, square face and graying hair under his campaign cap. The Ranger asked him, "Is that youngster in there always such a tin-plated bastard?"

Gresham sighed. "Don't take the major's attitude personally, Mr. Cody. He's got a lot to handle these days. There's still some Indian trouble from time to time, and now this bunch of outlaws has started causing problems. On top of that, there's folks around here who don't cotton to black boys wearing uniforms. Bad enough those uniforms are blue without the skin inside 'em being black."

"I know what you mean," Cody said. "Makes no never mind to me, but there's still some who haven't forgotten the War."

"Were you in the Confederate Army?" Gresham asked, his tone clearly indicating that he was just curious, not trying to start any trouble.

"Nope. My pa was dead, and there was a good-sized ranch to take care of. Couldn't leave it with my ma and three sisters. That's ten years and more gone, though. Ancient history when it comes to the frontier."

"Damn right. We got enough to worry about right here and now." Gresham leaned closer and lowered his voice even more. "Listen, if there's anything I can help you with, sort of unofficial-like, you just let me know."

"I'll do that, Sergeant," Cody said, equally quietly. "And thanks."

"And don't worry overmuch about reporting to me like the major said. I reckon you know what you're doing, or you wouldn't have lived this long out here."

Cody had to grin. "I was hoping you'd be a reasonable man, Sergeant. I can see now that I was right."

Gresham grinned back at him. "Hell, a good noncom's got to know how to get the job done in spite of his officers, not because of 'em." His expression became more serious. "You be careful hunting that Whittingham gang. That's a mean bunch, from what I've heard."

"I'll keep my eyes open," Cody promised him. "How about telling me what you've found so far in looking for them?"

"Be glad to."

He had just about broken even so far, Cody thought as Gresham began detailing the Army's efforts to locate the outlaws. Sheriff Randine looked to be fairly ineffectual, and Major Monroe was downright hostile under that smooth front. But having a man like Sergeant Rufe Gresham on his side could make up for all of that.

CHAPTER 3

Seth Williams sent his horse down the main street of the settlement in an easy walk. He was in no hurry. He'd never been to Fort Davis before, and he wanted to take in as many details of the place as he could. Besides, as the kind of itinerant cowhand he was supposed to be, it wouldn't do to get in too much of a hurry.

He pulled his mount to a halt in front of the Wild Rose Saloon. There was a pass through the mountains called Wild Rose Pass, Seth remembered. He had never seen it, but he'd heard Cody speak of it and seen its location marked on maps of the area. That was a mighty sweet name to give a narrow, hole-in-the-wall saloon, he thought. Even without going inside, he knew the place sure as hell wouldn't smell like wild roses.

He was right, he confirmed a moment later as he pushed the batwings aside and entered the saloon. It smelled like spilled beer, stale tobacco smoke, and piss. Not that bad once you got used to it, though.

The bar ran along the right-hand side of the room. To the left were several tables with no cloths covering their scarred wood, and in the back was a billiard table. There was no mirror behind the bar, just plain wooden shelves full of an assortment of bottles. No matter what the labels on the bottles said, they'd be full of the same panther sweat, probably mixed up by the proprietor in a dirty barrel out back. Said proprietor was a wizened little man in a gray apron, scurrying back and forth behind the bar to serve the drinkers lined up there. For the middle of the afternoon the Wild Rose was doing a good business. Most of the places at the bar were taken, and nearly all of the tables were full as well. A card game was going on at one of them, and from the rear of the room came the click of billiard balls as a couple of cowhands shot a game.

Seth looked back at the men along the bar and saw that, in fact, there were a couple of openings. Actually, there were gaps of several feet to either side of one of the men. This solitary drinker wore the uniform of the Eighth Cavalry, and the skin of his neck underneath the campaign cap was a rich brown.

Seth hesitated. He'd never had much to do with colored people, having grown up in the border country. But he had known and liked plenty of Mexicans, and he knew that some folks looked down on them just like they did blacks. Slavery and the War weren't really issues to him; he had been too young to fight for the Confederacy, and nobody in his part of the country had owned slaves or even wanted to. Besides, he was damned thirsty, and he wanted a beer even though he knew it would probably be warm and flat.

He stepped up to the bar to the right of the black trooper and motioned for the bartender to draw him a beer.

The soldier glanced over at Seth but didn't say anything. Neither did the young Ranger. He waited until the little man slid the beer across to him and croaked, "Two bits." Paying him, Seth picked up the glass. It was dirty, but not too bad. Just as he expected, the beer was warm and almost tasteless. But it was wet, and it cut the dust in his throat.

Gradually, Seth became aware that it was awfully quiet, especially considering the number of people in the Wild Rose. An occasional soft voice came from the table where the poker game was going on as the players bet and raised, but the men along the bar weren't talking, and neither were the ones at the other tables.

With a clatter the two cowhands playing billiards threw their cue sticks on the table, and out of the corner of his eye Seth saw them slouching toward him. No, not him, he realized a moment later. The man they wanted was the one standing beside him.

"See you're still here, nigger," one of the cowboys jeered.

"Looks like you ain't got the sense God give a jackass after all, or you'd'a got out like we told you."

Seth saw the trooper's fingers tighten on the glass of rotgut he held in his right hand. But that hand didn't tremble as it lifted the glass, and the soldier took another sip of the potent stuff.

"He ain't gonna talk to us, Newt," the other cowhand said with a grin. "Maybe he's deaf."

"He ain't deaf," the one called Newt said. "Just dumb. Like all the rest o' them niggers."

Two more cowpunchers stood up from a nearby table. They were both young, like the two who'd been at the billiard table. One was tall and gangling with a pleasantly ugly face, while the other was shorter, curly-haired, handsome. The taller one put out a hand and began, "No need to cause trouble, Newt—"

"I'm not the one causin' trouble!" Newt snapped. He pointed at the soldier. "It's that goddamned darky, thinkin' he can come in here and have a drink just like he's as good as white folks!"

From what Seth could see, four down-at-the-heels cowpokes didn't have any call to feel superior to a cavalry trooper, no matter what the color of his skin. Newt and his friend weren't going to be denied, though, and the other two didn't look like they were going to put a stop to it.

"Listen, nigger," Newt went on, "we done told you polite-like to haul your black carcass outta here. Since you ain't seen fit to do that, I reckon we'll have to throw you out."

The bartender held up trembling hands. "Please, Newt," he quavered. "Don't bust the place all up again."

"Don't worry, Augie," Newt assured him with a grin. "This boy ain't gonna give us no trouble." He abruptly stepped closer and gave the trooper's shoulder a hard shove. "Are you, nigger?"

Even though the soldier had to have been aware that trouble was coming, he was apparently unprepared for the swiftness of Newt's move. The push sent him staggering to the right, directly into Seth. The collision jarred the glass of beer out of Seth's hand, and the stuff splashed across the front of his buckskin shirt.

"Hey!" the young Ranger yelled.

The black man's head snapped around, and he asked in a taut voice, "You goin' to call me names, too, mister?"

Seth blinked, uncertain until that very second what he would do. Then he grinned and said, "Nope. But I *am* goin' to bust the son of a bitch who caused this right in the jaw."

He whipped around, his fist lashing out and crashing into Newt's face. He hadn't given it any thought, just reacted, and now the fight was on in earnest. Like it or not, he'd chosen his side.

As Newt stumbled backward from the force of Seth's punch, his companion leapt at Seth with a howl of rage, fists flailing. The other two young cowhands flung themselves at the trooper.

Seth ducked under the wild punches directed at him and stepped closer to his opponent to pepper the cowboy's belly with a flurry of blows. The saloon was anything but quiet now. The other drinkers, even though they weren't joining in the fight, were all on their feet and hollering, shouting encouragement to the four cowhands.

There was no time for the young Ranger to do anything except glance in the trooper's direction. The soldier had his hands full with the other cowboys, but Seth couldn't do anything to help him. He had to concentrate on blocking the punches of his own opponent and throwing some back.

Newt regained his balance and charged into the fracas. Seth took a blow on the side of the head from him, and his hat went sailing off. Stars twinkled in front of his eyes for a second; then his vision cleared and he darted aside from Newt's next punch.

So far the fight had been a clean one, not counting the uneven odds. Nobody had reached for a gun or a knife. If they had, Seth might've had a better chance, he reflected grimly. His relatively small stature was a disadvantage in a bare-knuckles brawl like this one.

Two against one was just too much. The other man managed to pin Seth's arms, and then Newt stepped in and slammed several blows to the youngster's belly. The beer Seth had drunk came right back up, and he took some bleak satisfaction in the way it splattered on Newt's pants and boots. But it just made Newt madder, made him hit harder.

After a couple of minutes Newt's arms must have gotten tired, because he said, "Take the bastard out and throw him in the street! Let him eat some dust!"

Seth was wavering between consciousness and oblivion. Vaguely, he felt himself being picked up and carried toward the entrance. His captor used him like a battering ram to knock the batwings aside, then planted a boot in his backside and shoved. With a mumbled "Whoa!" Seth went flying across the narrow boardwalk outside the saloon.

Images flickered across his vision in that fraction of time when he was practically airborne. He saw the stagecoach pulled to a stop in front of the building next door, saw the open door of the coach, saw the well-turned ankle beneath the hem of a blue traveling dress, and then he crashed onto the ground and rolled over several times before he came to a stop at the very feet of the woman who had just disembarked from the stage. Coughing and choking from the dust he had swallowed, Seth managed to lift his head and stare up into the horrified face of just about the prettiest girl he had ever seen.

Her beauty hit him like another punch, but this time he was jolted back to full consciousness. Sputtering, he climbed awkwardly to his feet and tried to find the words to apologize. The young woman just gaped, all big blue eyes and fair skin and thick brown hair that shone in the sunlight even though it was pulled back in a bun underneath her hat. Behind her, crouched in the door of the coach, caught midway in the act of getting out, an older man gave Seth an outraged glare and said angrily, "See here! What's all this?"

A whoop behind Seth made him spin around. The fight had spilled out onto the boardwalk from the saloon. The black trooper staggered into the open with one of the cowboys riding his back, legs clamped around the soldier's waist. The young cowhand had his left arm around the soldier's neck, and he was using his right to batter the soldier's head. Another of the cowhands danced around in front of them, looking for an opening for a punch.

The trooper suddenly reached up and back, tangling his fingers in the cowboy's hair, then bent forward from the waist, heaving with all his strength as he did so. The cowboy let out a screech of pain as he went sailing over the trooper's shoulders and crashed into his companion. The second cowhand was knocked backward by the collision and came off the boardwalk, out of control.

He was headed right for the girl.

Seth threw himself forward. There was no time to do anything except get between the young woman and the hurtling cowboy. Both men tumbled to the ground, Seth's teeth jarred by the impact—but at least he had changed the direction of the cowboy's plunge. They had both missed the girl.

He looked up in time to see the older man gripping the girl's arm and hustling her away from the stagecoach. They were headed for the Limpia Hotel across the street, the town's leading hostelry. As she hurried along, the girl threw one glance over her shoulder, and her eyes met Seth's for an instant. Then she was gone.

On the boardwalk the trooper, having rid himself of the cowboy on his back, spun toward the entrance of the saloon. He was a shade too late. Newt burst through the door, and for the first time in this ruckus a gun came into play when the cowhand slipped his six-shooter from its holster. It rose and fell, sunlight flickering on blued steel, and the barrel thudded against the trooper's head. With a groan the soldier slumped loosely to the boardwalk.

Still sprawled in the dusty street, Seth had turned his attention back to the fight in time to see the cowardly blow. Rage welled up inside him, and he reached for his own gun.

Before he could draw the Colt, a ring of hard metal was pressed against the side of his head. Seth froze, recognizing the touch of a gun barrel. "I wouldn't, mister," a breathless voice panted beside him. "Newt'd as soon kill you as look at you if you draw on 'im."

Seth darted his gaze to the side and saw that the voice belonged to the handsome young cowboy he had prevented from running into the girl. The man had twisted around and gotten his gun out from his own uncomfortable seat in the road.

Newt looked over at them. "Shoot him, Amos!" he urged.

The handsome cowboy shook his head. "No need. He's goin' to be reasonable." In a whisper, he hissed to Seth, "You'd damn well better be. Or I *will* shoot you."

Seth had to lick his lips and swallow a couple of times to get words past the dust clogging his throat. "Take it easy," he said. "Fight's over, far as I'm concerned."

"Now you're gettin' smart," Newt jeered from the board-walk. He prodded the unconscious trooper with a booted toe. "Smarter'n this nigger, anyway." He pointed the gun in his hand at Seth's face. "Next time you see me, nigger lover, you go the other way, understand? Or I'll kill you."

Seth jerked his head in a nod.

Newt holstered his gun and swaggered down the board-walk, followed by his billiard partner. The third cowboy, who was lying on the edge of the boardwalk, lifted his head and shook it groggily.

The man called Amos waited until Newt and his partner had gotten onto a couple of horses at the hitchrack and galloped out of town, heading west, before holstering his gun. He then rolled over and pushed himself to his feet, holding out a hand to the surprised Seth.

"Here, let me help you up."

Seth blinked at him. "A couple of minutes ago you were threatenin' to shoot me."

Amos shrugged. "That was just so *Newt* wouldn't shoot you. Come on. You fought pretty good. Let's get ol' Tug on his feet and go have a drink."

Seth hesitated a moment longer, finally taking the hand the young man was extending to him. Amos pulled him to his feet, then stepped over to the other young cowboy, who was sitting up now.

"You all right, Tug?" he asked.

"Reckon I will be," the lanky Tug replied. He massaged his scalp. "That feller like to ripped half the hair outta my skull. Felt like it, anyway."

Amos laughed and helped his friend to his feet.

Seth spotted his hat on the boardwalk. Somebody must have picked it up and tossed it out of the saloon. He scooped it up, pushed the dents out of it, and settled it on his aching head. Nodding at the fallen trooper, he asked, "What about him?"

"Oh, Sheriff Randine and a couple of his deputies'll be here in a few minutes, now that the fight's over," Amos said. "They'll take him back out to the fort. He'll be all right."

It went against the grain for Seth to leave an unconscious man lying there like that, but neither of the cowboys nor any of the townspeople looking on seemed particularly concerned about the situation. Seth knelt beside the trooper for a second and placed a couple of fingers on his throat to check for a pulse. It beat strong and steady against his touch.

"Reckon he'll be all right, like you said," Seth commented as he straightened up. He looked around quickly, as if a thought had just occurred to him. "There goin' to be trouble with the law about this?"

"Naw," Tug answered. "If Randine got worked up 'bout ever' fight in the Wild Rose, he wouldn't have no time to do his 'lectioneerin'."

Seth wasn't exactly sure what Tug meant by that, not having met this Sheriff Randine, but he accepted the cowboys' assurances that there'd be no trouble. He followed the two of them back into the Wild Rose, where they were confronted by the irate bartender.

"Take it easy 'fore you have a conniption fit, Augie," Amos advised the man. "You know Newt'll be good for any damages, next time he comes to town. Now, give us a bottle."

The proprietor sputtered a little longer, then sighed and handed Amos a bottle from behind the bar, along with three glasses. The handsome young cowboy led the way toward a table in the back of the room.

"Does Newt start fights like that very often?" Seth asked as he pulled out one of the rickety chairs beside the table and sat down.

"Often enough," Amos replied with a shrug.

"I reckon folks are gettin' used to it by now," added Tug.

"The four of you ride for the same spread?"

Amos shook his head. "Newt and Kelly ride for the Diamond RR. Me and Tug used to, but I guess you could say we're sort of between jobs right now."

"Footloose, that's us," Tug said with a smile.

Amos poured whiskey into the glasses, then set the bottle down in the center of the table and picked up his drink. "Not that we don't have some prospects," he said. He tossed back the drink, wiped the back of his other hand across his mouth, and, his voice dropping now, asked, "You ever hear of a fella called Barry Whittingham?"

Seth tried not to let his surprise show on his face. He forced himself to take a sip of the rotgut before he said, "Name sounds familiar. Some sort of outlaw, ain't he?"

Amos and Tug both chuckled. "Reckon you could say that," Amos replied. "He and his gang got the law runnin' in circles around here lookin' for him."

"We're goin' to join up with him," Tug added proudly.

Seth swallowed some more of the vile-tasting liquor and asked, "How do you intend to do that? Way you were just talkin', nobody knows where to find this Whittingham hombre."

"We can find him," Amos said confidently. "Nobody knows the Davis Mountains better'n Tug and me. We've ridden all over 'em, chasin' cows for this spread or that." He nodded slowly. "We'll find Whittingham, all right. And he's goin' to jump at the chance to have us throw in with him."

"How about you—" Tug broke off his question and frowned. "Say, I don't reckon we even know your name, feller."

Seth stuck his hand across the table. "Seth Williams."

"I'm Amos Bower, and this jug-eared galoot is Tug Mitchell."

Seth shook hands with both of the young drifters, then said, "You were about to ask me somethin', Tug."

The lanky cowhand exchanged a quick glance with Amos, who gave him a minuscule nod. "I was just about to ask if you'd like to ride with us for a spell, Seth," Tug said. "You seem like a pretty good sort, and you can handle yourself in a fight, no doubt about that."

Seth snorted. "I got the hell beat out of me, in case you boys didn't notice."

"Yeah, but that was a mighty good lick you got in on Newt," Amos said. "I reckon you'd have taken either him or Kelly if they'd come at you one at a time. You never had a chance the way they ganged up on you, though."

"Still should've taken them," Seth said with a self-deprecating shrug.

"You interested or not? Tug and me'd like to have you come along."

He had played out the hand long enough, Seth thought. Any more foot-dragging and he might make these two would-be hardcases suspicious. He smiled, downed the rest of his drink, and said hoarsely as the stuff set fire to his gullet, "I'm with you, boys."

With any luck they'd lead him straight to Barry Whittingham.

CHAPTER
4

Cody had spent a couple of hours being shown around the military post by Sergeant Rufe Gresham—not that there was that much to see—and most of the time they talked about Barry Whittingham and the robberies that had been pulled by the outlaw boss and his gang. As Sheriff Randine had said, the crimes had gotten more vicious as time passed, until now someone died in almost every job that was pulled by Whittingham's gang.

Usually the victims were stagecoach guards, ranchers, store owners—anyone foolish enough to fight back when they found themselves under the guns of the outlaws. A couple of times, though, innocent bystanders had been cut down by stray slugs, and once the gang's horses had trampled a small boy unlucky enough to get caught in front of them during a getaway. As Gresham's soft, deep voice detailed the atrocities, Cody felt his anger growing. It wasn't often that he thought about such abstract things as justice, law and order, and good and evil. Most of the time he just figured that he had a job to do and he did it as well as he could. But when he heard stories like the ones Gresham was telling him now, he knew there was such a thing as evil in the world, and it was up to men like him to oppose it.

"It's been a while since I've been around these parts much," the Ranger said to Gresham. "You reckon you could sort of show me around, quiet-like?"

"You mean assist in a civilian investigation?" The sergeant's voice took on a tone of mock horror as he asked the question. Then he grinned and said, "I'll be leading one of the regular cavalry patrols tomorrow up Limpia Canyon.

Why don't you meet us about half a mile east of here?
You'll be welcome to ride along."

"Won't Major Monroe hear about it?"

"You think the major hears anything the sergeants don't
want him to hear?" Gresham scoffed. He clapped Cody on
the back with a big hand. "I'll see you in the morning,
Ranger."

They had arrived at the hitching rail in front of the
headquarters building. Cody grinned at Gresham, swung
up in the saddle, and gave the sergeant a wave as he turned
the dun toward the settlement. He had been right in his first
impression of Gresham. As long as he could work with the
sergeant instead of Major Monroe, his mission had at least
a chance of success.

As Cody rode along the road at the edge of the parade
ground, he saw a buggy coming toward him from the direction of town. Two people were in the vehicle, and as the
buggy drew closer, Cody realized one of them was a woman. A damned attractive young woman, in fact. The Ranger
pulled the dun to the side of the road to give the buggy plenty of room to pass and noticed that a distinguished-looking
older man was handling the reins. The man didn't look any
too happy, and the girl's face, as she glanced at Cody when
they passed, was pale and full of worry.

Cody frowned thoughtfully as he leaned on the saddle
horn and watched the buggy proceed on toward the major's
office. He had no idea what business the older man and the
girl had with Monroe, but he silently wished them luck.
They'd need it in dealing with the major.

Continuing on his way, Cody rode back into town, wondering as he walked the dun down the street if Seth had
arrived yet. He didn't see the young Ranger on the board-
walks or in any of the buildings he passed, but that didn't
mean anything. Seth was probably around by now. They
had agreed not to make contact for a couple of days, just
to give each other a chance to work on their own.

After stabling the dun at a livery down the street, he took
a room in the Limpia Hotel—second floor front, to give
him a good view of the town. His bedroll, his rifle, and
his saddlebags were all he had in the way of belongings

besides what he was wearing, and when he had stowed them away in the hotel room, he paused to take a large watch out of the pocket in his jeans. He opened the catch on the turnip and glanced at the photograph of the pretty blond girl opposite the watch face. A quick twist on the ring holding the photo in place removed the picture from the watch case, exposing a hollow. Taking his Ranger badge from his pocket, he put it into the hiding place, which was exactly why he had bought the watch and had it modified in the first place. He didn't know who the girl was, but she was nice to look at so he had kept the picture.

He had decided on the way back into town that even though Seth was the one working undercover on this assignment, it wouldn't hurt for Cody to be discreet about his own status as a Ranger. Sheriff Randine knew who he was, of course, and so did several people at the fort, but if he could keep it from becoming general knowledge that a Ranger was poking around the area, it might help him catch up with Whittingham that much sooner. No need to put the outlaw on his guard. That was why he had unpinned his badge after leaving the fort. His vest was reversible and double-layered, too, so that he could even conceal the pinholes from the badge, but he didn't think it was necessary to go that far this time.

With his badge safely cached inside the special watch, Cody went back downstairs to get some supper. According to the desk clerk, the Limpia's own dining room was the best place in town to eat. That was the answer Cody would've expected from him, but he decided to give the place a try anyway.

The dining room was in a separate, adjacent building, connected to the Limpia's lobby by a covered walkway. A spacious, airy room with large windows, it had a lunch counter running along the back wall while tables covered with red-and-white checked cloths took up the rest of the space. Cody took a seat at one of the tables where he could keep an eye on the walkway, the street door, and the street itself through those big windows. The hour was still a bit early, and the dining room was only half full.

When a plump, pretty waitress came to his table, he ordered steak, potatoes with gravy, black-eyed peas, and cantaloupe. She smiled at him and went back to the kitchen, and Cody leaned back in his chair to wait for the food. Other than meeting Rufe Gresham, it had not been a particularly productive day, but Cody told himself not to be impatient. It might take a long time to run Barry Whittingham to ground.

Long time or not, though, he was going to do it. Cody was dead sure of that.

He sat up a little straighter as movement on the street outside caught his eye. The buggy he had seen approaching the fort earlier pulled up in front of the hotel, and the distinguished-looking gentleman got down from the vehicle, then turned to assist the lady. Cody got a better look at her as she stepped down from the buggy, and he saw that she was every bit as pretty as his first impression had told him she was. She was a little thing, probably not more than five feet tall, and though she was slender, the curves of her body were pronounced enough to tell the Ranger that she was full-grown. She wore a blue traveling outfit and a blue hat, and her thick, dark-brown hair was tucked up underneath the hat.

Cody passed a pleasant few seconds wondering what she'd look like with that hair taken down and loose so that it flowed around her pretty face and down her back. The thought brought a smile to his lips.

By that time the older man and the girl had disappeared from his view—going into the hotel, no doubt. Cody still wondered what they'd been doing at the fort, and he speculated also on the relationship between the two of them. Father and daughter? Uncle and niece? Lovers, maybe . . . ?

He shook his head. None of his business.

The waitress distracted him from those thoughts a moment later by appearing with a huge platter of food. Cody's stomach reminded him it had been a long time since the quick meal he and Seth had shared earlier on the trail, so with a grin and a "Thanks, ma'am" for the waitress, the Ranger picked up his knife and fork and dug in.

He had about half his steak eaten when the sound of

footfalls from the walkway between the hotel and the dining room made him look up.

The girl in the blue dress was coming toward him, accompanied by the silver-haired older man.

At first Cody thought that his impression was surely wrong. They were simply coming into the dining room to get some supper, he told himself, not to see him. But as they approached, he read determination in the girl's eyes and the set of her chin, and the man was frowning worriedly. Something was wrong, Cody sensed, and in a second he was going to be right in the middle of it.

Putting down his silverware and scraping his chair back, Cody stood up as the girl marched directly to his table. "Mr. Cody?" she asked firmly, tipping her head back to look up at him.

Her eyes dropped momentarily to his chin, and Cody realized he had dribbled some gravy. He quickly dabbed it off with his napkin, then said, "That's right, ma'am. What can I do for you?"

"We'd like to talk to you, if we may. Might we sit down?"

"Sure thing." Cody reached for one of the other chairs and pulled it out for her. "I'd be glad to have you folks join me."

The older man interrupted, "If you don't mind, Leigh, we agreed that I'll handle the talking." He smiled at Cody, but his eyes stayed hard and cautious as he extended his hand and went on, "My name is Josiah Breedlove, sir."

Cody shook the man's hand and then waved him into one of the other chairs. "Sit down, Mr. Breedlove. It appears you know who I am."

"We know you're a Texas Ranger," said the girl called Leigh.

As he sat down again, Cody said quietly, "I'd appreciate it if you'd sort of keep that under your hat, ma'am—though I see you're not wearing one now."

As a matter of fact, she had indeed removed the small blue hat, but her hair was still piled atop her head in an elaborate arrangement of curls. She frowned slightly in puzzlement at Cody's comment, then said, "I didn't know your identity was supposed to be a secret. Major Monroe out at the fort suggested that we talk to you. The clerk at the desk pointed you out to us," she added.

Cody nodded, then explained, "Well, I've decided not to wear my badge for a while. It's not really a secret, but I don't want to make a fuss about it, either."

"Just as long as we're sure that you're the right man," Breedlove said.

A smile tugged at Cody's lips. "I reckon that depends on what you folks want from me."

Leigh started to say something, but Breedlove held up a hand to stop her. "I'm an attorney from Dallas, Mr. Cody," he said. "I represent the interests of this young lady, who is Miss Leigh Gilmore, also from Dallas."

Cody nodded to her. "Pleased to meet you, ma'am." Lawyer and client was one relationship he hadn't considered when he was thinking about them earlier. For some reason he was glad the connection between them was just business.

Breedlove was a handsome, smooth-faced man starting to run a little to jowls, and everything about him from his shoes to his suit to the fancy stickpin he wore in his cravat said that he had money. There was an air of unease about him, though, as if he knew he was out of place here on the frontier. He laced his fingers together on the tabletop and said, "We have a business proposition for you, Mr. Cody."

The Ranger's eyes narrowed. "I'm paid by the state of Texas," he said, "and I'm not looking to go to work for anybody else, Mr. Breedlove."

"No, no, you misunderstand. We don't want to hire you away from the—from your present employer. We just have a very important job you might be able to handle in conjunction with your current assignment."

"It doesn't work that way," Cody said with a shake of his head. "Sorry I've got to turn you down without even hearing you out, but . . ."

Leigh Gilmore had been chewing her bottom lip, obviously having a hard time restraining herself while Breedlove talked to Cody. Now she couldn't hold her emotions back any longer. She leaned forward and said urgently, "It's my sister, Mr. Cody. She's gone, and you've got to help us find her!"

Cody blinked in surprise. He hadn't expected something like that. "Your sister?" he repeated.

"That's right." The attorney tried to hush Leigh again, but she hurried on, unwilling to be stopped now. "She was traveling on a stagecoach, going to visit some relatives of ours in El Paso, when her coach was stopped and held up by a gang of bandits. They . . . they kidnapped her, Mr. Cody. They took her with them when they rode off into the mountains, and poor Sara hasn't been seen or heard from since. You've got to help us find her!"

Cody leaned back in his chair, his mouth taut and his eyes bleak now. Nine times out of ten, a woman was safe anywhere in the West. Even the worst thief and killer would usually respect a woman and not dare to molest her. That didn't hold true for hostile Indians, who operated under a different set of rules, and there was a small percentage of white men who were even worse. Obviously Sara Gilmore had fallen into the hands of such men, and it was likely she was dead by now, used up and cast aside by her captors.

But how was he going to tell that to the sweet-faced young woman sitting across the table from him?

"Look, Miss Gilmore," he began, "I'm truly sorry about your sister, but I'm not sure I can help you. How long ago did this happen?"

"It's been two months since Sara was abducted."

"Two months is a long time, especially out here. This is hard country, Miss Gilmore, and lots of things can happen—"

Leigh cut in, "You're trying to say that Sara's probably dead, aren't you?"

Cody sighed heavily. "I think you've got to consider that a possibility. The men who took her—"

"No!" Leigh interrupted again, her voice rising so that some of the other diners glanced over curiously at Cody's table. "That's simply not possible," she insisted. "I'd know it if Sara was dead. She's alive, Mr. Cody, and I have to help her."

Cody looked at Leigh's pale, drawn, but still lovely face and reflected that he had rarely heard such conviction in a person's voice. She just wasn't going to let herself believe that her sister might not be alive.

Breedlove reached over and patted his client's arm, trying to calm her. "Please, Leigh," he said. "Getting upset isn't going to do any good. That's why I wanted you to let me handle this, why I insisted that I come along when you got the idea of traveling all the way out here to this godforsaken wilderness. . . ."

The lawyer was the second person today who had called this part of West Texas godforsaken. Breedlove and Major Monroe had to be blinded by their own prejudices, Cody thought. This was rugged country, sure, but it had its own wild, stark beauty. Given Breedlove's attitude, the man was probably collecting a hefty fee just for coming out here.

Leigh started to cry. Cody grimaced and pushed his plate aside. So much for getting back to his meal later. His appetite was gone now, chased away by the turmoil and pain the girl was going through. He was searching his mind for something to say, looking for some way to calm her down and make her see how hopeless it was, when Leigh said between sobs, "I wish I were a man! I'd get a gun and find that bastard Whittingham myself!"

Cody sat up straighter. "What did you say?" he asked sharply.

Leigh's hand went to her mouth. "Oh! I'm so sorry. I can't believe I said that. I wasn't brought up to curse. Mama would be so upset—"

Cody reached across the table and caught her other hand. "I mean about Whittingham," he said.

Breedlove supplied the answer. "The stage line told us that the man leading the gang that held up Sara's coach was tentatively identified as someone named Barry Whittingham. I understand from talking to Major Monroe that Whittingham is some sort of famous desperado around here."

"He's getting to be," Cody said, scowling. He was angry with himself. He should have seen this development coming. His brain must be slowing down in his old age, he told himself disgustedly.

"That's why we came looking for you," Breedlove explained with a sigh. "Major Monroe told us you were trying to find this fellow Whittingham and his cohorts."

"That's why I'm here, all right," Cody confirmed.

Leigh swallowed the last of her sniffles, and hope began shining in her eyes again. "Then you can find Sara when you find Whittingham."

"Maybe."

"And you can take me with you."

The bold suggestion surprised both Cody and Breedlove. The Ranger just stared across the table at her; Breedlove exclaimed, "Leigh! You can't be serious! It's bad enough you dragged both of us out here—"

"I can help you, Mr. Cody," Leigh said, ignoring the attorney. "I can help you find Sara, and when I do, you'll find that outlaw, too."

Cody shook his head. "Can't do that, Miss Gilmore. I reckon if you think about it, you'll understand why."

"But I don't understand at all!" Leigh was beginning to get angry now, and Cody wished they were having this discussion somewhere in private. It looked like discretion just wasn't something that was going to be possible on this assignment.

"Be reasonable, Leigh—" Breedlove began, but the girl cut him off again.

"I'm tired of being reasonable!" she snapped. "I'm tired of sitting in Dallas and hoping and praying that Sara will be all right. I didn't come all the way out here to sit and wait some more, Mr. Cody!"

Anger had put some color back in her cheeks, and Cody wanted to tell her she was even more lovely when she was mad. He didn't, though. Judging from her expression, she might well bite him if he said anything like that. Anyway, he had more important things to worry about at the moment.

"Listen, Miss Gilmore," he said, "if I run across your sister while I'm looking for Whittingham, I'll do everything in my power to help her. You've got my word on that, and Sam Cody keeps his word. But I'm damned if I'll let you traipse off out there into the mountains with me!

I'll have more to worry about than keeping you alive."

For a second he thought she was going to slap him or kick him, and it wouldn't have changed his mind if she did. But then she got control of herself with a visible effort, and after taking a deep breath, she cast her eyes down and said in a quiet voice, "You're right, of course. I . . . I wasn't thinking straight."

"Well, I reckon you're just upset," Cody said, "and you've got every reason to be."

She looked up at him again. "Do you really think there's a chance my sister could be alive, Mr. Cody?"

"There's always a chance," he replied without hesitation. A mighty slim chance in this case, he thought, but still a chance.

"Well, I'm certainly glad that's settled," Breedlove said with another sigh. "We will, of course, see that you're suitably recompensed for any efforts on our behalf, Mr. Cody."

The Ranger shook his head. "Told you, I draw my pay from the state of Texas."

"But surely it would be acceptable for you to—"

"Nope."

Breedlove just shook his head and looked at Cody as if the big man were some strange, unknown species. "Very well, Mr. Cody," he said. "Whatever you want."

Cody dropped a bill on the table to cover his meal and pushed his chair back. "If you folks'll excuse me, what I want right now is a drink." He picked up his hat from the floor beside his chair and got to his feet. "Good evening, ma'am. Mr. Breedlove. Reckon I'll be seeing you around."

Leigh's voice stopped him as he started to turn away. "Mr. Cody . . . thank you. I know you'll try to help."

Cody just nodded, gave her a half smile, and walked out of the dining room. He went through the lobby of the hotel and stepped out onto the street. Pausing there, he looked up at the sky. Dusk had settled in, and stars were beginning to twinkle into life in the darkening heavens.

"Barry, old hoss," Cody muttered to himself, thinking about the Englishman and Sara Gilmore, "when you crossed the line, you sure as hell went all the way!"

CHAPTER
5
||||||||||||||||||||||||||||||| ||||||||||||||||||||||||||||||

Knowing that cavalry patrols usually left the fort a little after dawn, Cody turned in early and set his mental clock to rouse him before sunup. He had trouble dropping off to sleep, though; he kept thinking about Leigh Gilmore and her plea for him to find her missing sister. Cody didn't hold out much hope that Sara Gilmore was still alive. And even if she was, she wouldn't be the same sister Leigh remembered. The things she'd have gone through by now would have changed her irrevocably.

Cody finally dozed off, and he was up again before dawn, as planned. The lack of sleep and the hard ride from the Rio Grande to the Davis Mountains had taken a toll on him. It took several cups of coffee in a café down the street from the hotel, plus a sizable plate of ham, eggs, and peppers, before the weariness in him began to ease. The Mexican who ran the place knew how to cook and didn't spare the jalapeños. Cody was grateful for that.

Breakfast taken care of, Cody reclaimed the dun from the livery stable just as the sun was starting to peek over the eastern horizon. It seemed to rise right out of the depths of Limpia Canyon. That was the way Sergeant Gresham's patrol would be riding today, and Cody squinted his eyes against the glare of the red orb as he rode out of town to keep his rendezvous with the troopers.

A mounted patrol kicked up a considerable amount of dust, so when Cody judged that he had covered the required distance, he stopped, hipped around in the saddle, and surveyed the sky to make sure there was no haze to indicate he had already missed the cavalrymen. The air was clear, so he drew the dun into the shade of a pine tree at the edge of the trail and settled down to wait for them.

It wasn't a long wait. Within a quarter of an hour Cody spotted the plume of dust rising into the morning sky to the west, and a few minutes after that he could make out the blue-uniformed figures riding at the base of it. As the troopers approached, the Ranger eased the dun out into the trail again and held up a hand in greeting to Sergeant Gresham.

The veteran buffalo soldier reined in and grinned at him. "Morning. You ready to take a look around?"

Cody nodded, all vestiges of tiredness gone now. He was alert and anxious to get started. "I appreciate this, Sergeant," he said.

Gresham motioned for Cody to bring the dun alongside his cavalry mount, and as the Ranger was doing so, Gresham turned in his saddle and said to the troopers behind him, "This gent's going to ride along with us for a while today, boys. He's a friend of mine, and I don't reckon Major Monroe has to know anything about this. That all right with you?"

The question drew smiles and nods from the company of black troopers, all of whom obviously respected their sergeant. Gresham turned around again and waved the group forward, Cody riding alongside as the noncom got his horse moving.

For pretty country the canyon they rode down that morning was hard to beat. Limpia Creek, which gave the place its name, ran through the canyon on its way to join Paisano Creek, a tributary of the Pecos River. Rugged upthrusts of rock shouldered their way along the sides of the canyon, but between those bluffs were areas of thick grass and wildflowers. Bluebonnets, Indian paintbrush, mountain laurel, and sunflowers all grew in profusion. The ridges were topped by oak and pine trees, and cottonwoods grew along the stream itself. Cody lost count of the number of deer he saw drinking at the creek and then bounding off as the riders approached. It was easy to see why the Apaches had fought for this land against the encroachment of first the Comanches and then the white man. Might have been better, Cody thought sometimes, if everybody had just left them alone with the mountains and the canyons.

It didn't do any good to look back, though. Looking over at Gresham, Cody asked, "Is there much Indian trouble hereabouts?"

"Not these days," replied the sergeant with a shake of his head. "Most of the Apaches have gone down into Mexico, and the Comanches are pulling back to the Staked Plains and the Panhandle. They still fight each other every now and then, and the outlying ranchers always have to be on the lookout for an occasional raiding party, but it's not like it was when we came here back in sixty-seven."

"I figure there'll be renegades and pockets of resistance for a long time," Cody commented.

"Amen to that. We won't have these mountains cleaned out of all the troublemakers for years." Gresham swept a big hand at the peaks rising all around them. "Maybe never, in country like this."

"Has Whittingham pulled any jobs up this way?"

"This is where he hit one of the supply trains," Gresham replied with a nod. He gestured toward the largest peak to the north and went on, "The gang took off toward Star Mountain there, and by the time the survivors got to the fort and we got a troop back out here, the trail was nearly gone. We followed the tracks a little way, but then they petered out on the rocks."

Cody sighed. His work was cut out for him, all right. Too many hiding places, too easy to lose any pursuit . . . It was no wonder that Sheriff Randine and Major Monroe's cavalry hadn't been able to run Whittingham to earth. Now the job had been handed to him, and he had to wonder if he was gnawing off a bigger hunk than he could chew.

But he'd never turned down an assignment yet, and damned if he was going to start now. He'd find Barry Whittingham or die trying—and in the meantime, it was a downright gorgeous day.

Seth Williams rolled over and groaned. If this wasn't the worst day of his life, he thought, he sure as hell didn't want to remember the one that was. There had been times in the past when his friend and fellow Ranger Alan Northrup had told him he looked like he'd been rode hard and put up wet, but that didn't even come close to describing the way Seth felt right now.

He tried to pry his eyes open again. The first time he'd attempted that, sunlight struck them like the blow of a sledgehammer and sent pain boring all the way through his head to explode out the back of his skull. That was what it felt like, anyway, and Seth didn't want that to happen again. He got a hand up to shade his face as he forced his eyelids apart. The muscles of his arm felt bloated and slow to obey his commands.

There. His eyes were open. He couldn't see anything except his trembling palm, but that was a start. Encouraged, he quickly lifted his head to look around.

Bad mistake, he discovered an instant later. His stomach lurched, every muscle in his body gave a twitch, and he found himself lying on his side, dry-heaving onto a dirt floor. He shook all over for a long moment until the spasms began to subside.

"Ohhhhh . . ." The agonized groan came from some-where nearby.

Getting his hands underneath him, Seth slowly—very slowly—pushed himself into a sitting position. His head pounded and the room spun dizzily around him as he adjusted to this new bearing. The slightest movement of his head set off more bells and whistles of misery.

Keeping himself as still as possible, moving nothing but his eyes, Seth looked at his surroundings.

He was in a shack somewhere. Between him and the door-way sprawled the forms of Amos Bower and Tug Mitchell, the two former cowhands and would-be desperadoes he'd fallen in with the day before. Seth recognized them right away, but for some reason he couldn't remember how the three of them had gotten here. This was the next morning, wasn't it? Suddenly, he couldn't be sure. And where the hell *was* here, anyway?

There was no door in the entrance, though the presence of hinges testified that there had been at one time. Likewise, the windows that Seth could see were also empty. The shack was made of planks nailed together haphazardly so that there were large gaps between some of them. Built as it was, the building wouldn't keep out any kind of varmint, certainly not scorpions and snakes.

And he had evidently spent the night here, oblivious to any creatures that might have curled up with him. He was damned lucky he hadn't been bitten by a rattler, he thought.

Amos and Tug were stirring around and making pained noises now, much as Seth had done a few moments earlier. All three of them were badly hung over, the young Ranger realized. This was about the worst headache he'd ever had—certainly the worst one from drinking. A few details of the night before were starting to come back to him now, and they weren't pretty.

Along with Amos and Tug, he had helped polish off that bottle of rotgut at the Wild Rose Saloon; then Amos had signaled little Augie, the proprietor, for another. Seth vaguely remembered protesting that maybe they'd had enough, but his two companions had overruled him. Wanting to stay on their good side, he had grinned and gone along with them.

Sometime during the evening either Amos or Tug—Seth wasn't sure which, but he knew for damn certain it hadn't been him—had come up with the idea of having a drink or two in every saloon in town. Seth had agreed. By then he was too drunk to argue.

Not many young men out here on the frontier reached even his tender age without taking a drink or two of whiskey. Generally Seth preferred a nice, cold beer, but he could handle hard liquor all right, too. At least he had always thought so. Now he wasn't so sure. He didn't like the way the events of the previous night were so damn blurry in his memory, and he sure didn't like the way he felt right now.

His right hand went to the broad leather belt at his waist. A pocket was stitched to the back side of the belt, just to the right of the big buckle. He'd had that pocket put there by a saddlemaker in Del Rio so that he could hide his Ranger badge if he ever worked undercover again. Cody had that

trick watch of his, and Seth wanted a good hiding place, too.
This job was the first time he'd had a chance to use it, and
he wanted to make sure now the badge was still there.

A surge of relief went through him as he felt the symbol
of the Rangers tucked safely away in the hidden pocket. He
had been fairly certain it'd still be there. If Amos or Tug had
discovered he was a Ranger, after telling him of their plans
to become outlaws, they wouldn't be lying here coming to
in the same hovel. They'd have probably either lit out for
the tall and uncut—or slit his throat and left him in a ditch
somewhere.

Seth's head and stomach had settled down a little now,
and he found that he could get to his feet if he was careful.
As he stumbled past the two cowhands, intent on getting
outside so that he could give back to the earth some of that
whiskey he'd drunk the night before, Amos and Tug sat up
shakily and peered around with the befuddled look of owls
caught out in the daylight.

Seth went outside and leaned on the wall of the shack as
he fumbled with his pants, hoping that the place wouldn't
collapse from his putting too much weight on it. Amos and
Tug joined him a moment later, staggering just as Seth had.
"Lord, my head hurts!" Amos said thickly, and Tug just
grunted his agreement.

After a moment Amos started to laugh, and he declared,
"We really put away the booze last night, didn't we?"

"How much did we drink?" Seth asked.

"Don't know, but I reckon there's still a few bottles left
in town. Want to go hunt 'em up? Or'd you rather get some
breakfast?"

The thought of food made Seth's stomach do flip-flops
again, and from the way Tug moaned and bent over, he
was feeling the same way. Some hair of the dog was the
most appealing alternative, but Seth knew that wouldn't
accomplish anything. He had to shake this hangover.

"Reckon we'd better . . . oh, God . . . get somethin' to
eat," he muttered.

"Yeah," Tug added, his normally boisterous voice weak
now, "just as long as I don't have to look at what I'm
eatin'."

Amos led the way from the shack. "Come on, boys. We got a big day ahead of us. Today's the day we start makin' our reputation as owlhoots."

That comment drove some more of the cobwebs away from Seth's brain. Obviously Amos and Tug had completely accepted him as one of them. If they were right and they could locate Barry Whittingham, that'd be the quickest and best way for Seth to infiltrate the Englishman's gang. Once he had done that, it'd be just a matter of secretly getting in touch with Cody and setting up some kind of trap for the bandits.

Seth glanced back over his shoulder at the shack. It sat by itself on the edge of Fort Davis, the legacy of an early settler who had abandoned it—or been killed—years earlier. Amos and Tug had apparently taken it over and claimed it as their own. Their horses were kept in the livery stable, along with Seth's, and the young Ranger remembered their saying something about how paying for the upkeep of the animals had taken just about all of the wages they had left from their last job as cowpunchers. They had enough money for some booze and a little food, and that was all. If it had been up to Seth, he'd have bunked in the stable with the horses, but evidently Amos and Tug didn't care for that idea. They fancied themselves above sleeping in a pile of hay.

So they had settled down in the abandoned shack instead. That was the wrong choice as far as Seth was concerned, but nobody had asked his opinion.

The hour was late and the sun was well up. Most folks had already eaten breakfast, so the café where the three young men settled down at a table was mostly empty. The sturdy Mexican man behind the counter poured cups of strong black coffee for them, smiled sympathetically at the pale faces and shaky hands, and promised that he had just the thing to fix them up. He retreated to the kitchen and emerged a bit later with a seemingly endless supply of food. Flapjacks, scrambled eggs, hashed brown potatoes, thick slices of bacon and ham. Seth looked at all of it, felt like a bucking bronco had taken up residence in his stomach and was trying to sunfish its way up his gullet, and damn near passed out face first in a pitcher full of syrup.

"Eat!" boomed the café owner, and he was right. After Seth had forced himself to choke down some food, he found his appetite returning. In fact, it came back with a vengeance, and he put away more of the meal than he would have thought possible a few minutes earlier.

He could tell by looking at Amos and Tug that they felt better, too. All three of them got refills on their coffee, then sat back and sighed. It was good to feel human again.

Tug took out a sack of makin's and started building a quirly. Seth shook his head when Tug offered him the tobacco, as did Amos. With a grin that was only a little shaky Seth asked, "Well, men, what now?"

"Reckon we'd better go check our horses," Amos said. "We'll be needin' 'em pretty soon."

Seth nodded. If they were going to ride into the mountains in search of Barry Whittingham today, they'd indeed need their horses.

They finished off their coffee, and Seth paid for the meal for all three of them. Amos and Tug thanked him heartily for his generosity, and then they went down the street to the livery stable.

Seth's horse was demonstrably glad to see him this morning, whickering at him and nuzzling his palm with its nose. The young Ranger patted the animal on the neck, then looked over at one of the other stalls to see that Amos and Tug were saddling their mounts.

"Come on, Seth, get ready to ride," Amos told him. "We got things to do."

"Sure," Seth said, reaching for the saddle blanket hanging over the side of the stall. He understood that Amos and Tug wouldn't want to say anything too specific about their plans while they were in here, not while the stable owner was nearby in his office.

All three of them had paid in advance, so there was no more business to conduct before they led their mounts outside. Seth expected them to swing up into the saddles right away, but instead Amos and Tug began leading their horses down the street. He fell in beside them. His first impulse was to urge them to mount up so that they could get into the mountains and begin looking for Whittingham that much sooner, but he kept silent, letting the other two young men take the lead. After all, this was their plan; he had merely been invited to come along with them.

"Let's tie 'em up here," Amos suggested as they drew even with a hitching post. He flipped the reins of his horse around the rail that had been split from a pine log. Tug followed suit, and with a frown of puzzlement, so did Seth.

"I thought we were headin' out of town to look for Whittingham," Seth said in a hushed voice.

"Pretty soon," Amos said. He slipped his Colt out of its holster and spun the cylinder, checking the loads. Tug did likewise. Both young men sheathed their guns and started walking across the street, toward the building opposite the hitching post.

It was a bank, Seth saw as he fell in beside them, hurrying to keep up with their long-legged strides. His stomach, which had finally settled down and felt contentedly full, now began doing dances again. He didn't like the looks of this, didn't like it at all. "What's going on, fellas?" he asked.

"Shoot," Tug replied with a grin, "you don't 'spect a feller like Whittingham'd take us on lest we'd proved ourselves, do you?"

"Yeah," Amos added, "we're goin' to rob us a bank to show him we got what it takes to be in his gang. You're comin' along with us, ain't you? We figured you understood."

Seth was stunned. Maybe he should have seen this coming, he thought, but he'd had no inkling of what Amos and Tug were really up to. His mind was a whirl of contradictory thoughts and emotions.

As a Ranger, he was supposed to prevent lawbreaking if possible, but if he stopped Amos and Tug from robbing the bank, then his best lead to Whittingham—his only lead so far—would go up in smoke.

Abruptly, he came to the only decision he could. He'd go along with them and try to prevent anybody from getting hurt during the holdup. Cody would probably have a few things to say about this later, not to mention Captain

Vickery if he found out, but Seth would have to deal with that when the time came.

Those thoughts took only a second of time. Forcing his mouth into a smile, Seth said emphatically, "Hell, yes, I'm comin' along. Sounds like a damn fine idea to me."

The threesome strode across the street side by side, and their spurred bootheels rang on the planks of the board-walk as they stepped up onto it. Quite a few pedestrians were around this morning, but none were paying any spe-cial attention to the three young men. Amos reached out, grasped the doorknob, and opened the front door of the bank.

Again, no one seemed to notice them as they went inside. Seth quickly assessed the scene. Over at the counter along the side of the room two tellers were currently working; the third window was closed. A couple of men, bank officers most likely, were seated at desks in the rear of the room in an area behind a low railing, their heads bent over papers spread out on their desks. A couple of customers were in line at each of the open teller's windows, but they paid no heed to the new arrivals.

But suddenly everybody noticed them when Amos jerked his gun from its holster, brandished it around the room, and called in a loud voice, "Nobody move! This is a holdup!" One woman stared at them and opened her mouth to scream, but Amos jerked the muzzle of the Colt toward her and ordered quickly, "No yellin', lady!"

Tug pulled a burlap bag from under his short jacket and headed for the tellers. "Fill it up, boys!" he demand-ed. He tossed the bag to the first of the bank employees, at the same time drawing his own gun and adding its menace.

Amos glanced over at Seth, who was watching grim faced, and hissed, "Help me out here, dammit!"

"Oh, yeah," Seth mumbled. He pulled his gun and helped Amos cover the employees and the customers. A strange, light-headed feeling of wrongness washed over him. He had never done anything like this before. Forcing himself to glare at the men at the desks, who had stood up and raised their hands over their heads, he told them, "You fellas just stand still and don't try anythin'." Then he glanced at the patrons. "That goes for all of you!"

The first teller had the bag partially filled with bills from his cash drawer by now, and he handed it across to the other teller in response to gestures from Tug's gun. The second man began emptying his own cash drawer.

Seth's pulse pounded heavily in his head. A part of his mind couldn't believe he was actually doing this. Time seemed to slow down for him, and it took forever for the second teller to fill up the bag with loot. Every detail burned itself into Seth's brain, from the faint smell of bay rum coming from one of the bank officers to the motes of dust dancing merrily in a shaft of sunlight coming through the big front window of the bank.

So far everything had gone smoothly, even though this was the first bank robbery any of the three young men had ever attempted. Seth kept an eye on the window, hoping that no one would come into the bank, see what was going on, and raise the alarm. If everything kept rolling along like this, maybe they could get away from the bank and out of town without any shooting or anybody getting hurt.

He'd take personal responsibility for the return of the bank's money, he promised himself. He'd recover the loot if possible, and if not, then he'd pay it back, no matter if it took every cent of his Ranger salary for the next twenty years—or even longer.

"Let's go," Tug said, turning away from the tellers and triumphantly lifting the bag stuffed with money.

Amos started backing toward the door and jerked his head to indicate that Seth should do likewise. "Nobody raise a ruckus in here till we're good and gone," he warned. "If you do, there'll be shootin', I can promise you that."

One of the bank officers, a stout, florid-faced man, couldn't stand it any longer. He said furiously, "You're nothing but a goddamned thief!"

Amos grinned. "Well, sir, I reckon you're right, and I ain't never shot a man yet for tellin' the truth. But I wouldn't push it if I was you."

The man paled.

Seth was at the door now. He reached behind him, found

the knob, and twisted it. As soon as they were outside, he thought, they could holster their guns, turn, and run across the street to their horses. The people in the bank would raise the alarm, of course, but with any luck he and Amos and Tug would be galloping down the street out of pistol range within a matter of seconds.

The moment he stepped out onto the boardwalk Seth heard the footfalls, but it was too late to change course. He collided with the man who had been striding quickly along the boardwalk.

"Watch it, son—"

The man's annoyed voice broke off sharply as Seth whipped his head around and stared into his face. He was a short, thick-bodied man with a graying beard—and the star of the county sheriff was pinned to his vest.

"Son of a bitch!" Sheriff Philo Randine yelled at the sight of the gun in Seth's hand. Amos and Tug were spilling onto the boardwalk now, both of them armed and an obviously full burlap bag clutched tightly in Tug's other hand. It didn't take a genius to figure out what the sheriff had literally bumped into. Randine grabbed for the pistol on his hip as he shouted, "Drop those guns!"

Seth saw Amos and Tug swiveling around, panic on their faces as they brought their guns to bear on the sheriff. Sheer desperation was about to squeeze those triggers and plow lead into the lawman unless Seth could do something to stop it.

He leapt forward, putting himself between the outlaws and Randine. The sheriff had cleared leather, and the barrel of his revolver was tipping up. Seth lashed out, cracking the barrel of his own Colt across Randine's wrist. The sheriff let out a howl of pain as his hand opened and the gun slipped from suddenly numb fingers. Before the gun had even hit the ground, Seth's other hand, balled into a tight fist, smashed into Randine's jaw. The sheriff went down, half on the boardwalk and half off, stunned by the blow.

"Get out of here!" Seth shouted to Amos and Tug, and they seized the opportunity to bound past him and sprint across the street to the horses. Passersby were starting to realize that something was wrong, even though no one else had emerged from the bank yet and the encounter with the sheriff had taken only a couple of seconds.

Taking just enough time to kick Randine's pistol away, sending it spinning down the boardwalk, Seth then followed Amos and Tug. Amos had also untied Seth's horse, which was a little skittish from the sudden commotion, and Seth jammed his Colt back in its holster and sprang for the saddle, grabbing the horn and throwing a leg over the back of the horse. The second his weight settled, he spurred the horse into motion. It pounded down the street, right behind the mounts of Amos and Tug.

Glancing back over his shoulder, Seth saw Sheriff Randine scrambling to his feet, his wits apparently restored. Bystanders were running up to him and shouting questions, and the people from the bank had come out and added their noise to the tumult. Randine shoved them aside, spotted his gun, and scooped up the weapon.

The gun in Randine's hand belched flame and smoke and lead. Slugs whined over Seth's head, too close for comfort. The sheriff was a good shot. But the three fleeing riders were rapidly putting themselves out of range—and just to be on the safe side, the young Ranger leaned forward over his horse's neck to present a smaller target.

Seth grimaced as he hung on for dear life and put the horse into a tight turn, following closely behind the pounding hooves of the other horses. He sure hoped this undercover gamble paid off before he wound up dead.

CHAPTER
6

The morning passed quietly as the cavalry patrol rode far up Limpia Canyon and then turned around to head back to the fort. Cody, Sergeant Gresham, and the troopers had encountered a couple of freighters and a few lone riders on the canyon trail, but there had been no sign of trouble from either Indians or desperadoes. If he hadn't known better, Cody would have said that this part of the country was downright peaceful.

The heat of the day was building as the patrol neared the fort. Gresham took off his campaign cap, wiped sweat off his forehead with the sleeve of his blue-woolen uniform tunic, and asked Cody, "What are you going to do now?"

"Don't know for sure," Cody replied with a shake of his head. "I didn't expect to have Whittingham and his gang handed to me on a silver platter. I reckon I'll spend a few days riding some of those trails you told me about."

During their time together this morning, Gresham had refreshed Cody's memory concerning the trails that ran through the mountains. Now he said, "You be careful up there. A man alone makes a tempting target for renegades—both kinds."

Cody nodded. "I'll keep my eyes open, don't worry about that." He angled the dun to the side, knowing that they'd soon be back within sight of the fort and not wanting Gresham to get in trouble with Major Monroe for letting the Ranger accompany the patrol. "I'll be seeing you," he said with a wave to the sergeant.

The dun hadn't been challenged all day, and his reserves of strength were great enough that he was a bit frisky on the way back to the settlement. Cody let him have his head and run for several hundred yards. He had just pulled the dun back to a walk when he noticed a group of riders coming rapidly toward him from the direction of town.

When a few moments had passed and the gap between Cody and the riders had shrunk, he recognized the man leading them as Sheriff Randine. The sheriff's bearded face looked grim and angry.

Cody reined in and let the posse come up to him—for he had no doubt that that was what the men were. All of them were armed, and in addition to their guns they wore the same expression as the sheriff. Randine pulled his own mount to a stop and demanded, "Where've you been?"

Cody didn't care for the lawman's tone of voice, but he made allowances for the fact that Randine was obviously quite upset about something. He noticed that the sheriff had a bandage tightly wrapped around his right wrist so that he was handling the reins a little awkwardly with his left hand.

"Been out for a ride, just taking a look around," Cody replied. "What's happened, Sheriff?"

Randine ignored Cody's question and asked another of his own. "Did you see three men riding hell for leather away from town?"

Cody shook his head. "Nope."

"Damn it! I know they came this way. Saw 'em with my own eyes."

"I was up Limpia Canyon way," Cody said. "Could be they turned off on another trail and headed either north or south."

Randine scowled and nodded. "North'd be my guess. Country's more rugged that way, more places to hide."

The Ranger felt his pulse quicken slightly as he thought about the implications of this encounter. "What did these three hombres do? Rob the bank?"

The sheriff looked at him sharply. "How the hell'd you know that?"

"I know a posse when I see one," Cody told him. "And as mad as you men look, I figured it had to be something pretty bad that brought you out." He paused for a second, then asked, "Was it Whittingham and a couple of his bunch?"

Randine spat on the ground, his disgust all too evident. "No, they're a pair of local cowhands and some new friend of theirs who just rode in yesterday. Youngsters, all three of 'em. Probably fancy themselves big outlaws now." He snorted. "They're not hardly old enough to shave."

Cody knew the type: young hotheads out to make a name for themselves as badmen. Most of the time they were even more dangerous than veteran owlhoots because they were quick to panic and start shooting when anything went wrong.

"Anybody hurt?" he asked.

Randine held up his bandaged wrist. "One of 'em damn near broke my wrist. Hit me with his gun just as I was pulling iron, then knocked me down. They didn't wait around to do any shooting, though. Just jumped on their horses and lit a shuck out of town. I reckon we were real lucky nobody was hurt worse."

Cody shared that opinion. Some outlaws would have stayed around long enough to pump a couple of slugs into a fallen lawman, just on general principles.

One of the posse members spoke up. "We're wastin' time, Sheriff. Bower and Mitchell and that other fella are gettin' a good lead on us."

Randine turned to glare at the man. "I know that, Ben. We'll be riding in a second." He switched his attention back to Cody. "How about coming along with us?"

Cody hesitated. This incident was unrelated to the job that had brought him here, but his duties as a Ranger didn't end with that one assignment, either. If he could lend a hand to Randine and the posse, he was beholden to do so.

"Sure," he said, turning the dun to fall in alongside the sheriff. "Let's go."

As the riders got moving again, Cody asked Randine, "What did that gent say were the names of those bank robbers?"

"Amos Bower and Tug Mitchell," the sheriff supplied. "Those are the two I know. It was the other one, though, the one who just came into town, who walloped me. I'd sure like to get him in my sights."

"You don't know his name?" Cody still hoped this holdup might have some connection with Whittingham, however indirect.

"One of the boys said Bower and Mitchell and the other one were out drinking all over town last night. He saw 'em in one of the saloons and said Bower and Mitchell called the third man Seth."

It took all of Cody's willpower not to snap his head around and exclaim in surprise. Seth was a common enough name, of course, but the sheriff had referred to the third outlaw as a young man. . . .

"What'd he look like?"

"Why are you so interested in this hombre?" Randine demanded suspiciously.

Cody shrugged. "Thought I might be able to tell you who he is. I've spent a lot of time studying the bible."

He wasn't referring to the Good Book, and Randine would know that. The Ranger bible was a listing of all the known owlhoots in the state of Texas, complete with descriptions and the charges against them, and sometimes even photographs of the lawbreakers. Rangers committed to memory as much of the information as possible because they never knew when they might run into an outlaw.

But in this case, of course, Cody had a special interest in the identity of that third bank robber. As Randine described a slender youth with long, fair hair and wearing a buckskin shirt, Cody's suspicion grew into a grim certainty.

Seth Williams was the third man.

Cody would've bet his life that Seth would never turn outlaw. The youngster had sided him enough times before now for Cody to know that he was as straight as an arrow and already a fine Ranger despite his tender years. But the sheriff had been face to face with the third robber and had no reason to lie about what he had seen.

Suddenly Cody realized what Seth was probably up to. The big Ranger's mouth grew taut under his mustache. Seth was taking one hell of a risk, but by establishing himself as an outlaw and fleeing into the Davis Mountains, he stood a good chance of hooking up with Whittingham's outfit. It

was a brash, daring plan, Cody thought—just the kind that
would appeal to Seth.

"That sound familiar to you?" Randine asked, cutting
through the Ranger's bleak thoughts.

Cody shook his head. "No, I reckon not. He's probably
new to the game, like Bower and Mitchell."

"Those two were always honest enough waddies, as far
as I know," Randine said. "A little shiftless, maybe, and
quick to jump in every time there was a fight in one of the
saloons, but not real troublemakers. I guess they got tired
of that kind of life."

"Did they get away with much money?"

"Almost five thousand dollars, according to the president
of the bank. Not a bad payoff for their first job." Randine
scowled and went on harshly, "But not worth swinging at
the end of a rope, and that's liable to be what happens to
'em if they put up a fight. They'd be better off to ride back,
turn themselves in, and give that money back." He sighed.
"I don't expect it to happen, though."

Neither did Cody.

As the hot day wore on and the posse searched for some
sign of the robbers, Cody found himself in an odd position.
He couldn't ever remember hoping that some bank robbers
would get away—but he did this time. Seth's plan had no
chance of succeeding unless he and his companions could
stay on the loose until they found Whittingham's gang,
which Cody was sure was what they were planning. Barry
Whittingham's infamy would be a magnet to a couple of
young cowboys with glorious dreams of being outlaws.
Cody could follow their reasoning just as clearly as if
they had laid it all out before him. They had robbed the
bank to prove themselves so that they could point to that
achievement when they tried to join Whittingham's gang.

Maybe he was wrong; maybe Whittingham didn't enter
into their thinking at all. But he wouldn't have bet money on it.

As Whittingham had proven over the last few months, it
was next to impossible to track anyone through these sce-

nic but rugged mountains. However, Randine had sharper eyes than Cody would have given him credit for, and in midafternoon the sheriff spotted a torn piece of burlap on the limb of a mesquite tree.

"I reckon that's from the bag they had the money in," Randine said, pointing at the scrap of material.

Cody had seen it a couple of seconds before the sheriff did, but before he could even start to consider whether he ought to keep the discovery to himself, Randine had noticed it, too. Now Cody had no choice except to say, "I reckon we're on the right track, all right."

The posse penetrated deeper into the canyons between the upflung mountains. From time to time now Randine called a halt so that they could listen intently to the silence, hoping to hear it broken by the faint click of hooves on stone. So far that hadn't happened.

The riders turned into a small side canyon near a peak Randine identified as Timber Mountain, its name, Cody judged, coming from the thick growth of pines on its slopes. This canyon leading past it had less vegetation. The floor of the pass was rather sandy, and great heaps of boulders littered the sides. Timber Mountain rose sharply to the south, but the northern rim of the canyon was less imposing. The slope on that side climbed more gradually to a rocky ridge. The canyon twisted and turned, and sometimes the posse couldn't see more than a quarter of a mile ahead and behind them.

Cody's instincts didn't like this place. It'd be too easy for somebody to set a trap here. He said to Randine, "I'll be glad when we get to the other end of this canyon."

The sheriff took off his hat and wiped away some of the sweat that had collected inside it. "Yeah," he agreed uneasily, "I don't much like it, either, but it's the quickest way to get over to Madera Canyon. Lots of hiding places there if somebody's trying to go to ground."

Cody nodded and urged the dun ahead. With Randine riding beside him he rounded a bend and found himself facing a long straight stretch of canyon. About two hundred yards ahead, in plain sight, were three men on horseback.

"It's them!" Randine cried.

Cody knew instantly the sheriff was right. His keen eyes picked out Seth's horse, and he spotted the youngster's hat and buckskin shirt, too. The three fugitives must have heard Randine's shout, because they twisted in their saddles to stare back at the posse for a second, then kicked their mounts into a gallop.

Randine jerked his Winchester out of its saddle boot, threw the rifle to his shoulder, and snapped off a shot as soon as he had levered a shell into the chamber, grimacing at the pain the recoil caused in his injured wrist. The Winchester's crack echoed back from the walls of the canyon, as did the whine of the slug as it missed its mark and ricocheted off. "Come on!" Randine ordered, spurring his horse forward.

Cody hadn't drawn his rifle, but he put the dun into a gallop right beside the sheriff's mount. The posse thundered along behind them, shouting with anticipation now that the quarry had finally been sighted.

There was a bad feeling in Cody's gut. This could turn ugly in a hurry, and he wasn't sure how willing Randine or any of the other men would be to listen to him when he started trying to explain that Seth was a Ranger. He had to do whatever he could to try to prevent the young man from being hurt—or worse.

Seth and his two companions were riding down the canyon like bats out of Hades. Randine and Cody had surged out in front of the other posse members, so the men behind them couldn't cut loose with their own guns. That was to his advantage, Cody thought. At least there wasn't a hail of lead storming after the three youngsters.

The fugitives whipped around a corner, and when Cody and Randine rounded the same corner a few moments later, they saw Seth, Bower, and Mitchell angling toward the northern side of the canyon. Bower was waving his arm as if he was giving orders. For a second Cody thought they intended to try taking their horses up that slope. That would be suicidal; though it was nowhere as steep as the other side of the canyon, it was still too rugged for horses, especially horses carrying riders. They might make it a few yards, but then the mounts would fall, likely crushing their riders.

To his relief Cody saw them yank the horses to a stop and throw themselves out of their saddles. They scrambled several yards up the slope, then ducked behind the cover of a cluster of boulders. Six-guns began to pop.

"They're forting up!" Randine shouted as he reined in. "Watch yourself!"

Cody pulled the dun to a halt and quickly dismounted. He led the horse into the shelter of some rocks. Randine was doing the same with his horse, and the sheriff waved for his men to follow his example. Slugs whined wickedly as the posse hurriedly sought cover.

Crouching behind a boulder next to Cody, Randine let out a bitter curse and said, "I was afraid they'd think of that. Now we've got to root 'em out."

Cody nodded. "It won't be easy," he told the lawman. "We can't get very close to them without losing our cover."

"Then we can sit here and starve them out!" Randine snapped. "Now that we've got 'em bottled up, we're going to keep them there!"

Cody hid his frown. There was nothing he could do.

The posse opened up on the fugitives with rifles and pistols, and the blast of gunshots bounced off the walls of the canyon until it was deafening. Return fire came from the boulders where Seth and the others were holed up. Cody had to believe that Seth was deliberately firing high, knowing that this was a posse and not wanting to hurt any of them. But the other two young men wouldn't be holding back. They'd be shooting to kill, and so were the other members of the posse.

Sliding his Colt from its holster, Cody edged the muzzle around the side of the rock and snapped off a shot, being careful to tip the barrel up so that the bullet would go high and wild. That was all he could do at the moment. If there was a lull in the firing, however, he intended to call out for Seth to get the drop on his two companions. That would ruin the younger Ranger's scheme, but Seth's plan had already been shot to hell. No point in the boy himself following it. As far as Cody could see, that was the only way to bring this disaster to an even partially satisfying close.

But with all the lead flying around, somebody was liable to get hurt first. Cody just hoped it wasn't Seth.

Ducking instinctively as a ricochet smacked through the air next to his ear, Seth crouched behind a boulder and wondered how things could've gone so wrong so fast.

He had been in gunfights before, and, anyway, he had never been under any illusions that being a Ranger was a safe and secure line of work. In fact, it was downright dangerous, and Seth knew it.

But he had never figured that he'd meet his Maker after being cut down by a bullet from a fellow lawman's gun.

Of course, Randine didn't know that Seth was a Ranger. He couldn't blame the sheriff. And he couldn't blame Cody, either. He had spotted his friend a few minutes earlier, crouched there in the rocks with the rest of the posse. He wondered if Cody even knew that he was up here. If he did, then surely he had figured out what Seth was doing with a couple of bank robbers. Surely . . .

The idea that Cody might think he had gone bad pained Seth more than any bullet could.

He took a deep breath. There was only one way out of this fix, as far as he could see. Amos and Tug weren't paying that much attention to him; all of their efforts were focused on the posse, naturally enough. He could get the drop on them, force them to throw down their guns. Then it'd just be a matter of revealing his true identity and turning Amos and Tug over to the posse. Cody would back him up. Seth was sure of that.

Tightening his grip on the Colt in his hand, Seth started to take a step back and swing the gun to cover his companions, hoping he wouldn't have to shoot either one of them. Just as he began to make his move, something slammed into the side of his head, staggering him and knocking his hat off. He felt his balance deserting him, felt himself falling as pain exploded through his skull. Hot wetness flooded down the side of his face.

He was hit, shot in the head. That realization burst through his brain. But it was the last thing he was aware of. Soft blackness closed in around him and cradled him, and he didn't even feel himself hit the ground.

"Amos!" Tug cried. "Seth's hit!"

Amos jerked his head around and saw the sprawled form of their new friend. Seth lay limply on the rocky ground, half of his face covered with blood.

"Goddamn it!" howled Amos. "The bastards've killed him!"

Kneeling behind a boulder, his face grim, Tug thumbed fresh shells into his pistol. Raising his voice over the thunderous gunfire from the posse, he said, "They're goin' to get us sooner or later, Amos. You know that."

"Yeah," Amos agreed, his face taut and angry.

"We gave it a good shot, hoss, but I guess we ain't cut out to be owlhoots. Question now is, do we give up—or do we go out shootin'?"

Amos reloaded his own gun. "I don't think we've hit any of those possemen. They probably wouldn't hang us, just throw us in jail for the next ten or fifteen years."

A shudder ran through Tug's lanky form, and he said, "I don't reckon I could stand that, Amos. I never did cotton to bein' locked up."

Managing a glum smile, Amos replied, "Neither did I." He snapped the loading gate closed on his Colt. "You ready?"

"We chargin' 'em?"

"Damn right."

"Then I'm ready," Tug said.

"Folks'll talk about this fight for years!"

With that, Amos surged to his feet, and Tug was right behind him. They were ready to charge toward the posse, determined that if they had to die, it would be in a blaze of sordid outlaw glory.

Suddenly from the ridge above them a volley of rifle shots rang out.

Cody glanced up sharply, a change in the sounds of the firing alerting him. He saw powder smoke floating above the rimrock, and he heard slugs whipping around him closer than before.

"Get down!" he called to the posse. "Gunmen on the ridge!"

The Ranger's warning came too late for a couple of the men from Fort Davis. Bullets punched through them, knocking them into lifeless heaps. Cody and Randine hugged the ground, the other members of the posse following their example.

Cody didn't know who the newcomers on the ridge were, but they had a commanding field of fire. Venturing a quick look around the rock he lay behind, he saw that Bower and Mitchell had retreated behind their cover again. For an instant they had gotten to their feet, as if they were about to come out shooting, but now they were hunkered down again while the shots from above clawed at the pinned-down posse.

Where the hell was Seth?

Cody hadn't seen him when Bower and Mitchell started to come out. Had he been wounded? Killed? Worry for his young friend gnawed at Cody, but there was no way for him to find out now. He and Randine and the others were going to have their hands full staying alive themselves.

"We've got to get out of here!" Randine said desperately.

The sheriff wasn't telling Cody anything he didn't already know. The rocks had protected them well from Bower and Mitchell, but the strangers up above had a lot better angle.

"We'll cover the others while they pull back to the horses," Cody said. Twisting around, he plucked cartridges from his belt and slid them into the Colt until the cylinder was full. "Get ready."

He glanced over at Randine, and the sheriff nodded. Randine was scared; the pale, haggard expression told him that. But anybody would be in a situation like this. Cody was scared as hell, in fact. In order to cover the other members of the posse, he and Randine would have to expose themselves even more to the fire of the ambushers.

Randine caught the eye of the other men, and with a combination of hand signals and a couple of shouted commands he told them to get to their horses as quickly as possible when he and Cody started occupying the attention of the riflemen. The possemen waited, tense, frightened, and flinching, as slugs thudded into the rocks around them.

"Now!" Cody ordered.

He came up on his knees and leveled the Colt at the ridge. The shots flew out from his gun as fast as he could work the hammer and trigger, the explosions blending into one long roar. A few feet away Randine was doing the same thing. Cody didn't dare glance behind him to see if the other men were making their escape. He concentrated on the rimrock and saw puffs of grit flying up where his slugs hit.

Then, as the hammer clicked on an empty chamber and Cody threw himself to the side, he heard rifles opening up from behind him. A couple of the possemen were laying down a covering fire with their Winchesters, trying to give Cody and Randine a chance to slip out of this deadly hole, too. Cody rolled over and over, blinded by dirt kicked into his eyes by the impact of a bullet, then jumped to his feet and sprinted toward the horses. He felt something tug at his sleeve, his hat, the leg of his pants. The bullets were coming that close.

Then he was behind a small bulge in the canyon wall with Randine panting and stumbling along beside him. The possemen who had covered them raced to their own horses. Cody reached the dun and grabbed the saddle horn to swing himself up. Randine clambered into leather, too, and waved the other men ahead of him. "Go! Go!" he shouted.

With the rifle fire from the ridge still searching for them, the posse members galloped back down the canyon. They were safe as soon as they rounded the first sharp bend, but most of them kept going. Cody couldn't blame them. Two of their friends and fellow townsmen were lying back there dead, victims of the devastating attack.

Cody slowed the dun and looked back, but from beside him Randine said, "Keep going! There's nothing we can do!"

Bitterly, Cody realized that the sheriff was right. Riding back down that canyon would be riding straight into the jaws of death. All he could do was keep going—and wonder what had happened to Seth.

Was the young Ranger still alive? Who had those deadly rifles belonged to? The answer to that question, at least, suggested itself to Cody right away.

The Whittingham gang.

Maybe if Seth was still alive his plan was just about to work after all.

CHAPTER 7

Was he going to wake up in heaven or hell? Seth wondered.

For the past few minutes he had been aware that he was coming steadily closer back to consciousness. But not for a second did he believe he was still alive. When he finally managed to open his eyes and look around, he'd be seeing what it was like on the other side of the grave. He was convinced of that. What awaited him? Billowy clouds and angels with big white wings and harps—or the stench of brimstone and the fiery pit? It was going to be mighty interesting to find out.

Something wet and blessedly cool touched his forehead. *I must be floatin' up through one of those heavenly clouds,* he thought, and a wellspring of relief surged up within him.

"So I says to him, 'You ain't nothin' but a goddamn, low-down, hydrophobia skunk, old son,'" a rough voice said.

Seth frowned. That didn't sound like any angel he'd ever imagined.

"Then he got his back up an' grabbed for his smokepole, but I got mine out first an' ventilated the son of a bitch." Harsh laughter. "Shot the shit out of him, for a fact."

No, definitely not an angel, Seth decided. Not unless heaven was a whole heap different than what preachers made it out to be.

"Are you going to wake up or not?"

There, that was more like it. The question came in a soft female voice that was as light and cool as that touch on his forehead. An angel for sure this time. Seth smiled and opened his eyes.

Son of a gun. He was alive. And a beautiful young woman was peering down anxiously at him, her head outlined by the starry night sky above her.

"Who . . . ?" Seth croaked. His throat felt as dry and rough as ten miles of dirt road.

Not only that, but the pain had come back, rolling through his head as inexorably as the waves of the Gulf of Mexico had rolled in to shore, that time he had gone over to Corpus Christi. With the hurting came memories of Amos and Tug, of the gun battle in the canyon, of being shot. . . .

Of being shot in the head! He groaned, remembering now. Was the bullet still up there, rattling around somewhere in his skull? He wanted to lift his hand and feel around on his head, looking for the hole the slug had left, but his muscles refused to obey him. All he could do was lie there and moan in pain.

"Please, just lie still," the girl said urgently, her soft touch on his shoulder making him cease his feeble struggles. "You've been hurt," she went on unnecessarily. "You'd better just rest."

There was something familiar about her. Seth couldn't see her very well, but one side of her face was lit by a faint glow that probably came from a campfire. Suddenly he realized where he had seen her before: back in the dusty main street of Fort Davis, lying at her feet where he had wound up after being tossed out of the Wild Rose Saloon.

Seth blinked in confusion, and even that hurt. How could the beautiful young woman he saw getting out of the stage in Fort Davis the day before have wound up here in these rugged mountains? It didn't make sense.

Things didn't get any clearer. The young woman picked up a cup from the ground and held it to Seth's lips. "Try to swallow a little of this," she urged.

Awkwardly, he took a sip of the cup's contents. It was coffee, he discovered, hot coffee laced liberally with whiskey. It started a few embers glowing in his stomach, and he drew strength from the warmth.

The night was cold, which wasn't unusual in these mountains. Something was spread over him, and when he finally got his fingers working enough again for them to stir against the covering, he decided it was a horse blanket. He could smell it now, too.

After several more sips of coffee he felt strong enough to try lifting his head. The pain was still there, but it had subsided to a dull ache. He was able to hold himself up on one elbow and look around.

He was in some sort of camp. A small fire marked its center, and sitting around the fire, swapping stories, were several men. The gravelly voice Seth had heard earlier belonged to one of them. Other men, at least a dozen altogether, moved around the camp, and there was a certain similarity among them. All of them were hard-faced, gun-hung hombres—outlaws if Seth had ever seen any.

"Please, you need to rest," the girl said again.

But Seth ignored her. Now that his muscles were working again, at least a little bit, he couldn't just lie there. Reaching up, he found a thick bandage wrapped around his head.

"Where's the bullet?" he rasped.

She smiled slightly and shook her head. "I don't know. You were just creased. The bullet didn't lodge in your head, if that's what you're worried about. I cleaned and bandaged the wound after you were brought in to camp. It looked a lot worse than it really was. But it was bad enough, and you'll have to really be careful after a knock on the head like that. It ought to heal up just fine if you're careful, though."

Seth was full of questions, but they'd have to wait. Right now he was still too muddleheaded to make much sense out of this. The last thing he remembered was being forted up in those rocks with Amos and Tug. How had he gotten here? Who had brought him to this lonely camp? For that matter, where were Amos and Tug now, and what had happened to Cody and the posse?

"I really think you should sleep some more, but if you're determined to stay awake, why don't you try to sit up, and I'll get you some stew. Perhaps that's what you need."

Seth nodded, and the girl moved to his side. She grasped his arm, and moving slowly and carefully, he pushed himself upright. For a few seconds dizziness engulfed him, and the surprisingly strong grip on his arm was all that kept him from falling over again. Then his head settled down, and he was able to scoot a few feet over to a small, rounded boulder that he could rest his back against.

"Looks like the pilgrim's feelin' better," one of the men beside the campfire said. "Takes more'n a bullet to dent a Texan's hard head, don't it, boy?"

Seth summoned up a weak grin. "I reckon," he replied.

The girl hurried over to a pot that was simmering on the fire and dished up a plate of stew. She brought it back to Seth and held out a spoon. "Can you manage," she asked, "or do I need to feed you?"

"I can handle it," he said, reaching for the spoon. No sooner had he grasped it, though, than a fresh wave of weakness went through him. The spoon slipped from his fingers and fell into the stew.

The girl picked it up and said firmly, "I'll take care of this for you." She began giving him small bites of the hot, spicy concoction.

As he ate, Seth listened to the conversation going on among the men gathered around the fire. The talk was full of murder, robbery, and assorted viciousness, punctuated by the kind of colorful profanity common to any camp of frontiersmen. The girl had to be able to hear the stories, and Seth expected her ears to start glowing red enough to light the night sky. But she seemed to pay no attention to them, concentrating instead on spooning the stew into Seth's mouth.

"There, you're feeling a lot better, aren't you?"

Seth was able to nod. The food and drink had made him stronger, even though his stomach was a bit unsettled now. Still, that beat being dead.

For the first time he took more notice of his surroundings. The camp was located in a hollow, and all around it rose steep slopes, looming only as dark, featureless bulks in the darkness. They were in the heart of the mountains, Seth knew. To his right was a narrow opening in one of the slopes, looking for all the world as if a giant hand had taken a knife and cut a gash in one of the peaks. That would be the way out of here, Seth figured. Beyond that opening in the stone wall was a simple rope corral containing quite a few horses.

On the far side of the clearing was a small cabin, built of logs that had probably been cut from the trees that dotted the edges of this hollow and extended up onto the slopes around it. As Seth watched, the door of the cabin opened, and four men emerged from it onto its small porch.

The young Ranger recognized Amos Bower and Tug Mitchell right away, but the two men with them were strangers to him. One of them, a tall, slender man with sleek blond hair and a small mustache, called out, "Come over here, Sara."

Quickly, the girl put down the plate of stew. Seth had eaten about half of it. She hurried over to the cabin, skirting the campfire and the men gathered around it, and Seth watched the graceful way she moved in the long, simple dress she wore. Thick brunette hair hung loose over her shoulders and back.

Now that he thought about it, Seth wasn't sure she was the same young woman he had seen back in Fort Davis or not. But if she wasn't, the resemblance was uncanny.

When she reached the porch of the cabin, the blond man spoke to her for several minutes in a voice too low for Seth to make out any of the words. A couple of times the girl half turned and gestured toward him, and he knew that he was the subject under discussion.

Finally the blond man seemed satisfied. He stepped down from the porch and strode across the camp toward Seth. Trailing him were the girl, Amos, Tug, and the fourth man, who was a lot like the other men in camp: beard stubbled, sullen faced, probably real handy with that big gun holstered on his hip, wearing a black Stetson and a cowhide vest over a grimy shirt. A hardcase if there ever was one.

The blond man was different. He was neatly shaven except for the mustache, and his face was pale, lean, almost gaunt. He was hatless and wore a white shirt and black whipcord pants tucked into high-topped boots. The difference was more than a matter of looks and clothes, though.

His eyes held an intelligence and a sophistication that was foreign to the other men here.

Despite that, as he approached, Seth sensed right away that he was just as dangerous as any of them—maybe more so. The well-worn walnut butt of the Colt he wore told Seth that the weapon had seen plenty of use.

When the man reached Seth's side, he knelt and said in a faintly accented voice, "Sara tells me you're feeling much better. I'm glad to hear it. We thought you were a goner when we first rescued you lads from that posse."

Seth blinked and licked dry lips. Given the circumstances, especially the man's voice, there was only one conclusion he could draw: This was none other than Barry Whittingham.

It had been a damned busy day, Seth thought wryly. He'd helped rob a bank, been shot in the head, and found the outlaw he and Cody had been sent here to the Davis Mountains to locate. Now all he had to do was recuperate from his wound, clear his name, and capture more than a dozen hardened owlhoots.

"Thanks," he responded, shoving his thoughts to the back of his mind since they wouldn't do any good right now. "I figured I was a goner, too. Only question was which place I was goin' to wind up."

"Reckon it would've been a mite hot," Tug put in with a smile on his ugly face. "Glad you didn't die on us, Seth."

"Yeah," added Amos, "you bled like a stuck hog when that slug grazed you. I don't know what we'd'a done with you if Barry hadn't come along."

"That's me," the blond man said. "I'm—"

"Barry Whittingham," Seth finished for him. Whittingham raised an eyebrow in surprise, and Seth went on, "I reckon just about everybody in this part of the country's heard of you. I figured if anybody showed up to save our bacon from that posse, it'a been you."

"Indeed." Whittingham inclined his head toward the hardcase who had drifted over to Seth's other side. "This is my second-in-command, Frank Parker."

"Howdy," Parker grunted, his tone neutral.

"Howdy," Seth replied. Parker's name rang a bell in his brain, but he couldn't place the man right away. He'd probably seen reward dodgers on him in the past, he decided.

"These young men"—Whittingham waved a long-fingered hand at Amos and Tug—"tell me that the three of you held up the bank in Fort Davis today. That was quite daring."

Seth shrugged. "Not really. We just wanted to show you we've got enough sand to ride with you, Mr. Whittingham."

The Englishman's thin lips curved in a smile. "Well, you certainly demonstrated your courage. It's a shame you didn't display an equal amount of intelligence."

Seth frowned. He was in no position to feel insulted by anything Whittingham said, and neither were Amos and Tug. But the bandit chief didn't have to take on such a superior air.

Whittingham went on, "You should have determined how close the pursuit was before you entered that canyon and closed yourself off from other options."

"Looks to me like you've only got one way in and out of here," Seth pointed out. "That cuts *your* options down a heap if somebody boxes you in here."

Frank Parker glowered at him, and Amos and Tug looked uneasy at this criticism, but Whittingham just chuckled. "It appears that way, doesn't it? Things are not always as they seem, however. There *is* another way out of here, even though it's not readily apparent. And there are always guards on that cleft so that it's impossible to take us by surprise in here. You'll find out all about these things—if you and your friends join our little band."

Seth felt his pulse begin to race faster. Even with all the misfortune that had befallen him, he was on the verge of accomplishing the first part of his mission. "That's what we came up here for," he said.

"Well, we'll talk about it in the morning," Whittingham said as he straightened up. "You need a good night's sleep, my young friend. By the way . . ." He held out his hand to the girl, and she immediately came over and took it, interlacing her fingers with his. "The angel of mercy who'll be charged with nursing you back to health is Miss Sara

Gilmore. She tells me you haven't been formally intro-
duced yet."

Seth nodded to the girl. "Pleased to meet you, ma'am. I
surely do appreciate what you've done for me."

"You're quite welcome, Mr. Williams," Sara said, adding
unnecessarily, "Your friends told us your name, in case
you're wondering. Now, why don't you lie back down and
take it easy? It doesn't pay to take chances with a head
wound."

"No, ma'am, I don't reckon it does."

Sara was still holding hands with Whittingham, and from
the way she stood so close to the outlaw leader and looked
up at him with wide, admiring eyes, it was readily apparent
that there was more than a little something going on between
them. None of the information he and Cody had been given
had mentioned anything about a girl. Whittingham probably
kept her hidden away here in this camp. The more Seth
thought about it, in fact, the more he was convinced that Sara
wasn't the young woman he had seen back in Fort Davis.

But if that was the case, who was that other girl who
looked so much like her?

Whittingham and Parker started to turn away, along with
Sara, but Seth stopped them by saying, "Mr. Whittingham?
Thanks for helpin' us out. Sure was lucky for us you fellas
happened along when you did."

"It wasn't entirely luck," Whittingham said with a smile.
"The three of you and that posse were making so much noise
it sounded like a war. These mountains are my domain, Mr.
Williams, and I believe in knowing what's going on in them.
But I suppose there was some element of luck involved."
He paused, then went on, "Let's hope it was a fortuitous
meeting for all of us."

It was nearly nightfall by the time Cody, riding with
Sheriff Randine at the head of the dispirited posse, got
back to Fort Davis. As they neared the settlement, Cody
could see lights twinkling in the gathering dusk.

The Ranger glanced over at Randine. It was clear that the
lawman was still furious, his bitter anger no doubt gnawing

at him all during the long ride back from the canyon. Added to his disappointment at having the outlaws elude him had to be the fact that two members of the posse had been left there, dead. There had been no way to retrieve the bodies in the face of that withering rifle fire. Randine, despite his shortcomings, was a conscientious lawman. Coming back with fewer men than he had left with would really stick in his craw.

"That was Whittingham's bunch," Randine said for what had to be at least the dozenth time. "Nobody else would've pitched in on the side of those bank robbers like that."

Cody had long since come to the same conclusion, but a contrary streak in his nature made him play the devil's advocate. "Could've been a band of Apaches," he said.

"Apaches would've sat up there on the rimrock and laughed at the white men shooting at each other," Randine said disgustedly. "You know damn well it wasn't 'paches."

Cody shrugged. "Reckon you're probably right."

"Even if those youngsters have joined up with Whittingham, it doesn't matter," Randine declared, also not for the first time. "I'll track down the bastards. They'll pay for what they've done."

Cody understood what the sheriff was feeling, but he was getting tired of listening to Randine. And he was worried about Seth. He wished he knew what had happened to the young Ranger.

"We'll have to ride back in the morning and get those bodies," Randine went on. "Hope the coyotes and the buzzards don't bother 'em too much till then. You going with us, Cody?"

"I'll have to let you know," Cody replied. "Don't wait around for me, though. Could be I'll have some other things I need to do."

Randine glowered at him, but Cody ignored the sheriff's expression. Randine could think whatever he wanted to about him. Cody couldn't help those dead men now—but he did still have a job to do. Besides, it could be Seth was still alive somewhere in those rugged peaks.

Cody saw the lights of the fort to the north. "I'll see you later, Sheriff," he said, turning the dun in that direction.

With a wave, he heeled the horse into a trot, not giving Randine a chance to object to his leaving the posse. Cody wanted to let Rufe Gresham know what had happened today and talk over the situation with the sergeant. Of all the people he had met since arriving in Fort Davis, Gresham seemed the most likely to be able to give him a hand.

The stars were coming out as Cody rode up to the guard post on the far side of the parade ground from the fort's buildings. He reined in and nodded to the pair of troopers who stood there holding carbines. "Evening, fellas," the Ranger said. "Can you tell me where I can find Sergeant Gresham?"

"You supposed to be on this post, mister?" one of the soldiers asked suspiciously. "What's your business?"

"Wait a minute, Zeke," spoke up the other trooper. "I know this man. He rode with us on patrol today. He's a friend of Sergeant Gresham's."

The first sentry lowered his rifle. "Well, I reckon that's all right, then. You'll find the sergeant in that barracks over yonder." He indicated the correct building with a pointing finger.

"Thanks. And where's Major Monroe tonight?"

"You wanna see the major, too?"

"Nope. Want to avoid him if I can."

Both troopers grinned. The second said, "The major, he done gone to his house there on Officer's Row for the night. Stay away from there, and you ain't likely to run into him."

Cody sketched a salute, touching his finger to the brim of his Stetson, then rode toward the barracks where Gresham was supposed to be. He swung down from the saddle and tied the dun to the railing in front of the building.

Several soldiers were sitting on the porch of the barracks, enjoying the cool breeze that sprang up when the sun had gone down. One of them was Sergeant Gresham. The noncom had a briar pipe clenched between his teeth, and around it he said, "That you, Cody?"

"Howdy, Sergeant," the Ranger replied. "Reckon I could talk to you for a few minutes?"

"Sure." Gresham got up from his chair and stretched.

Turning to the troopers, he said, "You boys go on back inside. This barracks could use some cleaning."

The soldiers let out a few groans of protest, but they went inside as asked. The sergeant came down from the porch and joined Cody beside the dun, his face solemn. "You must be here about what happened in town today while we were gone," he said.

"Heard about that, did you?" Cody asked.

"Hard not to. Everybody on the post was talking about it when we got back from that patrol. You ride right back out with Sheriff Randine and the posse?"

Cody nodded. "Yeah. Never got any lunch, and my belly's telling me about it. Important thing is, though, when we caught up to those bank robbers, somebody else took a hand. I think it was Whittingham and his men."

Quickly, Cody told Gresham about the battle in the canyon by Timber Mountain. Enough lantern light came through the open door of the barracks for Cody to see the sergeant's face growing dour as he listened to the tale. When Cody was finished, Gresham nodded and said, "That sounds like Whittingham, all right. He heard the ruckus, came to see what was going on, and decided to pitch in on the side of those young idiots."

Cody debated with himself whether to tell Gresham that one of those "young idiots" was actually an undercover Texas Ranger. The sergeant seemed more trustworthy than anybody else Cody had met so far on this mission, but he decided to keep the knowledge of Seth's identity to himself for the time being. If Seth was still alive—and that was a big if, Cody had to admit—and if he had indeed managed to hook up with Whittingham's bunch, the fewer people who knew who he really was, the better. Less chance of it being revealed—with potentially deadly consequences—that way.

"I figure it was Whittingham, too," Cody said. "And I plan on trying to pick up his trail tomorrow. Thought you might like to go along, since you've been poking around these mountains a lot more than I have."

Gresham puffed on his pipe for a moment, then took it out of his mouth and rubbed his jaw. "You mean just you and me?" he finally asked.

Cody nodded. "Seems to me like we might have a better chance of finding the gang by ourselves than if we took a troop of cavalry along with us. No matter how hard you try to be quiet, that many men make a lot of noise."

"And Whittingham probably spooks easy." Gresham nodded slowly. "I'll go with you. Major Monroe might not like it—but he doesn't have to know about it, either."

A grin stretched across Cody's weary face. "I was never in the Army, but I didn't have any idea you sergeants kept your officers in the dark so much."

"You tell your bosses everything you're doing?"

Cody thought about Lieutenant Oliver Whitcomb, the spit-and-polish second-in-command of Ranger Company C. Whitcomb was not as much of a "by-the-book" man as Major Monroe, but he made no secret of the fact that he thought most of the Rangers were severely lacking in discipline. Captain Wallace Vickery, on the other hand, was more interested in results than procedure.

"I see your point," Cody said. "We'll make an early start of it."

Gresham nodded again. "I'll leave right after morning formation. Meet you at the same place as this morning."

"Right." Cody loosened the dun's reins and mounted up. "Good night, Sergeant."

Gresham lifted a hand in farewell as Cody rode away from the barracks.

The big Ranger was tired as well as hungry. He had been in the saddle nearly all day, and when he hadn't been riding, he was being shot at, which could wear a man out by itself. He was looking forward to a hot meal, maybe a drink or two, and then the bed in his room at the Limpia Hotel.

Reaching town, he left the dun at the livery stable and flipped the hostler an extra dollar to see that the horse was well taken care of after this day's hard work. His next stop was the hotel dining room, where he put away a big plate of fried chicken, mashed potatoes, and peas, along with three slabs of cornbread and a bowl of peach cobbler to top it off. The food made him feel better, but he was still tired enough that he decided to skip the drinks and go on upstairs to his room instead.

Cody got his key from the clerk at the desk and trudged up the stairs. When he reached his room, he thrust the key in the lock, turned it, and opened the door to step inside.

His tiredness and the pleasant feeling of fullness from the meal had dulled his usual instincts, he realized as he stood in the doorway, because he hadn't immediately sensed that somebody was in his room. A soft footfall came from the direction of the window and a silhouette moved suddenly between him and the street.

Cody threw himself to the floor, his hand sweeping the Colt out of its holster.

CHAPTER

8

"Oh, my God! Who . . . ? What . . . ?"

Cody's finger eased its pressure on the trigger, and he grimaced disgustedly. The startled words had come from his shadowy visitor, and they were unmistakably the voice of a young, frightened female.

He got to his feet, holstered his gun, and shook a lucifer out of the small packet of matches he always carried. Scratching it into life, he squinted against the sudden glare of flame.

Leigh Gilmore stood there, looking as lovely as she had the night before—despite the spooked expression in her eyes. "Mr. Cody! You frightened me half to death!" she exclaimed.

Cody carried the match over to the lamp that sat on a small table. He raised the chimney and got the wick burning, then lowered the chimney and shook out the match as the lamp's yellow glow welled up and filled the room. As he turned back to face Leigh, he said, "You didn't do *my* ticker a whole lot of good, either, ma'am. I figured somebody was holed up in here ready to bushwhack me."

"Oh, no! I'd never . . . bushwhack you."

Cody took off his hat and tossed it on the bed. He faced Leigh squarely and asked, "Why *are* you here?"

She was wearing a silken dressing gown that looked almost as soft as the fair skin that was revealed where the neckline gaped open. Her hair was loose tonight, hanging around her shoulders and down her back. She smiled hesitantly and said, "I . . . I wanted to see you again. I got the clerk to let me in so that I could wait for you."

If she was trying to look seductive, Cody thought, she was making a fair stab at it. The whole effect didn't quite come off, though. Her youth probably had something to do with it—that and the innocence shining in her wide, doelike eyes.

Still, she was old enough to know what she was doing, and she was here alone in his room after dark. But he was damned tired, and right now he felt old enough to be this girl's grandfather.

Cody shucked his gun belt and put it on the bed next to his hat. He said, "You're here about your sister, aren't you?"

Leigh blinked in surprise. "You already said you'd help Sara if you found her. I . . . I don't know what else—"

"You still want me to take you up into the mountains, and you figured if you came here like this and stayed with me, I'd feel obligated to go along with whatever you want. Does that lawyer fella know you're here?"

"Mr. Breedlove? I should say not!" Leigh giggled, and she sounded more than ever like a little girl. "He'd be absolutely scandalized if he knew where I was right now."

"Then I reckon you'd better get back to your own room, so that he can't find out."

"But Mr. Cody . . ." Leigh stepped closer to him, close enough to reach up and rest both hands on his broad chest. "Surely we can discuss this." She let her body press against his, and there was just enough clumsiness in the move to let him know it was something she hadn't done very often—if ever. He could feel the warm softness of her body through the silken robe, and he figured she wasn't wearing anything under it.

Tired or not, he was still human. Damned if he was going to let this girl buffalo him, though. He caught both of her wrists and held them tightly as he growled, "Lady, I've got a saddle older than you."

With that, he shoved her away.

Leigh's eyes flared with anger as her face flushed. "You can't treat me like that!" she snapped.

"I'll do more than that," Cody warned her. "I'll turn you over my knee and give you the spanking you deserve if you don't get out of here, Miss Gilmore. I'm tired, and I don't have time for this foolishness."

"Foolishness!"

"That's right, foolishness." Cody reached out suddenly, grasped her arm, and steered her toward the door. "And if I have to throw you out, that's just what I'll do." He wrenched the door open, and a quick push propelled the startled girl into the corridor. Cody added, "If I was you, I wouldn't hang around out there too long, dressed like that."

He shut the door before she could say or do anything else.

Through the wooden panel, he heard another offended gasp from her, and then her small fist thumped against the door. "Let me in!" she cried.

"Nope," he told her through the door as he twisted the key in the lock. "And you're going to make a mighty big fool out of yourself if you stand around hollering like that."

"Ooohh!" She managed to communicate a considerable amount of outrage in that one syllable.

Then, to Cody's considerable relief, he heard the sound of her footfalls receding down the hall. Their quick pace reflected her anger.

With a rueful smile Cody stripped down to his long johns, hung his hat on one bedpost and the gun belt on the other so that the Colt would be easy to grab if he needed it, then blew out the lamp and climbed into bed. As he stared up at the darkened ceiling, he remembered the way Leigh had felt pressed up against him like that, and he sighed. Sometimes he was just too damned stubborn for his own good, he thought.

And with that he rolled over and went to sleep.

Cody hadn't said anything to Sergeant Gresham about Leigh Gilmore and the girl's missing sister, and he kept it that way the next day as they rode into the mountains to try to pick up the trail of the Whittingham gang. They'd gotten an early start, and Cody knew they'd reach the canyon before Sheriff Randine and the party coming out to recover the bodies of the slain possemen. Cody had planned it that way, even though that meant they'd have to ride past those corpses.

Gresham regarded the dead men solemnly. They weren't a pretty sight. Cody could have kept his eyes averted, but that wasn't his way. He'd always believed in looking bad news as well as good right in the face.

"You know those men?" Gresham asked when they were past the bodies.

"Nope," Cody said with a shake of his head. "Not really. But I know they were good men, or they wouldn't have come out here with that posse to chase some bank robbers. I reckon I've ridden with plenty just like them."

"Yeah. I served with some of the troopers who were killed when Whittingham raided those supply trains. We've both got some scores to settle with him."

Cody nodded. He rode on to the spot where Seth and the other two men had forted up in the boulders. Stepping down from the dun, he moved among the rocks, his eyes alert for anything the ground might tell him.

The first thing he saw was a large, reddish-brown stain on the rocks where blood might have splashed. His mouth quirked in a grimace. Bower and Mitchell had looked spry enough during that glimpse he had gotten of them. If one of the trio had been badly wounded—and from the looks of this, that was more than a possibility—it had to have been Seth.

But the boy's body wasn't here, and Cody was glad of that. There was at least a chance the young Ranger was still alive.

Gresham found tracks where a large group of horses had come up to the boulders, then turned and gone back the other way. That'd be Whittingham's gang, Cody thought as he studied the trail pointed out by the sergeant. He remounted the dun and said, "Let's go."

There were so many tracks that it was impossible to determine if three more horses had ridden away than had come up here. Cody figured that had to be the case, though. The trail led on down the canyon, which began to rise steadily and finally opened out into a tableland between several mountains. In the distance, Cody could see another

gash in the earth. That would be Madera Canyon, which
Sheriff Randine had mentioned the day before.

The tracks led in that direction. Cody and Gresham followed them to the rim of the canyon, where they reined in
and looked disgustedly into the wide, deep, rocky declivity.
The trail petered out on the stony slope leading down into
the canyon.

"I was afraid of that," Gresham said. "We've lost their
tracks more than once down there in Madera Canyon."
He glanced over at Cody. "Want to try to pick 'em up
somewhere farther on?"

Cody put the dun down the slope without hesitation.
"Don't have any choice," he said over his shoulder.

That was the beginning of a fruitless, frustrating search.
The Ranger and the cavalryman spent most of the day in the
saddle, not even stopping to eat lunch. They gnawed the
jerky and biscuits they had brought along and swigged
water from their canteens while on horseback. Their eyes
were never still as they rode slowly up and down the big
canyon; their gazes roved constantly, looking for some
sign that the outlaw gang had passed that way. During the
afternoon, they rode both rims of the canyon for several
miles in both directions.

Whittingham was good; Cody had to admit that. When
he had known the Englishman, there had still been some
rough edges to him; Whittingham had not totally adjusted
to frontier living. It appeared that now he had, that he
had mastered the techniques of surviving on the owlhoot
trail. Cody's anger and disgust grew as he realized that
Whittingham had given him the slip again.

When Gresham suggested that they might as well head
back to Fort Davis, Cody wanted to snap at him. But he
bit back the harsh words and merely jerked his head in a
bleak nod. They weren't doing any good out here.

It was a long ride back to town.

Leigh Gilmore sat in the lobby of the Limpia Hotel,
watching the street through the front window. Her hair
was put up again today, and she looked quite attractive

in a dark-blue dress. She was aware of the looks that some of the men who passed through the lobby gave her, but she ignored all of them.

There was only one man who interested her right now.

Sam Cody had to be the most frustrating man on earth, she thought, and she could have gladly shot him the night before—except for the fact that he still seemed to represent the best chance of finding poor Sara. Remembering the way the Texas Ranger had turned down her blatant invitation to take her, Leigh's ears and face burned. She was glad she was ensconced in a deep armchair where her mortification at her wanton behavior wouldn't be quite so visible to passersby. Still, she would do anything to help Sara—even throw herself at a man. And Sam Cody was very attractive, in a rough-hewn sort of way. . . .

Leigh had spent the afternoon here waiting for him after discovering that he was no longer in his room. Surely he was out searching for those outlaws, she had thought. But he had been gone a long time. Perhaps he wasn't even coming back to the hotel. Perhaps he intended to camp out in the mountains. Leigh decided she would wait for another quarter of an hour, then go find Josiah Breedlove and get some supper.

Less than five more minutes had gone by when she saw Cody riding down the street from the east.

He stopped at the livery stable and left his horse there, then came toward the hotel. Leigh was waiting for him when he opened the door and stepped into the lobby.

"Did you find them?" she asked quickly without preamble.

Cody stopped in his tracks, and Leigh saw the irritated expression that passed across his face. Then he sighed and said, "Find who?"

"The outlaws. You went out to the mountains to look for them today, didn't you? I'm sure it was Whittingham who rescued those bank robbers from the posse, aren't you?"

"You're well informed," he muttered, not responding to any of her questions.

"I have to be," she said a little haughtily, squaring her shoulders. "I want to find my sister, so I have to keep up with what's going on around here. I assume you were conducting a search today?"

Cody nodded. "I tried to follow them. Lost the trail after a while and never found it again."

Leigh felt her heart sink in her breast. Once more the Ranger had been stymied. She was more convinced than ever now that he needed her help.

"I can find my sister, Mr. Cody," she said. "I know my instincts will lead us right to her, and once we find her, the outlaws will be there, too. I'm sure of it."

"You may be sure of it, ma'am, but that doesn't mean you're right. Now, if you'll excuse me, I want to clean up and then get something to eat." He started to move past her.

Without thinking about what she was doing, Leigh grasped his arm and stopped him. "You're not going to listen to me, are you?" she asked, realizing that her voice was rising shrilly but unable to do anything about it. "You're going to continue to refuse my help, and you're going to let my sister rot in the clutches of those bandits!"

A mixture of annoyance and sympathy showed on Cody's rugged face. Gently, he disengaged his arm from her grip. "I'm sorry, Miss Gilmore," he said softly, and he sounded like he meant it.

Leigh turned away from him, no longer trusting herself to stay in control and not wanting to make a scene here in the hotel lobby. She hugged herself and stared out the window at the darkening street until she heard his booted footfalls moving away and knew that he was gone. When she finally turned around, he was just disappearing up the stairs.

A shudder ran through her. She had been postponing the next step, but now she knew she would have to take it.

After giving Cody enough time to reach his room so that she wouldn't run into him again, she went upstairs. She had intended to go to Josiah Breedlove's room in search of the attorney, but she found that that wouldn't be necessary. Breedlove was standing in front of her door, hand raised to knock. When he saw her coming, he smiled and lowered his arm.

"Ah, there you are, Leigh," he said. "I was just about to ask you if you were ready to have dinner."

"In a moment, Josiah." Leigh felt comfortable calling him by his first name. He had been her family's lawyer for many years in Dallas, and she had known him ever since she and Sara were children. "There's something we have to discuss first. Come in."

She opened the door of her room and entered it with Breedlove following behind her. The corridor was no place for the discussion they were about to have; she didn't want that Ranger accidentally overhearing any of her plans.

"What's this about, Leigh?" Breedlove asked once the door was closed.

"You know what it's about," she said as she turned to face him, her lovely face set with determination. "We can't wait any longer, Josiah. Mr. Cody isn't going to cooperate, so we have no choice but to seek out someone else to guide us into the mountains."

Breedlove frowned. "I thought you had given up on that absurd idea. We're city people; we can't go tramping around in the wilds. It was bad enough we had to ride that horrible stagecoach all the way out here!"

"I'm going to find Sara," Leigh snapped. "And I'm not going to let anything stop me—neither some stubborn Ranger nor your overly cautious nature!"

"But—"

"My father instructed you to give me your fullest cooperation, Josiah," she said coldly. "He also entrusted you with my safety. If you want me to find my own guide and go into the mountains on my own, that's up to you."

Breedlove sighed, and his smooth façade slipped a bit, making him look older. "All right," he said. "I should have known better than to argue with you. I'll ask around town and try to locate someone reliable who knows the area. If you want to poke around for a while, we'll give it a try. But I'm not promising to continue with this forever, Leigh. Remember that."

"It won't take long," Leigh replied confidently, smiling now that Breedlove had agreed to go along with her wishes. "You'll see, Josiah. We'll find Sara. I just know we will!"

• • •

If there was ever a better nurse than Sara Gilmore, Seth had never run into her. The girl spent a great deal of time with him while he was recovering from the bullet crease on his head. The gash on his scalp had healed quickly, a testament to the job Sara had done cleaning and bandaging it. For a few days Seth had been dizzy and headachy, but that passed and his full strength seemed to have returned. When he had insisted on doing his part of the chores around the camp, at first he tired easily, but after a day or two his stamina came back to him as well.

Sara seemed to enjoy sitting with him and talking. For one thing, he was closer to her own age than anyone else in the camp. There was nothing romantic about it, though; she was Whittingham's woman, that much was obvious. And she didn't really reveal much about herself in their conversations, either, giving Seth no idea how she had come to be here in this isolated outlaw camp. Instead, she wanted to know about him, and he told her as much of the truth as possible, relating stories of the days when he had grown up on a horse ranch over in the Concho River country. He left out the part about how he had joined up with the Rangers, of course, and tried to give her the impression that he had become unsatisfied with ranch life and started drifting instead. There was almost some truth to that—he hadn't been content to stay home and raise horses. The hunger inside him for adventure had led him to join the Rangers.

Amos and Tug were around a lot, too, and Seth could tell from the easy camaraderie between them and the other men that they had been accepted into the gang. As far as he could tell, he had been, too, though he sensed that the older outlaws were reserving judgment on all three of them until they'd ridden together on a job. That was especially true of Frank Parker. From time to time there was still suspicion in the eyes of the gang's second-in-command as he looked at the three newcomers.

The chance to prove themselves came sooner than Seth had expected. About a week after the battle with the posse Whittingham gathered the entire group—with the exception of the guards on the hideout's entrance—and spoke to them by the campfire. Sara stayed in the background but nearby as Whittingham sat down by the fire and laid out the details of their next job.

"I've been informed," the Englishman said, "that a pack train of mules will be bringing up a load of silver from the mines down in the Big Bend, bound for El Paso. This is supposed to be a bit of a secret, of course, but as you know, I have my ways of finding out such things."

That was one of the things Seth had learned during the time he had been there. Evidently Whittingham had a network of informants spread all over West Texas who got word to him anytime there was a suitable target in the vicinity of the Davis Mountains. It would probably be impossible to ever root out all the men who were on Whittingham's payroll, but if the bandit leader himself was killed or captured, along with the gunmen who rode with him, that would render his accomplices pretty much harmless.

Whittingham went on, "The drovers are traveling at night, and they'll be passing between Baldy Peak and El Muerto tomorrow evening. We'll hit them there."

"All of us?" asked Frank Parker, glancing at Seth, Amos, and Tug.

"All of us," Whittingham replied firmly. "This will serve as a baptism of fire, so to speak, for our new members. Not that they need one after the encounter with that posse." He looked directly at Seth, his eyes glittering in the firelight. "What about you, Seth? Is your wound healed sufficiently for you to take part in this little adventure?"

Seth didn't particularly want to accompany the outlaws, but he felt Parker's eyes on him and knew he had to take advantage of this opportunity to prove he was on the level. The more the gang trusted him, the better the chances he'd be able to turn the tables on them when the time came.

"Sure," he said. "I'm feelin' fine. Nothin's goin' to keep me from goin' along, boss."

"Excellent." Whittingham stood up and took Sara's hand. "Everyone get a good night's sleep, and take it easy tomorrow. We'll be quite busy, so you'll need your rest."

With that he turned and walked to the cabin, taking Sara

with him. The two of them slept there, while everyone else
in the gang curled up in bedrolls outside. Seth didn't mind
that; he'd had the stars for a ceiling many a time. But it
bothered him a little that such a young, seemingly innocent girl as Sara was carrying on so with a bloody-handed
outlaw, and an Englishman, at that.

Seth sighed. Sara Gilmore's virtue was the least of his
worries at the moment. Here he was a Texas Ranger, and
before another night was over he'd be taking part in hijack-
ing a silver shipment.

He tried to take Whittingham's advice and get a good
night's sleep, but it sure wasn't easy.

About the middle of the next afternoon the outlaws rode
out of the hideout, following the great gash in the earth
through its twists and turns into an even larger canyon.
This was Madera Canyon, Amos told Seth as they rode
with Tug near the rear of the group. The two young former
cowhands pointed out other landmarks to him, such as
Timber Mountain to the south. The group rode southeast,
through a wide valley between towering peaks. This was
wild, majestic country, and Seth would have enjoyed the
journey—if he hadn't been on his way to a scene of murder
and robbery.

Somehow he kept a jaunty smile on his face most of
the way. The trail they were following began curving even
more so that they were riding almost due south as the sun
lowered toward the western horizon. The mountain called
El Muerto was over there, and Baldy Peak, the tallest
mountain in this range, was to the east. Next to it was the
jagged, picturesque summit of Sawtooth Mountain, which
was even more imposing despite the fact that it didn't reach
quite as high an elevation as its neighbor.

Whittingham led the outlaws to a rocky ridge overlooking
the trail. The pass between the mountains narrowed down
at this point so that when the mule train arrived from the
south, the animals would be forced to proceed through it
one or two at a time. The caravan would be stretched out—
easy pickings for an ambush.

Following Whittingham's commands, the gang members positioned themselves among the rocks with their rifles. As Seth settled down behind a boulder, a Winchester in his hands, he fought down the sickness that threatened to overwhelm him. It was as much a spiritual pain as a physical one, probably more so. Men were going to die tonight at the hands of his companions, and there wasn't a damn thing he could do to stop it. He told himself to look at the bigger picture, reminded himself that eventually Whittingham and the others would pay for their crimes.

That knowledge didn't help a hell of a lot right now, though.

Darkness fell, but an early moon was rising, casting silvery light over the trail below. Still, Seth heard the pack train before he saw it. The sound of plodding hoofbeats and the tinkle of bells tied to the mules came to his ears and made him stiffen in his hiding place. All along the line of outlaws the same thing was happening. Men lifted their rifles and got ready to kill.

The mules appeared in the pass, bulky shapes made even more so by the silver-laden *aparejos* slung over their backs. The contents of the packsaddles would add up to a small fortune. Mexican drovers in big sombreros walked alongside the mules, their white pants and shirts showing up vividly in the bright moonlight. Riding at intervals along the line were white men carrying rifles; these horsemen were the guards hired by the mine owners to get the silver safely to El Paso. Unfortunately, that precaution wasn't going to do any good.

The gang waited. When the entire pack train was stretched out along the trail under the guns of the outlaw gang, Whittingham suddenly rose from his crouch and shouted, "Now!"

Flame geysered from the muzzles of the hidden Winchesters. Blast after blast pounded against the rocky slopes and echoed back in a cacophony of noise. Lead thudded into flesh—human, horse, and mule flesh. Some of the men died silently, while others screamed as slugs knocked them out of the saddle or drove them to the ground. Dark flowers of blood blossomed on the white clothes of the drovers.

The animals shrieked from pain and fear, adding to the appalling scene.

Above it all, Seth Williams felt a heartsickness stronger than any he had ever known before.

He watched, fighting his horror as innocent men were cut down by bushwhacker lead. The rifle in his hands bucked against his shoulder as he fired again and again, as fast as he could work the lever, but as he had done during the fight with the posse from Fort Davis, he deliberately missed each time he pulled the trigger. It was little consolation—the men with the pack train were being slaughtered anyway—but it was all he had.

The killing didn't take long. Only a few minutes after the firing began Whittingham called a halt to it and motioned for his men to follow him. They came down off the ridge, sliding on the rocky slope, and quickly took charge of the mules that hadn't been killed. Most of the beasts were unharmed, because the outlaws had tried to miss them. They would need the mules, after all, to carry the silver back to camp. A few of the mules had been hit and killed by stray bullets, and the silver they had packed would be split up among the saddlebags of the gang.

"Outstanding work, men," Whittingham told them, smiling amidst the carnage. "This will be our best payoff in a long time. When we get back to camp, we'll keep some of the mules for ourselves, and I'm sure Naztache will appreciate the others."

Seth knew from talk he had overheard in the past week that Naztache was the chief of a band of renegade Apaches who were still in the area. Whittingham bribed him from time to time to leave the outlaws alone, and the gift of more than a dozen mules would be greatly appreciated by the Indians. To an Apache, Seth remembered, mule meat was mighty tasty.

Leaving the bodies where they had fallen, the outlaws gathered up their loot and hit the trail again. It would be a long ride back.

And Seth carried with him a burden he knew would never completely lay down—because he knew he'd never forget what he had seen tonight.

CHAPTER 9

▮▮▮▮▮▮▮▮▮▮▮▮▮▮▮▮▮▮▮▮▮▮▮▮ ▮▮▮▮▮▮▮▮▮▮▮▮▮▮▮▮▮▮▮▮▮▮▮▮

It wasn't long before dawn when the outlaws reached their camp, but despite the fact that they had been up all night, nobody was in a hurry to go to sleep. They were laughing and talking, still full of excitement from the killing and the loot they had garnered. Sara came out of the cabin to greet them, and the two men who had been left behind to guard the camp hurried over from their posts to get the details of the attack.

Whittingham stepped down from his horse, cuffed back his flat-crowned black hat so that it hung behind his neck from its chin strap, and gathered Sara into his arms. He kissed her passionately, then turned to the other men, who were dismounting, and grinned.

"Break out some bottles of whiskey from the supply in the cabin, Frank," he said to Parker. "I think a bit of a celebration is warranted."

Parker nodded crisply. "All right, Barry." Normally Whittingham kept a fairly tight rein on the men's drinking, preferring them to be sober in case of trouble. But apparently the gang leader had gauged the mood of the owlhoots, and right now they were ready to cut loose and howl at the fading stars for a while.

Amos and Tug were as caught up in the hilarity as any of the other men. Seth tried to act like it, too, but it was difficult. Maybe the whiskey would help, he thought. But he knew it wouldn't erase the memories of the massacre he had witnessed and indirectly taken part in.

He unsaddled his horse and got it into the rope corral with the others. As he turned back toward the cabin, Parker emerged, carrying several bottles of whiskey. The outlaws pounced eagerly on the rotgut, passing around the bottles and taking healthy swigs. When one of the bottles came to Seth, he took it without hesitation, lifted it to his mouth, and swallowed some of the fiery stuff.

Whittingham and Sara were standing on the porch of the cabin, holding glasses in their hands. No drinking from the bottle for them, Seth thought. And from the looks of what was in those glasses, it was wine rather than homemade panther sweat.

Lifting his glass, Whittingham called out, "Gentlemen! A toast to us—and to our success!"

The gang shouted out its agreement and downed some more whiskey. Whittingham drained his own glass, tossed it aside, and led Sara back into the cabin. From the looks of it, he intended to do some celebrating that didn't involve drinking.

The rest of the outlaws settled down to putting away the whiskey. Seth found a place to sit near the fire with Amos and Tug. As the hardcases began to feel the liquor, they got more and more boisterous. A couple of them linked arms and began dancing a clumsy jig while some of the others sang a bawdy song and clapped out the tune for the dancers. Seth contented himself with an occasional sip of whiskey and listening to the low-voiced conversation between Amos and Tug.

"Well, we did it, partner," Tug said. "I reckon we're sure-'nuff desperadoes now."

"Yeah," agreed Amos, tilting up a bottle and letting its contents gurgle down his throat. When he lowered it, he went on, "I figured it might bother me to shoot them drovers and guards, but it didn't. Not one damned bit."

"Me, neither," Tug said, but he didn't sound completely sincere to Seth.

Amos, on the other hand, seemed genuinely unconcerned about the butchery and his part in it. That knowledge just added to the cold knot in Seth's guts. He had thrown in with Amos and Tug in order to locate Whittingham, but he had found himself liking the two young cowhands despite their goal of becoming outlaws. Now Amos had crossed the line all the way, whatever conscience he'd had dying along with those men earlier. Tug had done his part, too, but at least he seemed to feel a trifle guilty about it.

Not that it really mattered, Seth supposed. Both of them were outlaws now, and sooner or later they'd have to face justice in the form of a hangman's rope or a lawman's bullet.

He just hoped he wasn't the one who'd have to take them.

Suddenly, he became aware of a pair of boots right in front of him. He'd been brooding and hadn't noticed the man stopping to glare down at him. He looked up into the sullen face of Frank Parker.

"You want somethin'?" Seth asked after a moment.

"I want to know what the hell you think you're doin'."

Seth glanced over at Amos and Tug, who had fallen silent at Parker's harsh declaration. He shrugged and said, "As far as I can tell, I'm not doin' anything except sittin' here. That all right with you, Parker?"

"I mean what are you doin' pretendin' to be a member of this gang—"

Seth's heart seemed to freeze for an instant. Had Parker found out he was really a Ranger? The badge was still secure in its hiding place, Seth was sure of that.

"—when you're nothing but a low-down coward," Parker continued.

Seth flushed angrily, even though he was incredibly relieved. Parker never had liked him, and now the hardcase was trying to pick a fight.

"I don't know what the hell you're talkin' about," Seth snapped.

"I saw the way you was shootin' over the heads of those drovers. What's the matter, boy? Too damn lily-livered to kill anybody?"

Seth uncoiled and came to his feet, no longer willing to let Parker tower over him. He said, "Lead was flyin' all over the place. How do you know my bullets didn't hit somethin'? How could you tell who shot what?"

"I could tell by the angle of your rifle barrel, dammit! You were deliberately shootin' over the heads of them men, and it ain't no use you denyin' it."

"Now wait just a minute, Frank," Amos spoke up. "It was dark—"

"There was plenty of moonlight," Parker sneered.

"And like Seth said, there was a heap of shootin' goin' on," Tug added. "It ain't like there was just one of us up there with a rifle."

Parker spat at Seth's feet. "I still say you're chicken-hearted, boy. And I don't think there's any place for a coward in this gang."

Seth took a deep breath, about to frame an angry reply, then hesitated when a slight movement he saw over Parker's shoulder caught his eye. He looked across the camp at the cabin and saw that Whittingham had come out onto the porch again. Sara wasn't with him this time, and the outlaw leader's shirt was unbuttoned almost to his waist. He held the bottle of wine now instead of just a glass, and he lifted it to drink, watching the confrontation between Seth and Parker with keen interest.

Seth realized that Whittingham wanted to see how he was going to react to Parker's prodding, and he wondered for a second if the Englishman had set up this encounter. He could have easily ordered Parker to confront Seth. It didn't really matter who was behind the argument, though. The only thing that counted was what he did next.

He'd keep a tight rein on his temper, he decided. Parker was trying to goad him into a fight, so if he started throwing punches, the hardcase would have accomplished his goal. With a sneer of his own, Seth said, "This ain't worth fightin' over. I never heard anythin' more ridiculous in my life." He started to turn away.

Parker ripped out a curse and grabbed Seth's shoulder. "Nobody turns his back on Frank Parker when he's talkin' to 'em, goddammit!" As Seth staggered, Parker launched a blow at his head.

Seth ducked frantically. After just recovering from that bullet crease, he didn't think his skull could stand much more. Parker's fist whipped harmlessly over his head.

But Seth knew that wouldn't be the end of it. Parker wasn't going to back off now. Quickly, Seth took a step that brought him closer to the big hardcase. Setting himself, he slammed a right and a left in succession to Parker's midsection.

Parker was taller and heavier, but Seth's blows were well aimed and had all of the young Ranger's strength behind them. Besides that, Seth let the anger that had been dammed up inside him come out with the punches. Fate had forced him to watch the killing of all those men earlier tonight, and now he was striking back.

The other outlaws came to their feet and let out yells of surprise as Parker was knocked backward. His boots slipped on some rocks, and he lost his balance and went down hard on his back. Rolling over, he gasped for the breath that had been knocked out of him by the impact, and as he pushed himself to his feet, he grinned coldly at Seth.

"Thanks, boy," he rasped. "You just gave me an excuse to beat the hell outta you."

He lunged.

Seth tried to get out of the way, but he was a little too slow. Parker grabbed him and both men went down, rolling over and over on the ground. Seth's hat flew off. He blocked the punches that Parker aimed at his head, but that left him open for blows to the body. He grunted in pain as the bigger man's fists slammed into him.

The rest of the gang gathered around quickly, most of them shouting out words of encouragement to Parker. He had been with them for a long time and was Whittingham's *segundo,* while Seth was a newcomer, a relative stranger. The only ones supporting Seth in this fight were Amos and Tug, who shared his status. Tug yelled out, "Watch it, Seth! Don't let him bite you!" and Amos cried, "Rip his head off, Seth!"

Parker wound up on top, his big hands wrapped around Seth's throat. For a second Seth was afraid that Parker would start pounding his head on the ground, but it looked like the man was going to be satisfied with choking him to death. Blood roared in Seth's ears, and his eyesight began to dim and blur.

He used a trick Cody had taught him. His right leg came up, and he twisted his body enough to bring his foot around in front of Parker. He caught it under Parker's chin and then straightened his leg, and Parker had to release Seth's neck and go with it or get his own head torn off. Parker fell off to the side, and Seth rolled desperately in the other direction.

Gasping for air, Seth came to his feet and saw Parker lumbering toward him again. This time Seth was able to elude his charge, and as the outlaw went past him, Seth clubbed his hands together and slammed them against the back of Parker's neck. The outlaw stumbled. Seth dropped to the ground, catching himself on his hands as he drove both of his heels into the small of Parker's back. Parker fell hard, his face smashing against the rocky ground.

Seth scrambled back to his feet, and this time he came upright before Parker did. The bigger man had slowed down some, and as he turned toward Seth again, the young Ranger saw the blood welling from his nose. There was a nasty cut above Parker's left eye, too. Parker shook his head back and forth and bellowed like a maddened bull. He came at Seth swinging huge, looping blows that would have taken Seth's head off if they had connected.

None of them did. Seth stepped inside again and brought his right up from his boot tops in an uppercut that had all of his energy behind it. He knew it was the last punch he'd throw, because he was done in. If this didn't put Parker down, then the outlaw would just have to beat him to death, Seth supposed.

His fist cracked cleanly against Parker's jaw. Parker's head jerked back and his eyes rolled up. He toppled like a tree and stretched out motionless on the ground.

The sound of languid clapping came to Seth's ears as he stood there gulping down great lungfuls of air and staring in surprise at Parker. He had actually knocked the man out. Seth looked up to see that the applause came from Barry Whittingham, who sauntered forward.

"Bravo," the outlaw leader said casually. "That was quite a display of fisticuffs, my young friend. If Frank was accusing you of cowardice, I'd say you proved him wrong."

"I'm no coward," Seth said, still puffing a little, "but I didn't want this trouble, either."

"I saw that you tried to avoid violence, and I'll speak to

Frank—when he's coherent again—to make sure there are
no repercussions against you." Whittingham put a hand on
Seth's shoulder. "Congratulations."

As if that was a signal, the rest of the gang crowded
around him, clapping him on the back and congratulating
him on his victory. Amos and Tug were in the forefront
of the well-wishers, obviously proud of him. Seth accepted
the compliments as graciously as possible.

But as Frank Parker pushed himself onto hands and
knees and shook his head to clear it, the young Ranger
saw the look the man gave him. It was a look of pure,
blood-freezing hatred. Seth had won the fight, but he had
also made an enemy for life.

He had actually made it through a week without Leigh
Gilmore pestering him, Cody thought as he left the dining
room of the Limpia Hotel one morning after breakfast. He
knew that she and the attorney, Josiah Breedlove, were still
in town because he had seen them around Fort Davis from
time to time. Leigh had gone out of her way to avoid him,
though, and wouldn't even meet his eyes when they both
happened to be in the hotel dining room at the same time.

There was nothing like the wrath of a woman scorned,
the old saying claimed. Cody reckoned that was probably
true. He had thought more than once about Leigh and the
way she had looked and felt that night she waited for him
in his room, and he had to sigh a little when those memories
crossed his mind. Still, he knew he had made the right decision. There was no way he could have taken the girl into the
mountains with him on his search for Whittingham.

Not that she would have been in any real danger, Cody
thought ruefully as he walked toward the livery stable to
check on the dun. He had spent every day riding the mountain trails, sometimes with Gresham, sometimes alone, and
he hadn't found a damned thing that led him any closer
to Whittingham. The closest he had come to trouble was
having to shoot a couple of diamondback rattlers. He had
seen one mountain lion, too, but it left him alone and he
did likewise.

The main thing that worried him now was that he hadn't heard a word from Seth. If the youngster was alive, he'd get word to Cody and let him know what he was doing sooner or later; the big Ranger was confident of that. The long silence didn't mean Seth was dead, but the chances of that were increasing every day.

Cody had almost reached the livery stable when he heard screams and cries coming from the west end of town. He stepped out into the street and peered in that direction to see what was causing the commotion.

A man was stumbling along the road, a man in clothes that had once been white. Now they were covered with blood. The man tottered down the street, obviously badly injured.

Cody joined the townspeople running forward to intercept him. The man collapsed before anyone could reach him. Somehow he had found the strength to get this far, but now it had deserted him. By the time Cody got to him, a couple of the passersby had reached him and rolled him over onto his back.

Cody dropped to a knee beside him. The man was a Mexican, and from the looks of the bloody, jagged holes in his clothes, he had been shot half a dozen times or more. Skin that would normally be swarthy was pale from exhaustion and loss of blood. Breath rasped in the man's throat.

"Somebody fetch the sheriff and the doctor," Cody said, and the tone of command in his voice made a couple of men hurry off on those errands. The Ranger leaned over the injured man and asked, "What happened, mister?"

The man muttered something in Spanish, and Cody switched to that language, repeating his question quickly and urgently. How the man had lived this long was a miracle, and surely he wouldn't be able to hang on much longer. Cody's instincts told him that the man had the answers to some important questions.

He had to lean closer and closer to the man's feebly moving lips as the grim story unfolded. Cody heard about the pack train loaded with silver that had skirted Fort Davis and moved on through the mountains, avoiding the settlement in the interest of secrecy. Obviously that hadn't been enough, because the caravan had been ambushed by thieves. The bushwhackers had killed everyone except this lone man, and apparently they had thought him lifeless, too, when they saw his limp, blood-splattered body. A spark of life had still been beating within his chest, though, and when the bandits were gone with their loot, he had pushed himself to his feet and started walking toward Fort Davis. He had walked all night, only half conscious most of the time, but some Providence had brought him to his destination.

Sheriff Randine arrived during the Mexican's story, but Cody curtly motioned him to silence when he tried to interrupt with blustering questions.

"Did you see who did this thing to you and your amigos?" Cody asked when the man fell silent.

"*Sí.* A tall man . . . with yellow hair and a mustache. He . . . he was a very bad man."

Yeah, that went without saying, Cody thought. Barry Whittingham, without a doubt. He wanted to ask about Seth, but he couldn't very well do that with Randine hanging over his shoulder and listening intently to every word.

The doctor hurried up to them then, and Cody stood aside to let him minister to the Mexican. With Randine beside him, Cody moved off a few feet away.

"You're thinking what I am," the sheriff said. "Had to be Whittingham."

Cody nodded. "This is his worst job yet. He slaughtered a couple of dozen men, to hear that herder tell it."

"I'd better ride out there and see how bad it really is," Randine said with a sigh.

"I'll go with you. And I'd like to let Sergeant Gresham from the fort in on this, too."

Randine glanced at him sharply. "I know Gresham. What's he got to do with this?"

"He's been helping me out, sort of unofficial-like."

The sheriff was able to summon up a smile. "Going behind Monroe's back, I imagine?"

Cody shrugged. "He'd like to catch up to Whittingham just like the rest of us."

"Gresham's a good man," Randine said, nodding. "Get your horse ready to ride. We'll go by the fort and see if he wants to go with us."

As it turned out, Rufe Gresham was more than willing to accompany them. He was drilling a cavalry troop on the parade ground, but he turned that duty over to a corporal and quickly saddled his horse. From what Cody told him of the wounded Mexican's story, he had a pretty good idea where the ambush had taken place.

The three riders reached the spot before noon, and the scene that greeted them was every bit as bad as Cody had expected it to be. Buzzards flapped off into the sky as the horsemen approached, and flies filled the air with their buzzing. Cody, Randine, and Gresham reined in and sat looking at the carnage with almost unbelieving eyes. All three men had fought Indians before and seen some things that would shake the strongest stomach, but this was damn near as bad.

"I'll head back to town and get some wagons," Randine finally said in a hushed voice. "We'll need 'em."

"Rufe and I are going on," Cody said. "We'll try to pick up Whittingham's trail. That all right with you, Rufe?"

The sergeant nodded wordlessly, his dark eyes filled with pain for all the dead scattered before him.

The three men split up, Randine heading back toward town, Cody and Gresham riding deeper into the mountains, and as the Ranger rode, he thought that after this there was no way things could get any worse.

Josiah Breedlove gestured at the man standing beside him and said, "Leigh, this is, ah, Mr. Hanrahan."

"Howdy, Miss Gilmore," said the white-whiskered, buckskin-clad old-timer. He gave Leigh a toothless grin and went on, "They call me Jinglebob."

Leigh blinked, unsure what to say. She had told the attorney to locate a guide to take them into the mountains, but she had never expected Breedlove to find someone like this.

Jinglebob Hanrahan was sixty-five if he was a day. His untidy brush of whiskers was pure white, and the skin that showed above the beard was burned a deep, permanent bronze by a lifetime of sun. His face had been lined and ravaged by time, but the surprisingly blue eyes were still alert. Like Jinglebob himself, his clothes had seen better days. The buckskin pants and shirt had been patched repeatedly, and the battered hat with the brim pushed up in front was covered with grime and unidentifiable stains.

After a moment's silence the old man went on, "I reckon yer wonderin' why they call me Jinglebob." He turned his head to display his left ear, and Leigh had to stifle a gasp when she saw the way the ear had been split across the middle so that the two halves of it flapped back and forth when Jinglebob shook his head. He pointed at the grotesque sight and said, "See? Just like a jinglebob notch on a cow's ear. Comanch' did that to me a long time ago, and folks got to callin' me Jinglebob."

"Josiah . . ." Leigh quavered, "have . . . have you already hired Mr. Hanrahan to be our guide?"

"He's the only one I've been able to find, Leigh," the lawyer answered quietly. "Everyone else around here is too worried about Indians and outlaws."

Leigh looked back at the bizarre old man. "You're not afraid to go into the mountains, Mr. Hanrahan?"

He shook his head, making that ear do its ghastly trick again. "No, ma'am," he croaked. "Oh, we may be headin' into trouble, I ain't a-goin' to deny that. But 'twon't be the first time I took a chance. I've fit Injuns from hell to breakfast, missy, and I've done my share o' cowboyin' and prospectin'. Ain't nothin' in them mountains I'm afeard of."

Leigh glanced past Jinglebob and looked at Breedlove again, who just raised his eyebrows and shook his head.

A few times in her rather sheltered life Leigh had encountered dime novels, though her mother would have been horrified if she knew that Leigh had read those lurid tales of the Wild West. Jinglebob Hanrahan was like a character out of one of the worst of those dime novels—yet here he was standing in front of her, a real person rather than the creation of some scribbler with a mind fevered by deadlines and cheap wine. The smell of him alone was enough to tell her that he was real.

"Very well," she said, gathering her courage. If Jinglebob was the best guide—the only guide—available, then they'd just have to make the best of it. She went on briskly, "We'll be leaving as soon as possible. I shall rely on you, Mr. Hanrahan, to provide us with mounts and see to gathering whatever supplies we'll need. Money is no object. Mr. Breedlove will go with you and pay for anything you require."

"I warn you, though, sir," Breedlove added, "don't try to take advantage of Miss Gilmore's generosity."

"Oh, no, ma'am, I'd never do that," Jinglebob declared. "Ain't never cheated a woman yet, 'specially not a young, purty one."

Leigh steeled herself and put out a hand to touch the old man's arm. "I know Mr. Breedlove must have told you why I want to go into the mountains."

Jinglebob nodded. "Yes, ma'am. Said we was a-goin' to hunt for your sister. We'll find her, ma'am. You can bet yer ass on that."

With that blunt guarantee he clapped his disreputable hat back on the thinning white hair and turned toward the door. Leigh blinked and swallowed as she watched him go. Breedlove gave her a dubious look and followed the old man.

Perhaps she was making a terrible mistake, Leigh thought, but she had no choice. Sara was out there somewhere, and Leigh was convinced now that she was the only one who could find and rescue her sister.

And to borrow one of Jinglebob Hanrahan's expressions, she would search from hell to breakfast if she had to.

CHAPTER
10

Neither Cody nor Sergeant Gresham was willing to turn back. Having found the tracks left by the outlaws as they had led the silver-carrying mules away from the site of the massacre, they followed the trail northeast, passing Baldy Peak, Sawtooth Mountain, and several smaller crags by nightfall. They were heading back toward Madera Canyon, confirming the Ranger's hunch that Whittingham's hideout was somewhere in that area. But they wouldn't be able to reach the spot before dark.

"I don't mind spending a night on the trail," Cody told Gresham when they stopped at a creek to refill their canteens and eat some jerky. "Done it many a time before. But you'll be missed if you're not back at the post."

"Don't give a damn," Gresham said firmly. "Not after what we saw this morning. Somebody's got to put a stop to Whittingham before this whole country runs red with blood."

Cody could understand the way the sergeant felt. He was starting to experience some of the same thing himself. When you were a lawman, it usually didn't pay to hate the lawbreakers you were after. But considering the rampage Whittingham's gang had been on, it was hard to avoid a little good, healthy hate.

"Well, if you're sure you can handle Major Monroe, I'd be glad of the company," he told Gresham, and the noncom threw back his head and laughed, a deep, booming sound.

"Worst the major can do is get me thrown out of the cavalry. And if he did that, I might be forced to go back to Illinois and sit on the porch of my daughter's house and watch her young uns scamper around my feet. No, sir, Cody, don't you worry about me and the major."

Remounting, they rode on for another couple of hours, still following the trail of the outlaws. From the looks of the tracks, Whittingham hadn't done anything to try to hide the signs of their passage. Of course, that would have been hard to do, considering there were over a dozen horses and nearly that many mules in the group. The Englishman had to be mighty confident that they were heading for a place where pursuit couldn't follow them, Cody thought.

They finally quit for the day when it became too dark to see any tracks. Looking for a place to camp, they found a sheltered spot in a grove of cottonwoods beside another creek. The two men talked little. Exhausted as they were, sleep came quickly and easily.

Cody and Gresham were both up before dawn to push on, and around midday the tracks they were following wound up at Madera Canyon, just as Cody had expected. He and the sergeant reined in and sat their horses on the edge of the canyon.

"Has Whittingham made for here every time?" Cody asked.

"He hasn't run for this canyon after every single job," Gresham replied, shaking his head. "Leastwise, not from what I've heard. You've got to remember I haven't trailed him after any of his civilian jobs until now. The times I've tracked him, the trail usually peters out somewhere around here, but I reckon he's got two or three different hidey-holes."

"But the main one's down there somewhere," Cody said, nodding toward the vast canyon.

"I'd say that's a good guess."

Cody sighed. "We've been through there once. Nothing left to do but head down there again."

They found a slope shallow enough to negotiate and entered the canyon. Cody kept his eyes on the rocky walls as they rode along. Everything looked different from the way it had when he was here the first time. That was characteristic of these mountain canyons, he knew. He'd heard plenty of stories about lost treasures that got lost because the folks who hid them couldn't ever find them again, even with maps and good memories. The mountains sometimes guarded their secrets jealously, and it took a keen eye to spot things that seemed to be right out in the open—once you knew where they were.

It turned out to be another frustrating day for the Ranger. For a while he and Gresham were able to follow the tracks in the canyon itself, but then they vanished as if all those horses and mules had disappeared along with them. Late in the afternoon Cody was forced to admit that they were riding in circles and not accomplishing a damned thing. As difficult as it was to accept, there was nothing left to do but return to Fort Davis.

"We'd better head back," Cody finally said, putting into words what neither of them wanted to say. "You don't want to be away from the post another night."

"Yeah, I reckon it'd be best to get back," Gresham agreed with a sigh. He tried to sound encouraging as he went on, "We'll find them one of these days, Cody. They can't stay hidden forever."

Cody just grunted. He was starting to wonder. There had been plenty of times since he'd joined the Rangers when he hadn't known if he was going to come out of a tight spot alive. But this was the first time he felt that he might absolutely fail in his mission. He didn't like the feeling, didn't like it one damned bit.

One more mark, he thought, to chalk up beside Barry Whittingham's name. If he ever did catch up to the Englishman, it was going to take a while to even the score.

As usual, Cody and Gresham parted company before they reached the fort. The Ranger skirted the military post and rode on into the settlement, and as he walked the dun down the street, he thought that things were quieter than usual this evening. The folks he saw out and about had sort of a glum look to them, and he figured it was because of all the bodies Sheriff Randine must have brought in by now. There had probably been a mass funeral and burial today for the slain drovers and guards from the mule train, and that was enough to sober up the whole town.

In no mood to face Randine and report his lack of success, Cody avoided the sheriff's office and went straight
to the Limpia Hotel. A good hot meal in the dining room
made him feel a little better. So did the fact that Leigh
Gilmore wasn't waiting in the lobby to waylay him as
soon as he came in. In fact, he didn't see the girl or her
attorney at all.

After he had eaten, Cody strolled down the street, still
postponing his report to Randine. He turned in at a small
saloon he had patronized a couple of times during his stay
in Fort Davis. The younger cowboys tended to avoid it,
leaving it to the older hands and the townspeople. That
made it a quieter place than some, and after the last couple
of days he could use a nice peaceful drink, Cody thought.

As he had expected, there were a few veteran cowpunchers leaning on the bar, and some of the tables were
occupied by townies. At a table in the rear of the place,
instead of a poker game such as one found in many saloons,
a leisurely game of dominoes was going on between some
of Fort Davis's old-timers. Cody had grown up with the
friendly sound of dominoes being shuffled and played,
and after he had gotten a beer from the bartender, he
wandered over to the table to watch the game for a few
minutes.

"Well, I reckon I'll set you up, Mose, but I'll put that
double-four out there anyway," one of the players said. He
played the domino, then glanced up at Cody. "You need
somethin', young fella?"

Cody shook his head. "Nope. Just thought I'd watch the
game for a while, if that's all right with you gents."

"Sure." The man looked at the player to his left. "You
goin' to put that double-six out there or not?"

"Who said I had double-six?" asked the second old man.

"I know you got it."

"Then why'd you play that double-four?"

"Reckon I just felt generous."

The man called Mose shook his head. "Nope, I know
you, Howard. You're tryin' to trick me somehow. But it
ain't goin' to work. I'll just play that double-six and make
my twenty-five."

"Thirty!" exclaimed the next player, slapping down a double-five.

Howard leaned back and grinned at his partner. "Figured you had that double-five, Alvy," he said.

The fourth man frowned at the dominoes laid out on the table and shook his head. "With all them spots out there, I ought to be able to make somethin'. But durned if I can see what it is."

"Jinglebob'd figger out a way if he was here," one of the other men said. "I never saw anybody who could make somethin' out of nothin' in a domino game the way he can."

"Where is ol' Jinglebob tonight?"

"Got him a job."

"A job? Jinglebob? You sure about that?"

The other man nodded. "Yep. He signed as guide for a couple of tenderfoots. He's goin' to take 'em into the mountains on some fool's errand. Ought to be up there now, in fact." The speaker laughed. "Heard tell one of the folks he's workin' for is a female."

The other three men shook their heads. One of them said, "Jinglebob workin' for a female . . . That's hard to believe, boys."

Cody had been listening with only half an ear, but suddenly the conversation caught his attention. He leaned forward, hoping these elderly gentlemen wouldn't think he was intruding by asking some questions. He was starting to have a bad feeling about what he had just heard.

"Who's this fella Jinglebob you're talking about?" he asked.

"Friend of ours," Mose replied, looking up at the Ranger. "Jinglebob Hanrahan's his name. Old Injun fighter and prospector; knows the mountains like the back of his hand. Better, I reckon."

"You know anything about the people who hired him as a guide?"

The old man shook his head. "Nope. Jinglebob said he was goin' to rent some hosses for 'em, though, so you might ask around down at the livery stable. What business is it of your'n, young feller?"

"I don't know yet," Cody answered honestly. He drained the rest of his beer and set the mug on the table. "Thanks, men," he said as he turned away.

On the way out of the saloon he paused at the bar long enough to hand the bartender a coin and tell him to take a round of beers to the domino table, then hurried out and turned toward the livery stable.

Alarm bells had gone off in his mind as soon as he heard mention of how two tenderfeet—one of them a woman— had hired the old man called Jinglebob to take them into the Davis Mountains. Folks weren't traveling much in those mountains these days, with good reason. It'd take an even better reason for a couple of greenhorns to do it.

Like the search for a missing sister.

Cody strongly suspected that the two people who had hired Jinglebob Hanrahan were Leigh Gilmore and Josiah Breedlove. When he reached the livery stable, a conversation with the hostler at the stable confirmed that suspicion. Both of the visitors from Dallas had come to the stable with Hanrahan to pick up their mounts, and the hostler described them accurately, especially Leigh. That wasn't surprising; the hostler was a young man, and Leigh was an exceptionally pretty girl. And the youngster had also noticed that Breedlove seemed quite uncomfortable about the whole thing, as if he thought they were making a bad mistake.

On principle Cody hated to agree with lawyers, especially lawyers from someplace like Dallas, but in this case Breedlove was right. It was a bad mistake for them to head into the mountains.

His rugged face grim, Cody asked the hostler, "Have you got a good horse I can rent? My dun's been ridden too far in the past couple of days. He's worn out, needs some rest and grain."

"Sure, Mr. Cody. How about that roan over there in the second stall? He's a mite feisty sometimes, but he's got sand."

Cody looked at the horse. Calling the animal feisty was probably an understatement. The roan had a downright mean look in his eye. But he was also tall and sturdily built, and he looked like he could handle a hard ride into the mountains. Cody nodded and said, "Saddle him up for me."

"You're leaving again? I thought you just got back to town a little while ago."

"Don't have any choice," Cody said. "I'm afraid the decision's been taken right out of my hands."

By a foolish girl, a lawyer, and an old man, he added silently to himself.

Sergeant Rufe Gresham was met at the edge of the parade ground by a corporal and several troopers, all of whom grinned broadly when they recognized him.

"Glad to see you're back, Sarge," the corporal said. "We done covered for you last night, but I ain't sure we could've got away with it again."

"Thanks, Johnny," Gresham said as he swung down from the Army-issue saddle and led his tired horse across the parade ground. Gresham's shoulders were slumping with weariness. The other soldiers followed him eagerly.

"Major Monroe wants to see you," the corporal went on.

Gresham looked sharply at him. "The major doesn't know I was gone last night, does he?"

"Nope, this is about something else," the corporal said with a shake of his head. "Like I said, we made sure nobody knew you was gone, Sarge. When the major sent word you was to come to his office, we told the orderly we'd find you as soon as we could."

Gresham clapped the man on the shoulder and then handed over the reins. "Take care of my mount, Johnny," he said. "And thanks again for covering for me. I reckon I'd better go see what the major wants."

Summoning up some more energy, Gresham tramped toward the headquarters building, where lamps were still glowing brightly in the windows. Major Monroe was working late again. That wasn't unusual; Gresham didn't care for a lot of Monroe's ideas, but there was no denying the young officer was a go-getter.

Monroe's orderly was still on duty, too, and he leapt to his feet as soon as Gresham came into the outer office. "Where've you been, Sergeant?" he hissed. "Major Monroe's been waiting for you!"

"Been busy, son," Gresham told the young white corporal. "Just let the major know I'm here if you would, please."

The orderly hurried over to the door of Monroe's office and rapped on it. Opening it without waiting for a response, he said crisply, "Sergeant Gresham reporting as ordered, sir."

"Well, show him in, show him in," ordered Monroe's peevish-sounding voice from inside the office.

Gresham stepped into the room and gave the major a smart salute, which Monroe returned just as smartly. "Sergeant Gresham reporting, sir," the veteran noncom said.

"It's about time," Monroe snapped. "I haven't seen much of you around here the past couple of days, Sergeant. You haven't been neglecting your duties, have you?"

"No, sir!" Gresham answered truthfully. The way he saw it, tracking down the outlaws who had looted a couple of Army supply trains and killed a dozen troopers was more his duty than anything else.

"At ease, then, Sergeant." Major Vance Monroe leaned back in his chair. He picked up a piece of paper from his desk and went on, "I received a wire from the War Department this afternoon. Another supply train will be arriving here at the post in a few days." Monroe paused meaningfully. "Along with the usual supplies, it will be carrying the garrison's payroll."

Gresham blinked. Sending a payroll along with supplies was an unusual procedure. Obviously Major Monroe recognized it as irregular, too.

"The thinking is that with all the outlaw trouble we've had around here recently, the payroll would be too tempting a target," Monroe continued. "So the paymaster is sending it with the supplies and not adding any extra guards to the caravan in hopes of fooling this man Whittingham." He added with a sigh, "I think this is a mistake."

"Yes, sir," Gresham said, once again replying honestly and thinking how unusual it was for him to agree with the major like this. Whittingham was too sharp to be fooled that way. The outlaw chieftain seemed to know everything that went on in the area.

"However, it's too late to increase security. The supply train has already left from San Antonio. So I'm going to do the next best thing. I'm going to send out a patrol to meet the supply train and accompany it on to the fort. The paymaster may not like it, but I won't be disobeying a direct order. There was nothing in the telegram saying that we couldn't furnish some guards of our own."

That was pretty smart thinking on the major's part, Gresham had to admit. He was prepared for Monroe's next statement.

"I want you to go along with that patrol, Sergeant."

"Of course, sir," Gresham said. "I'd be honored."

Monroe nodded. "Very good. We'll ride out at daybreak tomorrow."

Gresham started to salute and turn away, but then the full import of Monroe's words sank in. "*We,* sir?"

"That's right." Monroe looked up at him. "I'll be leading this patrol, Sergeant. Surely you didn't think I'd leave something this important to my subordinates, did you? I'm taking personal responsibility for the safety of that payroll."

Gresham didn't say anything. There was nothing *to* say. He couldn't very well tell the major what a damned stupid idea it was for Monroe to go along on the mission. If he opened his mouth now and expressed his true feelings, he'd probably wind up being busted back to private. And at his age Gresham wasn't sure he could stand that.

Finally he made his mouth work enough to say, "Yes, sir, I understand."

"Very good. You'll be in charge of picking the men for the patrol. Dismissed, Sergeant."

Gresham saluted again and left when Monroe had returned it. His steps were even slower and more plodding as he headed for his barracks.

With Monroe in charge, there was a good chance all of them might wind up dead, the sergeant thought. But maybe not. Maybe with some luck, he'd still retire in a few years to that front porch and those grandkids.

But right now Gresham wouldn't have bet money on it. And he sure as hell wouldn't have bet that payroll. . . .

Leigh wouldn't have believed it was possible for one man to talk as much as Jinglebob Hanrahan did. By the time she, Breedlove, and the old man had spent part of one day, a night, and most of the next day on the trail, Leigh thought that surely her hearing would abandon her under the constant assault of profane stories. Not to mention the fact that Jinglebob seemed to insist on riding within smelling distance, no matter how much she tried to shy away from him.

She couldn't complain about his services as a guide so far, however. He obviously knew the mountain trails quite well, and he had fixed the three of them a comfortable camp beside a creek the night before.

Now it was late afternoon of the second day. Leigh was tired and sore from riding, but she had often gone horseback riding in Dallas, so that helped. Josiah Breedlove, on the other hand, was in utter misery. The attorney hadn't ridden a horse in years, and though he kept his complaints to himself in a gloomy silence, Leigh knew he had to be suffering the torments of the damned. Of course, to Jinglebob, who had spent most of his life in a saddle, the ride was no more taxing than a leisurely Sunday stroll.

If only he would put an end to the endless stories, Leigh thought.

He had started with his birth on a farm in Georgia in 1810, then continued up to the present day, explaining how his family had come to Texas when he was just a baby so that he knew no other home than the Lone Star State. Then there were battles against the Mexicans who had owned the place; Jinglebob had been one of the few survivors of the Goliad Massacre and had gone on to fight at San Jacinto with General Sam Houston. After that there had been Indian fighting, then more battles in the Mexican War, then the time of the great Comanche raids in the bloody sixties. Jinglebob had grown old drifting west, and the past few years had been spent prospecting with unspectacular results in the Davis Mountains, the Big Bend, and the Guadalupes farther west. He had settled down to an uneasy retirement in Fort Davis, and he was just winding up a lament about how there was little for an old man to do these days except play dominoes and remember when the West had been really wild.

"It must have been a lonely life," Leigh said, feeling an obligation to at least try to make conversation with him. "No wife, no children . . . always living alone and doing all that fighting."

"Never said I didn't have no wife," Jinglebob replied. "Shoot, I been married six times, little lady. Lost track o' how many kids I had along the way."

"Married six times?" Breedlove said, probably trying to take his mind off his own miseries.

"Yes, sir. And there was even two of 'em what was white. Two white women, two squaws, and two Meskins. I always did believe in not playin' no favorites."

Leigh stared at him, saw that he was absolutely serious, then shook her head. She had never met anyone like Jinglebob Hanrahan before.

And with any luck, once she left the Davis Mountains she never would again.

As dusk approached, Jinglebob found another good campsite next to one of the many creeks that flowed through these mountains. Leigh was grateful when the old man called a halt, but not as grateful as Breedlove. The attorney climbed down stiffly from his horse and walked to the creek with tentative little steps. He looked at the water for a long moment, then said fervently, "If I wasn't a gentleman, I swear I'd take down my pants and sit right in that stream."

Despite the fact that they were in the middle of a wilderness, looking for a band of vicious outlaws who had kidnapped her sister, Leigh had to laugh. Breedlove flushed almost as red as the setting sun, and Leigh knew he must really be in pain to compromise his dignity by such a comment. That thought made her turn solemn.

"I appreciate your coming with us, Josiah," she said. "I know you didn't think it was a good idea to come out here—"

"And I still don't," Breedlove put in.

Leigh went to his side, came up on her toes, and brushed her lips across his cheek. "Thank you for everything you've done," she said softly.

"Just doing my job as your family's attorney," he replied in a gruff voice.

Leigh knew better than that. Tramping around these mountains was hardly one of his duties as the Gilmore family lawyer.

"How 'bout gatherin' me some firewood, missy?" Jinglebob called from the other side of the clearing beside the creek. "Once we got a fire goin', I'll fix us some grub."

"All right," Leigh replied. One other thing she had discovered about Jinglebob: He was a surprisingly good cook. The meal the night before had been plain enough—biscuits and bacon and beans, the staples of a frontiersman's diet—but Jinglebob had made it taste better than it should have. The skill came from being on his own so much of the time, Leigh supposed.

She started picking up twigs and branches from the ground, gradually moving farther and farther away from Jinglebob and Breedlove. Night fell quickly out here once the sun was down, she had noticed, and shadows were already closing in. She stepped up beside a clump of mesquite to see if there were any fallen branches under the scrubby trees.

The figure that materialized in front of her was almost as formless as a shadow at first. Leigh stopped in her tracks, her breath catching in her throat. The shape resolved itself into that of a man, a tall, slender man—with a gun in his hand.

"Don't worry," he said in a deep voice. "I won't hurt you."

Leigh wanted to scream, wanted to turn and flee, but something held her there, still and silent. Unnoticed, the branches she had gathered slipped from her hands. The man with the gun moved forward into the last fading light of day, and when he saw her face he stopped just as suddenly as she had done.

"Sara," he breathed, his voice husky with shock.

That was when Leigh screamed.

She whirled around, darted away from his reaching hand, felt his fingers brush her back. The touch gave her added speed as she sprinted toward the campsite.

Then she stopped again, terror making her heart pound wildly in her chest. Jinglebob and Breedlove were standing motionless, their hands raised to shoulder level, as the hard-faced men around them covered them with six-guns.

"Don't give 'em no trouble, missy," Jinglebob advised in an angry voice. "They done got the drop on us."

The man who had startled her so caught up to her with a couple of long strides. He grasped her shoulder and turned her around, not roughly but inexorably.

Then he stared down at her from his great height and demanded in as confused a voice as Leigh had ever heard, "Who *are* you?"

CHAPTER
11

Seth Williams was wondering the same thing. The girl was a dead ringer for Sara Gilmore.

"My . . . my name is Leigh Gilmore," the young woman finally said when she was able to talk again. Her voice quivered with fear and shock.

Seth couldn't blame her for that. She and her companions were surrounded by as dangerous-looking a band of cutthroats as could be found in these mountains . . . or, for that matter, anywhere else. She probably figured she was only moments away from death—or worse.

The night before, one of Whittingham's men had returned to the outlaw camp to report seeing a campfire some distance away. Travelers had become pretty scarce around here, so out of curiosity Whittingham had decided to see who these pilgrims were. That morning he had ridden out from the camp with several men, Seth among them, and picked up the trail late in the day. Now they had closed in, but what they had found was nothing like what they had expected. A young woman, an old man, and a middle-aged tenderfoot—an unlikely trio to be out here in the middle of nowhere.

Especially when the girl looked just like somebody else.

"Gilmore," Whittingham repeated softly. He nodded. "I understand now. You're Sara's sister. I knew she had one, but I didn't know that the two of you—" He broke off his comment and shook his head. "Never mind. Come along. I know you've had a long ride today, but I have to ask you to indulge me."

Leigh Gilmore found her voice again. "You're him," she said accusingly. "You're Barry Whittingham."

"That is correct," he murmured.

Suddenly, she was on him, screaming curses that she shouldn't have even known, given her ladylike appearance, and pounding her tiny fists against his chest. Whittingham grimaced and tried to back away from her. He said, "Wait, please! There's no need for this!" The girl ignored him, though, just as she ignored the threat of the guns all around her, swept away as she was by her fury. Whittingham snapped, "Someone get her off me!"

Seth was the closest. Leaping forward and at the same time holstering his Colt, he grabbed the girl's shoulders and pulled her back, away from Whittingham. When she tried to wrench away from him, he bear-hugged her, pinning her arms to her sides. She was strong for a little thing, Seth thought as he struggled to hang on to her and regretting having to do so. He enjoyed having his arms full of a squirming young woman, but only when she wanted to be there. This wasn't fun at all.

"Let her go, damn you!" That was the tenderfoot. He was trembling with anger, but the outlaw guns pointing at him kept him from doing anything except shouting angrily.

"You're nothin' but a bunch of polecats lower'n a snake's belly!" the old man added. "Why, if I was ten years younger, I'd thrash the lot o' yuh! Mebbe I'll do it anyway!"

"You'd better settle down," Seth hissed at the girl. "If you don't, your friends are liable to get hurt."

"Ooohh!" she exclaimed in a mixture of dismay and rage. "You leave them alone!"

"We'll leave 'em alone, lady, but you got to stop fightin' like this," he warned.

Seth's urgent words must have gotten through to her, because she suddenly went limp in his arms. That didn't feel particularly good to him, either.

"This is ridiculous," Whittingham said impatiently. "Get them on their horses. I want to get back to camp and find out what's going on."

So did Seth. He was afraid that the presence of these three was only going to complicate his job that much more.

The old jasper and the greenhorn got back on their horses grudgingly, the greenhorn sputtering out his name and the fact that he was an attorney and threatening to see them all at the end of a rope for this. The girl was more trouble. She hadn't fainted, but she had a stunned, faraway look on her face now, and she didn't cooperate, either. Seth had to practically pick her up and put her in her saddle. Of course, as small and slender as she was, that wasn't too difficult a chore. Once she was mounted, he got his own horse out of the brush where it was concealed across the creek and rode up alongside her. He was going to keep a close eye on her to make sure nothing happened to her—and to make sure she didn't go crazy again.

Full dark had settled by now, and Seth was glad Whittingham knew where he was going. He'd have been good and lost if he had been by himself. But the gang rode at a brisk clip despite the darkness, keeping the prisoners moving by surrounding them. Less than an hour later they reached Madera Canyon and descended into it.

How Whittingham found his way now, Seth didn't know. He'd have had enough trouble finding the entrance to the hideout in broad daylight. The gang moved through a jumble of massive boulders and then rode single file through the jagged switchbacks leading into the cleft that eventually opened out into the hollow where the camp was located. Seth knew from experience that you could stand ten feet from the opening and not see it unless you happened to be at exactly the right angle.

When they finally emerged at the hideout, the usual fire was burning in the center of the camp, and Sara was standing on the porch of the cabin. As the riders entered the circle of light cast by the flames, Seth saw Sara stiffen in surprise at the sight of the prisoners. She took a couple of tentative steps down from the porch, then suddenly broke into a run. "Leigh!" she cried.

Life came back into Leigh Gilmore's eyes. Seth grabbed the reins of her horse to steady the animal as Leigh slid down from the saddle. Whittingham made a curt gesture, telling his men not to interfere with her. The two young women ran toward each other, and as they embraced, Seth saw that what he already suspected was true. They were identical twins. Sara's hair was a little shorter and they wore different clothes, of course, but those were the only ways the young Ranger could tell them apart.

Whittingham rode up to them and reined in, crossing his hands on the saddle horn and watching the tearful reunion with a sardonic smile on his face. After a moment he said, "You told me you had a sister, Sara, but you didn't say anything about the two of you being twins."

Sara looked up at him and said, "Where did you . . . ? How . . . ?" She turned her attention back to Leigh and went on, "What are you *doing* here?"

"Looking for you," Leigh replied. "I *knew* you were still alive. I *knew* those outlaws who kidnapped you hadn't killed you."

Sara caught her bottom lip between her teeth and gnawed on it for a moment, obviously upset about something. She looked past Leigh and saw the other two prisoners, seemingly for the first time. "Josiah!" she exclaimed, recognizing the lawyer.

"Are you all right, Sara?" Breedlove asked anxiously.

"Of course I'm all right. You and Leigh came all the way out here to look for me. . . . I can hardly believe it."

"Well, what were we supposed to do?" Leigh demanded. "You get carried away into the mountains by some bandits, and you don't expect your sister to come after you?"

"No, I didn't." Sara took a deep breath. "You see, Leigh, the truth is I wasn't kidnapped. I *wanted* to go with Barry."

Seth saw the stunned look on Leigh's face, saw it mirrored on Breedlove's puffy features. The old man in buckskins just shook his head and muttered, "Well, if that don't beat all."

Whittingham told his men to dismount and take care of their horses. When Seth swung down from the saddle, Amos and Tug came up to him. Tug reached for the reins and said, "We'll take care of your hoss for you, Seth."

"Looks like you come back with quite a prize," Amos added, grinning at Leigh Gilmore. "Or do you think Barry'll want to keep her for himself, too? That could get mighty excitin', havin' both those gals in your bunk at the same time, lookin' just alike the way they do."

Seth scowled as Tug led the horse away toward the rope corral. Amos had been spending a lot of time with Frank Parker lately, and the influence of the hardened outlaw was beginning to show.

"I reckon Barry'll do whatever he wants to," Seth snapped. "He usually does."

Amos raised his eyebrows in surprise at Seth's tone. Seth didn't care. It was getting harder and harder to stomach the masquerade he was trapped in.

Sara led her sister onto the cabin's porch, with Whittingham and Parker following. Seth meandered over that way, too, anxious to hear what was said between Sara and Leigh. He had a feeling he was about to learn something.

"I don't understand any of this," Leigh was saying, her distress obvious. "You *wanted* to come with this . . . this outlaw?"

"Barry and I are in love," Sara declared. "We have been ever since we met in El Paso two years ago, while I was visiting Aunt Ruth and Uncle Peter out there."

"I remember that trip. You . . . you seemed the same when you came back."

Sara smiled. "I had to hide the way I felt. Mother and Father never would have understood if I told them I was in love. They would have said I was still just a child, that I didn't know what I was talking about. But Barry and I kept in touch, and we planned for the day we could be together again."

"Then that wasn't just a random holdup when the outlaws stopped the stagecoach you were on?" The question came from Breedlove, who had been brought over to the porch by a couple of members of the gang.

"Not at all, Josiah. Everything was arranged ahead of time. I pretended to everyone that I was going out to El Paso for another visit. We just gave the appearance of a kidnapping so that no one would stand in my way."

Leigh said, "But this man's an outlaw!"

Sara shrugged, then looked her sister in the eye. "I didn't know everything about Barry," she admitted. "But I'd rather be here with him, no matter what he is, than be stifled in a boring existence back in Dallas." She took Whittingham's hand. "I love him, Leigh. And I don't like you judging us. I didn't ask you to come out here, after all."

Leigh looked crestfallen. "You're right. I guess I've made a terrible mistake."

Breedlove massaged his temples. "This is dreadful, just dreadful. What are we going to do now?"

"You're going to stay right here, sir," Whittingham said. "Now that you know where our sanctuary is located, we can't have you scurrying back to Fort Davis to inform the authorities."

The old man had wandered over in time to hear that part of the conversation. He had been disarmed, and though a couple of the owlhoots were keeping an eye on him, he didn't seem to be a threat. "He means they're goin' to kill us, sonny," he said now to Breedlove.

"No!" Sara cried, turning to Whittingham. "You can't mean that, Barry."

"Not at all," Whittingham assured her, though from the glance he cast toward Breedlove and the old-timer, it was obvious that he'd have cheerfully plugged both of them. "But we have to keep them here for the time being, Sara. I have some big plans, and we can't allow anything to jeopardize them."

"But surely you can let my sister go."

Whittingham shook his head. "That's just not feasible right now. Besides, you wouldn't want me to release her without her two companions. She'd hardly be safe out here on her own."

That answer made sense to Seth, and it seemed to satisfy Sara, too, because she didn't protest anymore. She just stepped over to Leigh, took her sister's hand, and said, "I'm sorry. But everything will be all right. You'll see."

Leigh didn't look convinced, and Seth didn't feel too certain of that, either. Also, he was wondering exactly what those big plans were that Whittingham had just mentioned.

No sooner had he posed the question to himself than it looked like he was about to find out. Whittingham called everyone over to the cabin, and as he gazed down at the assembled gang, he said, "Some of you are already wondering what our next undertaking will be. Based on information I received earlier today, before we left, I can now tell you that we'll soon be in a position to realize our most lucrative results yet. One of my contacts has informed me that an Army payroll will be arriving in this area in the next few days, concealed in a regular supply caravan such as the ones we've raided twice before."

That announcement brought on a stirring among the outlaws. The silver they had captured a couple of nights earlier had been quite a haul, but an Army payroll could add up to even more.

Whittingham held up his hands for quiet, and when the men had settled down, the Englishman continued, "I don't know exactly when the supply train will be arriving in the vicinity, but I intend to send out teams of men far enough along the trail to watch for it and then give the rest of us plenty of time to await its arrival. We shall set up an ambush just as we did with the others. It shouldn't be too difficult."

No, not difficult, thought Seth. Just murderous. He felt sure none of the soldiers with the pack train would come through alive.

He couldn't let that happen again. The memories of what he had already seen would prey on his mind for the rest of his days. Somehow he had to find a way to stop this raid from going off as Whittingham planned.

The bandit chieftain dismissed his men and went into the cabin, taking Sara and her sister with him. Breedlove and the old man were left to sit on the porch with a man standing guard nearby. The other outlaws wandered off and went about their usual business, which consisted mainly of eating, telling stories, and playing cards. When they weren't off killing and looting, they weren't such a bad bunch of fellows, Seth thought—at least most of them weren't. Frank Parker was always unfriendly, even more so now that Seth had defeated him in their fight. That hadn't affected Parker's status as Whittingham's lieutenant, but it had deepened the hatred that Parker felt for the young Ranger. Seth was sure of that.

Amos and Tug came up to him as he sat down cross-legged with his back against a rock. "You look a mite down in the mouth," Tug said. "What're you broodin' about, Seth? Things are goin' just fine."

"I'm wonderin' what Whittingham's really going to do with that girl and the other two," Seth said with a sigh.

"Yeah, me, too," Amos said. He wiped the back of his hand across his mouth. "One thing's for sure. He can't let 'em out of here alive. And where that gal's concerned, it's going to be a damned shame to have to kill her."

Inside the cabin Sara Gilmore sat her sister down at a rough-hewn table and handed her a plate piled high with food. There was stew from the pot on the cooking fire outside, plus cornbread and beans and a pot of coffee. Leigh picked up her fork and began eating without enthusiasm. Sara wished she could say or do something to cheer her up, but she was afraid her sister would never understand. Leigh wasn't at all the impulsive type; that was why making a perilous journey into the wilds of West Texas was so unlike her. As a child Leigh had always been the calmer of the two, the one more likely to want to please their parents. Sara had been just the opposite. She had wanted her own way, and she had been prepared to do whatever was necessary to get it.

Things really hadn't changed much since then, Sara thought as she watched her sister.

A figure suddenly filled Sara's peripheral vision, and she looked over to see Whittingham standing impatiently in the doorway of the cabin's lone bedroom. Excusing herself to her sister, Sara joined him, and he shut the door behind them. She thought from the look on his face that he had love-making on his mind, but that turned out not to be the case.

"I'm sorry about your sister," he said to her in a low voice that wouldn't carry to the other side of the wall. "If I had known who she was, I never would have told the men to capture those travelers. I'd have let them wander around out here to their heart's content. They never would have found us."

"I don't understand why you can't let them go," Sara protested. "I know my sister, and I know Josiah Breedlove. If your men took them back nearly to Fort Davis and then released them, they'd never find their way back here. Never."

"That old man might," Whittingham mused. "He's called Jinglebob Hanrahan, and I know of his reputation. He's quite a talented scout. He could find this hideout again, I'm sure of it."

"Then hold him and let Leigh and Josiah go. They're not any threat."

Whittingham shook his head. "I'm sorry, Sara. I can't take that chance." He came closer and let his hands rest on her shoulders as he looked down at her. "Listen to me. This next job will provide us with a great deal of money. With the loot we already have cached, we'll have enough to last us a long time, perhaps the rest of our lives. How would you like to leave here and go somewhere else? San Francisco, perhaps, or Mexico?"

She let her head rest against his chest and replied truthfully, "I'd love it."

"Then be patient with me. Soon, very soon, we'll be able to do that. Until then, we'll keep your sister and her friends here. But don't worry about them. They'll be safe; you have my word."

And he was a man of his word. Sara knew that, and she felt a bit better. Leigh would have to endure a few days of captivity, but then Whittingham would arrange her release. Then, with Sara at his side, he would leave this part of the country and leave his outlaw past behind him as well.

She had to cling to that hope. It was all that sustained her now.

By the next night, nothing had changed, and Seth was feeling the frustration growing within him, not to mention the confusion that kept his mind racing constantly.

The best solution would be to slip away from the hideout, get back to Fort Davis, and warn Cody and the other authorities about the ambush Whittingham planned to spring on the Army supply train. But it was hardly an ideal solution.

For one thing he hadn't yet come up with a way to get out of the closely guarded camp, and for another, if he *did* get away, there was a good chance Whittingham would kill Leigh, Breedlove, and Jinglebob Hanrahan. Seth had to weigh their lives against the lives of the troopers who would surely be killed when the gang bushwhacked the caravan. It was a decision that had had him agonizing sleeplessly long into the night before and yet again—or was it still?—this one.

Finally in the gray light of approaching dawn he came to the conclusion that he had to get away and carry the warning about the planned raid. But that was a whole hell of a lot easier said than done.

The entrance to the hideout was always guarded, of course. Men were coming and going a lot of the time, as Whittingham sent out relays of riders to keep an eye on the trail the pack mules carrying the payroll would follow. Seth had hoped to be one of those riders so that he'd have a chance to slip away, but so far Whittingham had tapped other men for that job. Seth couldn't volunteer without looking too suspicious, like he wanted to get away from the camp. He had to bide his time. Amos and Tug hadn't been picked for that assignment, either, and it was only to be expected that Whittingham would choose the men who had been with him the longest and the ones he trusted the most.

With the exception of Frank Parker. Parker seldom left the camp unless Whittingham was with him. That was poor tactics, Seth thought. Chances were, if anything happened to one of them, it would happen to the other one, too. That could leave the gang without a leader.

But maybe that was what Whittingham wanted. Maybe he didn't fully trust Parker.

That evening Seth discovered that Whittingham had plenty of reason to distrust his second-in-command.

The young Ranger had just spent some time talking to Jinglebob Hanrahan. The elderly frontiersman reminded him of Captain Wallace Vickery and some of the other old-time Texans Seth had known. Jinglebob was eccentric, and he could have used a bath, but seeing the way he

watched the outlaws all the time just waiting for a chance
to strike back told Seth that the old man had a dangerous
core underneath the colorful exterior.

He hoped that Jinglebob, as well as Breedlove and the
girls, made it through this alive.

Strolling over to the corral to check on his horse, Seth
heard the faint sound of voices coming from behind a
clump of bushes beside the enclosure. He moved closer,
now being careful not to make any noise. Sam Cody had
taught him how to walk quietly, like an Indian, and Seth
was putting that lesson to good advantage. Within moments
he was close enough to make out what was being said on
the other side of that screening brush.

"You sure about this, Frank?" a voice was asking. "If
everything don't go right, Whittingham'll kill us all."

"Whittingham won't have a chance to kill anybody,"
Frank Parker replied, the scorn he felt for his leader evident
in his voice. "He'll never expect a double cross. He won't
know what hit him."

Seth felt his heart begin to pound faster. If the gang fell
apart around him, spurred on by Parker's ambition and
resentment, it might be the best thing that could happen.
On the other hand, it could get Seth and all three of the
prisoners killed if Parker wound up in charge. He could
murder all of them without blinking.

That wasn't what Parker had in mind for the Gilmore
sisters, though. He went on, "Once Whittingham's out of
the way, we'll get word to the family of those girls back
in Dallas. I hear they're mighty rich. I reckon they'll pay
a big price to get 'em back. 'Course, they don't have to go
back in exactly the same condition as when they got here."
Parker chuckled.

Seth felt his jaw tightening in anger. Parker was long
overdue for a .45 slug through the brain, and Seth would've
given a lot to have a chance to put it there. But he couldn't
make his move yet.

"What about the old man and that lawyer?"

"We won't need 'em," Parker said. "Reckon we'll have
enough money so's we can afford a bullet for each of
'em." He laughed again. He sounded like he was in a

better mood than Seth had ever seen him in. Plotting to murder people was what had cheered him up, the young Ranger supposed.

He didn't wait to hear any more. Still moving quietly, Seth headed away from the corral and toward the cabin. An idea had occurred to him. If he exposed Parker's treachery to Whittingham, the Englishman would probably start to trust him a lot more. And that added trust could only work out to Seth's advantage.

Josiah Breedlove was sitting near the fire, a forlorn expression on his face. Beside him Jinglebob was spinning a yarn, oblivious to the fact that Breedlove was ignoring him. Seth looked past the two of them and saw Leigh and Sara sitting on straight-backed chairs at one end of the porch. Whittingham was at the other end, smoking a cigarette.

Seth came up to the porch and looked at Whittingham. "Talk to you for a minute?" he asked.

"Of course, Seth. What's on your mind?"

Seth stepped up onto the porch and sauntered over to the railing next to the Englishman. He perched a hip on it and said quietly and casually, "I thought you might like to know that Frank Parker's over there behind the corral with some of the men, and they're plannin' to kill you and take over the gang. Once they've done that, they're goin' to kill Breedlove and the old man and hold the girls for ransom."

Whittingham listened to the bold statement with no change in the expression on his face. He lifted the cigarette to his mouth, drew on it deeply so that it flared bright red in the shadows, then dropped the butt and ground it out under his bootheel. "Quite so," he said.

"Quite so," Seth agreed, although the expression sounded funny to him, coming out of his mouth.

"Am I supposed to believe this?"

"It's the truth," Seth insisted.

"Why don't I find out?" Whittingham nodded toward the corral, and when Seth looked over there, he saw that Parker and the other men had come out of hiding. For some reason he was glad that Amos and Tug weren't among the others.

"You can ask him about it, but don't expect him to tell you the truth," Seth warned.

"On the contrary," Whittingham said coldly, and Seth began to realize that he had misjudged the man. Whittingham wasn't as smart as he had thought. "I *do* expect Frank to tell me the truth. We've been together for quite some time, at least as far as men such as us measure these things. Whereas you I hardly know, Mr. Williams." Whittingham lifted his voice and called, "Frank! Would you come over here, please?"

Parker said, "Sure, Barry," and ambled over, thumbs hooked nonchalantly in his gun belt. For a man who had just been plotting against his boss, he looked awfully cool, Seth thought.

And that wasn't a good sign at all.

"Mr. Williams has been telling me an interesting story," Whittingham said as Parker came up onto the porch.

"Oh?" Parker glanced at Seth, the venom in his eyes plain to see.

"Yes, he claims that you and some of the other men have been plotting to overthrow me. A mutiny, as it were. What do you have to say to that, Frank?"

"A double cross?" Parker laughed harshly. "You know me better than that, Barry." He swung to face Seth, though he continued speaking to Whittingham. "This little son of a bitch has had a grudge against me ever since I pointed out what a coward he is."

"You mean the time I beat the hell out of you," Seth snapped, knowing it was unwise but unable to restrain himself.

For a second he thought Parker was going to draw then and there, and he was ready for the outlaw's hand to dip toward his gun butt. Seth was more than willing to match his own speed against Parker's. But Whittingham intervened, moving between them and saying, "That's quite enough. Frank, do I have your word that there's nothing to the story young Williams is telling?"

"There's not a damn word of truth in it," Parker growled.

"Good enough for me." Whittingham turned to face Seth. "You'd better walk lightly around here, my friend. Any more attempts at troublemaking, and I'll be forced to decide that we can dispense with your membership in our little organization."

Which meant they'd kill him, Seth knew. He looked one more time at Parker's smug grin, then nodded to Whittingham. "Sure. If that's the way you want it."

"It is."

Whittingham turned away, and Seth knew he had been dismissed. He stepped down from the porch, ignoring the looks from the other members of the gang, whose attention had been drawn when Whittingham called to Parker. He strode past them, heading for the fire and a cup of coffee.

The decision had been taken out of his hands, he thought as he hunkered beside the flames. Now he had another reason—as if he had needed one—to get out of here before Whittingham ambushed that supply caravan. If he waited, he'd never come back alive from that raid. Parker would see to that just as he intended to dispose of Whittingham.

Seth had to get out now—tonight if he could.

CHAPTER

12

The young Ranger waited until the camp was asleep to make his move. Of course, the place was never completely asleep. There were always guards. But most of the men had curled up in their bedrolls for the night, and the fire had died down to glowing embers.

Seth had spent the time debating exactly what he should do. The smartest course would be to try to slip out alone, but that would leave the prisoners at Whittingham's mercy. And somehow Seth didn't trust that to keep them alive—at least not Breedlove and old Jinglebob. Whittingham probably wouldn't kill Leigh, but he might turn her over to the rest of the gang. Death would no doubt be a better alternative than that.

The only thing he could do, Seth figured, was try to take the captives with him.

Jinglebob and Breedlove had bedrolls and slept outside like the rest of the men. Leigh was going to be the problem; she was inside the cabin with Sara and Whittingham. But Seth thought he could manage—if he had a distraction to occupy the outlaws. And he had just the thing in mind.

Sliding out of his bedroll, he picked up his boots and headed in his socks toward the corral. The gang's saddles were kept next to the corral on makeshift sawhorses, and Seth paused beside his saddle and lifted off the coiled rope. The rope, of twisted manila hemp, was thirty-three feet long, the standard length for a cowboy's lasso here in Texas. Seth wished it were a bit longer, but it would have to do. He carried it over to the steep slope on one side of the hollow, pausing to slip on his boots when he got farther away from the sleeping outlaws.

This wasn't going to be easy in the dark, but he had to give it a try. He set his feet, shook out a small loop, and began twirling the rope over his head, building up some speed with it. After a moment he flicked arm and wrist and sent the loop sailing up the rock-littered slope.

It slithered back down to him a second later.

His mouth set in a determined line, Seth tried again and then again. Finally on the fourth cast the loop caught on something. The young Ranger gave it a quick tug to set the loop, then gradually put more and more weight on the strand, feeling a slight give under the pressure.

Good. He didn't want it caught on anything strong enough to support his weight. That'd ruin everything.

The rope slipped again, and a tiny grating sound came to his ears. A rock moving, he decided, and a faint smile came to his face. He took a deep breath. Now he was as ready as he'd ever be.

He hauled back on the rope with all his strength.

There was another rasping sound, and suddenly the rope went slack in his fingers. Seth staggered back a step, thrown off balance by the abrupt release of tension. He caught himself and heard the clatter of the rock he had pulled free bounding down the slope, taking other rocks with it. The rockslide wasn't much of an avalanche, but it was the best he could do. He turned and started to open his mouth to yell out a warning.

The shout died in his throat. Two figures stood there, pointing guns at him. Tug Mitchell asked, "Seth, is that you? What in blue blazes are you doin', pard?"

"He's not our pard," Amos Bower put in coldly. "He's trying to double-cross us, just like he accused Frank of doin'."

For a second the sound of the rockslide grew to a small roar, and clouds of dust billowed into the air. Around the camp men sprang to their feet, shouting questions. Seth had planned to use this confusion to his advantage, but under the guns of Amos and Tug he had no chance to.

"Listen, fellas, you've got to let me get out of here," he said quickly. Friendship was the only weapon he had left. "It's important. Please don't try to stop me."

Even though he couldn't see their faces very well in the shadows, he sensed that Tug was wavering. "Amos?" asked the lanky former cowboy. "What should we do, Amos?"

"Only one thing we can do," Amos answered without hesitation. The barrel of his gun never wavered as he went on, "Nobody who's really one of us'd go to this much trouble to try to get outta here. Come on, Williams. Let's go see Barry and Frank."

The moment had passed, Seth knew. There was no way he could free the prisoners now. But he could still make a break, maybe get away and bring back some help.

He grabbed for his gun, twisting aside to dodge the flame that burst from Amos's Colt when the outlaw pulled the trigger and gave a startled curse at the same time. Seth's gun slithered out of leather and started to come up.

Tug leapt forward, lashing out with his pistol as Seth had done back in Fort Davis when he ran into the sheriff. The barrel of the gun slammed into Seth's wrist with numbing force. Tug batted Seth's revolver aside and shoved him down, landing on top of him with his own gun muzzle pressed up under Seth's chin. "Maybe I should've let Amos shoot you," Tug growled. "You best be still, Seth, or I'll ventilate you myself."

He was caught good and proper, Seth knew, and he stayed motionless on the ground until several more of the outlaws had run up to see what was going on. Then Seth was hauled to his feet and stood up in front of Whittingham and Parker. Somebody had gotten the fire going again, and one of the outlaws carried a torch that threw garish red light over the scene.

"Somehow I suspected you might be behind this commotion, Williams," Whittingham said.

"He was tryin' to escape," Amos said. "I reckon *he's* the one who planned to double-cross you, Barry."

"That's what I said all along," Parker snapped.

"I'm tired of this trouble," Whittingham said harshly. "I've got more important things on my mind right now.

Tie him up. Tie up the old man and the lawyer, too, so that we can stop worrying about them." He holstered his gun and stalked off toward the cabin.

"You heard the man," Parker said with a wicked grin. "Let's get 'em hog-tied." He stepped up to Seth and leered at him. "Reckon I'll tie you up myself. When I get through with you, mister, you won't be goin' anywhere—except to hell."

"The long way around, I hope," Seth muttered.

He saw the angry look flash across Parker's face, saw the gun come toward his head. But he couldn't get out of the way of the blow in time. The gun barrel smashed against his skull and sent him spinning to the ground. He felt himself hit, tasted dirt in his mouth.

Those were the last things he knew for a while—along with the fleeting thought that Cody was his only chance now.

Cody was tired. Once again back in the saddle, he had been riding up and down the mountain canyons for a couple of days, and he hadn't seen hide nor hair of Leigh Gilmore, Josiah Breedlove, and the old man they had hired to guide them. It was as if the three of them had just up and vanished.

Sort of like the way the Whittingham gang had disappeared.

That thought made Cody frown. Could Whittingham have grabbed them and taken them back to his hideout? Cody had to admit it was a possibility. More than that, really, considering the way Whittingham seemed to keep up with everything that went on in these mountains. He'd want to know what three strangers were doing out here, especially when one of them was a pretty girl.

After Cody had rolled out of his sugan that morning, he had eaten a cold breakfast and then mounted up, heading toward Madera Canyon. It wasn't that far from his campsite, and sometime during the previous night he had been roused from sleep by his warning instincts just in time to hear a faint rumble fading away. The sound of a rockslide, maybe? A few moments after that a gunshot had sounded, a single blast that hadn't been repeated.

Something was going on over there, Cody had decided; he had also decided it wouldn't be a good idea to go blundering in on it in the dark. He had waited until morning to start.

Now he was at the edge of the canyon. Reining in the rented horse, he looked out over the rugged terrain. Nothing looked different from the last time he had been here . . . yet *everything* looked different. That was the way of the mountains.

With a weary sigh he started the roan moving down into the canyon.

The column of troops moved smartly in the bright sunshine. The men were well trained and well disciplined, Rufe Gresham had to give them that. Of course, he could take credit for some of that, since he was one of the noncoms who had whipped the soldiers into such good shape. Major Monroe looked good at the head of the patrol, too, his uniform still crisp and not too dusty. The boy didn't even seem to sweat, Gresham thought.

They had left Fort Davis early the previous morning, heading east on the main trail through Limpia Canyon. That was the route the mule train would take, Gresham knew. It was the easiest approach to the fort, the one the supply caravans usually took. And the Army paymaster's bright idea had been to make everything look as normal as possible.

The patrol had brought enough rations along to stay out in the field for several more days if necessary, but Monroe said to Gresham when they were about an hour away from where they had made camp the night before, "I think we'll meet that supply train today, Sergeant. I have a feeling in my bones that they're close by."

"Didn't know there was anything in the regulations about following hunches," Gresham commented.

"What's that?" Monroe asked sharply, looking over at the sergeant riding beside and slightly behind him.

"No offense, sir," Gresham replied quickly. "Just didn't figure you were the type to play a hunch, sir."

"Well, perhaps you have me 'figured' all wrong, Sergeant."

"Yes, sir," Gresham said. Maybe the major was unbending a little, he mused. But if trouble came, he still expected Monroe to follow the book, regardless of the circumstances.

Only problem was that out here on the frontier trouble usually didn't follow any rules at all.

Seth had a headache when he woke up. It wasn't as bad as the pain he'd had when he came to after suffering that bullet crease, but it was bad enough. He moaned and tried to shift around, only to discover that he couldn't move.

When he finally forced his eyes open, he found that he was tied to a tree. A few feet away Josiah Breedlove and Jinglebob Hanrahan were in the same fix.

"Still alive, are you, boy?" Jinglebob asked. "Wasn't sure 'bout you; thought maybe Parker busted your head open when he clouted you with that hogleg."

"I'm alive," Seth told the old man. "I hurt too much to be dead."

Jinglebob let out a cackle of laughter. "I hear that. Felt the same way m'self, many a time."

Seth lifted his head and looked around. It was bright daylight, and he and the other two captives seemed to be alone in the camp. That wasn't possible, he told himself. Whittingham wouldn't have gone off and left the prisoners alone, not even tied up like this.

"What happened?" he asked hoarsely. "Where is everybody?"

A footfall sounded behind him, and Amos Bower appeared, walking past Seth to swing around and look down at him with a smug grin. "Don't worry, Williams," he said. "You ain't alone. Barry left Tug and me here to keep an eye on you while he and the others go get that Army payroll. One of the men out on patrol spotted that caravan this mornin'."

Across the camp the door of the cabin opened, and Tug Mitchell emerged from the building, followed by Leigh and Sara Gilmore. Tug hurried down the steps and over to the trees where the captives were tied.

"You all right, Seth?" he asked anxiously. "I saw Amos talkin' to you and figured you was awake. We was afraid Frank'd killed you by hittin' you so hard."

"I'm not goin' to die from being knocked out," Seth replied coolly. He knew Tug's concern was genuine, but under the circumstances it seemed sort of strange. "I'll die when Parker comes back and shoots me, though."

"Barry won't let that happen," Tug said. "He'll figure out some other way to take care of this so's you and these fellers don't get hurt. You wait and see."

Seth snapped, "Whittingham won't be back. Parker and some of the others plan to kill him as soon as the raid's over."

Amos snorted in disgust. "Are you still tryin' to get somebody to believe that story? Hell, Frank Parker's been in the outlaw game a long time. He wouldn't try to double-cross Barry."

"Yeah, Parker's been an owlhoot for a long time," Seth agreed. "But how many gangs has he been the leader of? None! He's always been the second-in-command, hasn't he? Don't you reckon he's gettin' a mite ambitious by now?"

"I don't want to listen to this," Amos said sharply. "Frank's a good man. Anybody can see that."

Anybody who wanted to shut his eyes to the kind of low-down skunk Parker really was, Seth thought. Amos had clearly convinced himself that Parker was trustworthy. Tug looked less sure of that, however, and Seth knew that if he had any hope of convincing one of them to help him, it'd be the lean, homely Tug.

Amos stalked off angrily, but Tug came over to the prisoners and knelt in front of Seth. "Don't be too mad at Amos, pard," he said quietly. "The way it looks to him, when you tried to run off last night, you didn't just cross Whittingham, you crossed us, too. I don't rightly see it like that, myself."

"Then you'll let us go?" Seth asked in little more than a whisper.

Tug shook his head regretfully. "Well, I can't do that, neither. I know you must've had a good reason for what you done, Seth, and if it was up to me . . . Ah, hell. It ain't up to me, and we both know it. Whittingham and his bunch saved our lives back in that canyon, when that posse had us bottled up. We just can't go against 'em."

Seth sighed heavily and nodded. "I understand, Tug," he said.

And he did understand. There were such things as loyalty and honor, even in outlaws. He couldn't expect Tug to go against his partners, even though he might be sympathetic to the spot Seth found himself in.

Leigh and Sara were still on the porch, and Seth could tell from the glances they sent toward the prisoners that they were upset by the situation. He didn't think Sara would cross Whittingham, since she was in love with the outlaw, but if Leigh got a chance to help them all escape, surely she would take it.

But she wasn't likely to get such a chance. Amos sauntered over toward the cabin and grinned up at the young women. "Mornin', ladies," he said. "Barry said Tug and me was to watch out for you, so if there's anythin' you need, you just let us know."

"We're fine," Sara said, folding her arms across her chest and looking away.

"How about you, little lady?" Amos asked Leigh, moving closer to the porch. "You look a mite upset. Maybe some lovin' would make you feel better."

"Leave me alone," Leigh said hollowly, her voice quivering. "I wouldn't have anything to do with a . . . a desperado like you!"

Amos grinned smugly. "You might change your tune after you've been here awhile. You'll need somebody to look out for you, like Barry looks out for your sister."

"That's enough," Sara snapped. "If you keep bothering us, I'll be sure and tell Barry about *that*."

Amos chuckled. "You do that, ma'am," he said with a smirk. "You just do that."

Seth saw the expression on his face and heard the arrogant tone in his voice and knew right away that something else was wrong. The threat Sara had just uttered should have carried some weight with Amos—unless he knew that

Whittingham wouldn't be coming back from the ambush on the mule train.

The knowledge hit Seth like a hammer. Amos's defense of Parker was just for Tug's benefit. Parker must have let him in on the planned double cross and told him to keep Tug in line. It made sense.

Sara was staring angrily at Amos. She demanded, "What do you mean by that?"

"Oh, nothin'. It's just that I'm not worried overmuch about nothin' you might tell Whittingham."

"He'll believe me," Sara insisted. "Just because he didn't believe that young man doesn't mean he wouldn't believe me."

"I reckon he would," Amos said with a careless shrug, "if he was comin' back." As soon as the impulsive words were out of his mouth, he grimaced at the obvious realization that he had said too much.

Sara came down quickly from the porch, followed by Leigh. Both of them looked frightened. Across the camp Tug had been listening, too, and he said tentatively, "Amos . . . ?"

Amos's head jerked around, and his face twisted in a snarl. "Oh, hell, what's the use of lyin'? Seth was right, Tug. Frank's takin' over the gang. But it don't matter. We'll be just as well off, maybe better. Frank's as smart as Whittingham. Hell, he's smarter. He's grabbin' the chance to take over, ain't he?"

"You're a damned liar!" Sara said, her voice shaking with rage and fear. "Barry wouldn't let himself be betrayed by a thug like Parker."

"I wouldn't talk that way about Frank when he gets back, ma'am," Amos advised her. "You're goin' to be his woman, you see." He grinned at Leigh. "And I reckon the rest of us'll have to make do with you."

Leigh raised her hands to her mouth and let out a muffled scream.

Sara moved suddenly, taking Amos by surprise. Darting across the camp, she headed toward the prisoners. Seth saw a small knife appear in her hand, plucked from a pocket in her dress, and he knew she intended to free him. He leaned forward eagerly, wishing he were already loose.

"Stop her, Tug!" Amos yelled.

Tug hesitated, uncertainty on his face. It was apparent that he didn't know which side of this conflict to come down on. But then he acted, moving swiftly to intercept Sara before she could reach Seth. She slashed at him with the knife as he got in her way, but he avoided the blow and easily caught her wrist. A quick twist brought a cry from her lips and sent the knife clattering to the rocky ground. Tug wrapped his arms around her and lifted the struggling female form until Sara's kicking feet dangled several inches off the ground.

Meanwhile, Amos grabbed Leigh's arm and began to drag her toward the trees. "We'll tie up these twin hellcats, too," he said, grinning at Tug. "That'll keep 'em out of trouble till Frank gets back."

It was with obvious reluctance that Tug brought Sara over to one of the small trees and began tying her to it with a length of rope that was lying nearby, left over from when Seth, Breedlove, and Jinglebob had been bound. Amos picked up another piece of rope and began performing the same task with Leigh, demonstrating considerably more enthusiasm for his work than his partner did. When Leigh suddenly tried to break away from Amos before he got the rope knotted, his rough palm cracked across her face in a brutal slap. "Don't give me trouble, girl," he warned. "It'll just go harder for you later on if you do."

Leigh subsided and began to sob. Sara was crying, too, but it was clear from her expression that there were tears of fury mixed in with hers.

Amos straightened and put his hands on his hips with a self-satisfied grin. "Well, that's a good job, if I do say so myself."

"It'll be the last thing you say, you son of a bitch."

The cold, hard voice came from Sam Cody as he stepped around the corner of the cabin, a Winchester in his hands.

Seth and the other prisoners gaped at the tall, rugged Ranger as Amos and Tug whirled around in shock. Their guns were pouched and Cody had the drop on them, but that didn't stop Amos from grabbing at the butt of his Colt.

The rifle flashed to Cody's shoulder with blinding speed as Amos's gun emerged from its holster. The young outlaw had barely started to lift his revolver when the Winchester cracked. The slug punched into Amos's chest and burst out his back in a spray of blood and gristle. Lifted off his feet by the impact, he flopped backward, his gun discharging harmlessly into the air as he fell. He landed almost at Sara's feet, dead eyes staring sightlessly upward.

Amos's death took only an instant. Tug was still trying to draw his gun. Seth cried, "No, Tug!" as he twisted toward the lanky young outlaw. Seth's feet and legs were free, and by stretching, he was able to kick Tug in the back of the right knee. That leg buckled from the kick, and Tug went down. By then Cody had levered another shell into the Winchester's chamber, and he had the sights lined on Tug's head.

"Don't do it, son," the big Ranger warned. "Just leave that gun right where it is for now."

"All right, mister," Tug panted. "I reckon you got me."

Cody started across the clearing, striding past the now-dead campfire. He kept the Winchester trained on Tug, lowering it only when he was a few feet away. "Slide the gun out slow and then roll away from it," he ordered.

Tug nodded. "Yes, sir." He put his hand on the gun butt again and started to follow Cody's command, then abruptly yelled, "You killed Amos!" He snatched the Colt out and tried to bring it to bear.

Cody struck with the rifle, slamming the butt against Tug's wrist. There was a sharp crack of bone snapping as the pistol was knocked away unfired. Tug clutched the injured wrist to his body and rolled over, his face contorted in pain.

"Damn right I killed Amos," Cody growled. "Looked to me like he deserved it, too." He stepped over beside Seth, holding the rifle in one hand and using the other to slide his bowie knife from its sheath. One slash of the razor-sharp blade parted the ropes binding Seth to the tree. "You up to holding a gun on that fellow?" Cody asked.

Seth nodded. His hands, arms, and shoulders were slightly numb from being tied up for hours, but he could manage.

Cody gave him the rifle, then cut everyone else free in a matter of seconds.

"How'd you find us?" Seth asked.

"Been looking for you for several days now, ever since Miss Gilmore and Mr. Breedlove left Fort Davis with this fella." Cody grinned at the old man. "You'd be Jinglebob Hanrahan, I reckon."

"Heard of me, have you?" Jinglebob asked proudly as he rubbed circulation back into his hands and arms. "Well, I ain't surprised. There ain't many folks in this part o' the country who ain't heard o' Jinglebob Hanrahan. I reckon I'm just about the most famous Injun fighter and scout in these parts."

"Actually, the old boys you play dominoes with told me about you," Cody said with a chuckle. He swung back to Seth and helped the youngster to his feet. "I've thought for a week now that Whittingham's main hideout was somewhere around Madera Canyon. While I was camped last night, I heard a noise from this direction, then a gunshot. Seemed like it'd be worth checking out."

"Well, I'm glad you did," Seth said fervently. "I'm still not sure how you got in here, though."

"Found a cave around on the other side of that ridge," Cody said, jerking a thumb at the slope behind the cabin. "Turned out it was more like a tunnel. It led straight through to this side and came out behind some bushes. I used the cabin for cover until I'd overheard enough to know what was going on." He pointed toward the cleft that led out of the hollow. "That's the other way in and out, I reckon, and what I found was Whittingham's bolt hole."

"Yeah," Seth agreed. "I remember him telling me there was another way out, but I wasn't ever able to find it."

Cody nodded. "The entrance on this end was covered up with brush. You'd never know it was there unless you knew what you were looking for—or unless you came through from the other direction, like I did. Are there any guards on the front door?"

"I don't know," Seth replied, shaking his head slowly.

"Usually there are, but you'd think they'd've showed up by now, what with all the shootin' in here."

Jinglebob spoke up. "Heard that Whittingham feller sayin' he was goin' to take ever'body with him 'cept them two younkers." He pointed at Tug and Amos. "Said they'd need all their guns to take that payroll."

"What payroll?" Cody asked with a frown.

"You didn't know about it?" Seth was surprised.

"Like I said, I've been gone from Fort Davis for several days. Maybe you'd better tell me."

Quickly, Seth did just that while Breedlove ushered the sisters into the cabin, away from the gruesome sight of Amos's body. Jinglebob knelt next to Tug and used a couple of short branches to splint the young outlaw's broken wrist. "This'll hurt a mite," he said cheerfully as he grated the fractured bones back into place. Tug turned pale and let out a shriek. Jinglebob chuckled. "Reckon I was wrong. Guess it hurt a hell of a lot." He tore off several strips from Amos's shirt and bound the splints into place. The material was stained with the dead man's blood, but Jinglebob didn't seem to care.

Cody listened to Seth's story about the Army pack train Whittingham planned to ambush, then nodded as the young Ranger wrapped up his account. "Have Whittingham and his bunch been gone long?" Cody asked.

"Since early this mornin'," Jinglebob supplied. "You fixin' to go after 'em?"

Cody frowned in thought, then shook his head. "It's too late to catch up with them. If Major Monroe knew about that payroll coming in, hopefully he had enough sense to send a patrol out to meet it. If so, maybe they were able to drive Whittingham off. Either way, Whittingham will head back here."

"You mean Parker will," Seth said. In a few sentences, he explained the planned double cross.

Cody nodded thoughtfully. "Doesn't make any difference. This is where the gang will end up, regardless of who's leading them and whether or not they got the payroll. So this is where we'll wait for 'em. They won't be expecting trouble when they ride in, so we'll be able to surprise 'em."

"I don't like leavin' the girls here," Seth protested. "If something happens to us, they're just as bad off as before, probably worse."

"They're not going to be here," Cody said. "I want them and that lawyer to start back to Fort Davis."

"Reckon they'll be able to find their way?" Jinglebob asked dubiously. "That gal Sara may know her way around, but them other two don't."

"They'll be safer on the trail than they would be here," Cody pointed out.

Seth said, "I reckon you're right. I'll tell them, then help them get saddled up."

"What about me?" Jinglebob asked.

"I'd send you back with the others—" Cody began.

"Hell, no!"

"—but I'll need you here to help us with those outlaws," Cody finished with a grin. "You up to fighting some bandits, old-timer?"

"Just gimme a gun," Jinglebob said excitedly. "I'll show you young whippersnappers some *real* fightin'!"

CHAPTER
||||||||||||||||||||||||||| **13** |||||||||||||||||||||||||||

U nlike the canyon where the silver shipment had been ambushed, the trail followed by the Army supply mules led through broad and shallow valleys and didn't lend itself to bushwhacking. Barry Whittingham knew that, so he was careful about where he placed his men. Some he positioned on either side of the trail, taking advantage of what cover there was, and the rest of the gang was concealed in a draw to the south of the trail. He and Frank Parker rode with that group, since they'd be taking the biggest risk when the time came to confront the caravan.

"Goin' to be quite a haul, ain't it?" Parker asked in a quiet voice as they waited with the other men.

Whittingham nodded. "I hope so. If my information is correct—and I'm confident that it is—we're going to be very rich men, Frank." For a second he toyed with the idea of telling Parker about the promise he had made to Sara. When he and Sara were gone—to California or Mexico or wherever they decided to go—Parker would be left in charge of the gang, free to make the decision whether to continue with its activities or to disband the group.

It would probably be better if they split up, Whittingham thought. Parker was a good man, but Whittingham had serious doubts about his leadership ability. Besides, Parker was too brutal, too quick to kill. That was another reason Whittingham had for getting out of this outlaw life now, while he had a chance. He was afraid that too much of Parker's viciousness might be rubbing off on him.

Strange the way life worked out, he mused. If things had

been different, he'd be back in London now, leading the life of a wealthy, titled young man.

But then he never would have met Sara.

He wouldn't say anything to Parker about his plans, he decided. There'd be time enough for that, once they all got back to camp. He'd also have to deal with the problem of the prisoners then. Leigh could live, of course, but Whittingham didn't see any real way out for the other three.

Movement on a nearby hill caught the Englishman's eye. He took a pair of field glasses from his saddlebag and peered through them to see one of his riders halted atop the hill. The man waved his rifle in the air in the signal they had agreed upon.

"The supply train is coming," Whittingham announced as he lowered the glasses. "They'll be here within a half hour."

He waved his own rifle in response to the signal, and the rider on the hill started down it, ready to rejoin the gang now that he had alerted them. Whittingham slipped his Winchester back into the saddle boot and went on, "Everyone be prepared. There won't be any time to waste once those mules get here."

The gang members checked their guns, even though there was no real need. All the weapons were fully loaded and ready to spit flame and death at their victims.

Whittingham and Parker rode to the head of the draw, the Englishman stopping just before he reached the top so that he could see the trail without being too visible. He leaned forward in the saddle, listening intently. Time seemed to crawl by. None of the outlaws spoke behind him, fearful of breaking his concentration. He was tensed, his whole body ready for action.

Finally, sounds came to his ears. The Army mules in the caravan didn't have bells on them, as the Mexican drovers in the silver trains preferred their animals to wear, but there was still the rattling and popping of harness to be heard, along with the plodding hoofbeats and the calls of the herders.

Whittingham slid his Colt from its holster and raised the

gun over his head. He waited until the tension seemed stretched to the absolute breaking point, then suddenly slashed the air with the pistol and yelled, "Now!"

The outlaws swept up out of the draw, following closely behind Whittingham. The gun in his hand cracked, and one of the Army outriders toppled from the saddle. From the hills on both sides of the trail the hidden bandits opened fire, and more blue-coated troopers spilled from their horses. Spooked by the gunfire, the mules tried to bolt, but their herders kept them in line while at the same time trying to fight back.

Whittingham shot another soldier, then shouted, "Surrender! Surrender and you won't be harmed!"

The troopers ignored him. Their carbines and handguns boomed their only response. The outlaws spread out as they attacked, peppering the soldiers all along the line of mules. More men went down. Whittingham's gang wasn't escaping unscathed, however. A couple of the outlaws were sagging in their saddles, clutching bullet-shattered shoulders.

Suddenly the firing began to die away as the soldiers realized the futility of fighting. They were surrounded and outgunned, and further resistance would just mean that all of them would be wiped out. The captain in charge of the detail ordered his surviving men to lay down their arms, and as the dust settled and the gun smoke blew away, the outlaws rode in, covering the soldiers who were now their prisoners.

Whittingham felt a fierce exultation as he trained his pistol on the officer and said, "You've made the intelligent choice, Captain. No sense in you and any more of your men losing your lives over something as trivial as money."

"Goddamn you, sir!" the captain burst out. "I know you. You're Whittingham!"

The Englishman inclined his head in acknowledgment. "Correct, Captain. And if you've heard of me, you know that I won't hesitate to kill you if you interfere with me." He twisted in the saddle and called to Parker, "Find that payroll!"

The hardcase *segundo* nodded and gestured to several of

the outlaws to start searching the packs on the mules. Parker also joined the search himself. A few minutes later he was rewarded with the discovery of bundles of cash in one of the packsaddles.

"Here it is, Barry!" he called.

"Make sure there's not any more," Whittingham ordered.

Within ten minutes all the mules had been searched and the entire payroll accounted for. The two packsaddles containing the money were stripped from the mules and fastened over the backs of Whittingham's and Parker's mounts. Meanwhile, some of the other outlaws had collected all the guns from the troopers.

"Are you going to keep your word and not harm the rest of my men?" the captain asked angrily when the outlaws were through with their looting. "Or are you going to murder us in cold blood?"

"I am a man of my word, sir," Whittingham said. He holstered his gun. "If you'll allow us to depart without offering any further resistance, you won't be harmed."

"I say we kill 'em all," Parker growled.

Whittingham shot him a sharp glance. He wasn't used to being contradicted like that. "I said there'll be no more violence," he snapped.

"Well, you're makin' a mistake," cautioned Parker. "We're liable to regret leavin' these bluebellies alive."

"I doubt that," Whittingham said scornfully. He'd have to have a talk later with Parker. The man was getting too bold for his own good.

Suddenly Whittingham wondered if there had been anything to Seth Williams's story about Parker planning to betray him. Whittingham still couldn't bring himself to believe that, though.

"Somebody's comin'!"

The cry of warning came from one of the other outlaws. Whittingham whirled his horse around and saw the dust cloud to the west where a sizable force was galloping down the trail. Blue-coated figures were visible at the base of that dust cloud, and the sound of a bugle blowing the charge filled the hot, dry air.

The United States Cavalry had arrived.

• • •

This was all wrong, Sergeant Rufe Gresham thought. But he and his troopers had no choice except to try to make the best of it.

When they had heard all the shooting a few minutes earlier, Gresham had known right away what was happening. They were too late to head off Whittingham's attack on the supply train carrying the hidden payroll. But Major Monroe knew that, too, and he'd immediately cried out, "Bugler, blow the charge!"

"Sir!" Gresham exclaimed. "We can't just go galloping in there, sir! Why don't we try to circle around the outlaws and pin them in?" This was the closest he had gotten to Whittingham, and he wanted the gang leader so badly he could feel it in his bones. If Whittingham got away now . . .

"Our fellow soldiers are under attack, Sergeant!" snapped Monroe. "I intend to come to their aid without delay. Bugler, I ordered you to blow the charge!"

"Yes, sir!" the private replied, glancing momentarily at Gresham before lifting the bugle to his lips.

Now the entire patrol was racing down the trail toward the spot where Whittingham had ambushed the pack train. Riding right into the guns of the outlaws, Gresham thought. He unsnapped the holster at his waist and drew his Army revolver. He tasted dust and grit in his mouth.

A sudden volley rang out from the outlaws, and Gresham heard lead whine past his ear. He lifted his revolver and fired, even though the range was still a little long for a handgun. Major Monroe was shooting, too, but the troopers behind the officer and the noncom had to hold their fire.

Gresham twisted in the saddle and waved for the men to spread out. As he did so, he heard a cry of pain and jerked around in time to see Major Monroe swaying in the saddle. Gresham jammed his pistol back in its holster and spurred his horse up alongside Monroe.

"Hang on, Major!" he called, putting out a hand to steady the wounded officer. He saw a bloody patch spreading on Monroe's uniform tunic, and the major's face had gone deathly pale.

The outlaws were on the run now, Gresham saw when he glanced at the pack train—but they had inflicted quite a bit of damage before hightailing it. Several of the patrol's mounts were riderless, and motionless figures were sprawled along the trail where they had been spilled from their saddles by owlhoot bullets.

The sergeant reined in his horse as he reached the halted mules. There were dead men here, too, he noted grimly. Quickly, Gresham dropped from the saddle and caught Monroe as the major started to fall. Monroe was only half conscious and in no shape to command.

Holding up the sagging major, Gresham lifted his head to bawl, "Set up a perimeter in case those outlaws come back!"

The captain in charge of the pack train came hurrying up to him. "I'm Captain Britten," he said curtly. "Is this your commanding officer, Sergeant?"

"Yes, sir. This is Major Monroe from Fort Davis. But I don't reckon he's in any shape to do much commanding right now! Do you have a doctor with you?"

Britten shook his head. "We didn't bring along a medical officer. We have plenty of wounded of our own, though. Can you do anything, Sergeant . . . ?"

"In a minute," Gresham grunted, not worrying overmuch about military protocol right at the moment. He lowered Major Monroe to the ground and ripped open his tunic, grimacing at the sight of the bloody, black-rimmed bullet hole in the major's chest. The wound was high, which was probably good; it had missed the heart and probably the lungs. Monroe's collarbone was busted for sure, though.

First thing to do was stop the bleeding, Gresham thought. The bullet would have to come out sooner or later, but that'd have to wait till they got back to Fort Davis. It was a job for the post surgeon. For now Gresham fashioned a bandage and pressed it to the wound. "Hold that there," he told Captain Britten.

Britten's face was taut, and Gresham knew he probably resented being told what to do by a noncom, especially a black noncom. But there was no time to worry about that now. Gresham left Britten with the major and hurried to check the other wounded men.

He patched them up as best he could with the skills learned in two decades of soldiering. Two of the men died as he was trying to stop their bleeding, and his face reflected his distress. Those two dead men joined about a dozen others.

God, he hated death and dying! Most good soldiers, Gresham had found, felt the same way. Some folks couldn't understand that, couldn't see how a man schooled in violence was the one who hated it the most *because* he understood it.

No time for thoughts like that, Gresham told himself with a shake of his head. He had to get the situation here squared away and get the survivors of the two battles started back to the fort along with part of the patrol.

As for himself and the rest of the men . . . well, they still had some damned murdering outlaws to catch.

"Are they following us?" Whittingham called to Parker as they galloped into the mountains at the head of the gang.

Parker twisted in his saddle and checked their back trail. "No dust!" he reported. "I reckon that patrol stopped to treat their wounded and check on the pack train."

Whittingham's mouth stretched in a ruthless grin. That had been a bit of a close call, he thought. If that cavalry patrol had proceeded a bit more intelligently instead of blundering in full speed ahead, he and his men could have been trapped. They might have been able to fight their way out, but escape would have come at a terrible cost.

Instead, his luck had held once again, and they were free, with only two men suffering wounds. And the payroll was theirs as well.

Whittingham was filled with a sense of victory as he rode hard along the familiar mountain trails. Finally, he was on the verge of freedom from this life of banditry. He and Sara could take the money and get away, start a new life somewhere else, someplace where he could forget all the blood that had been spilled in the past year. . . .

For one of the few times since he had become an outlaw, Barry Whittingham allowed his mind to wander, letting his thoughts play with the way things would be when all this was far behind him.

"We'd better rest the horses."

Frank Parker's voice cut into Whittingham's pleasant musings, and the Englishman realized suddenly that they were high in the mountains, still heading toward Madera Canyon and the hideout. He had led them here without even thinking about where they were going. With a rueful smile, he reined in his horse. "You're right, Frank," he said. "If we run our mounts into the ground, we'll only be cutting our own throats."

"Yeah," Parker grunted. "That's what I was thinkin'."

They had come to a halt on a narrow shelf at the foot of one of the mountains. A shallow ravine ran along the other side of the shelf. Whittingham swung down from his saddle and stepped over to the edge, peering down. A small stream trickled along the bottom of the cut some thirty feet below.

Taking a deep breath, the Englishman lifted his eyes and looked out across the valley beyond. His keen gaze searched for any sign of movement that might mean pursuit. But the valley and the mountains were still. Either the cavalry patrol had not come after them, Whittingham thought, or they had given the troopers the slip.

He smiled faintly. Yes, his luck was holding, just as it always had.

"Barry."

Something in Parker's voice made Whittingham stiffen slightly. He turned slowly and said, "Yes? What is it, Frank?"

Parker had his gun in his hand, and he was holding it loosely pointed in Whittingham's direction. Beyond him several other members of the gang had also drawn their guns.

"I'm takin' over," Parker said harshly.

Whittingham's smile became more sardonic. "Mutiny, is it?" he asked quietly.

"Call it whatever you want. All I care about is that I'm givin' the orders now."

Whittingham shook his head. All he had to do was explain that he and Sara were leaving and that he intended to turn the leadership of the gang over to Parker anyway. "You don't need to do this, Frank. I'm going to—"

"Shut up!" Parker rasped, bringing the gun up abruptly. "I'm tired of you tellin' me what you're goin' to do and what you're not goin' to do. You're not givin' the orders anymore, you goddamned Britisher! You understand?"

"Yes, I'm afraid I do," Whittingham murmured. "I thought you were my friend, Frank. I thought I could trust you." His eyes narrowed and turned icy with rage. "I can see now I was wrong."

"Yeah?" Parker leered at him. He flashed a sidelong glance to his partners in the double cross who were keeping the other members of the gang neutral with their guns. Then he focused all his attention on the slender figure of the man he had grown to resent and despise. He asked, "What are you goin' to do about it?"

The Englishman's face had settled into a bleak, fatalistic expression. "This," he answered softly.

His hand streaked toward his gun.

He was fast, and this draw was the fastest he had ever made. Despite the fact that Parker's gun was drawn, cocked, and aimed, Whittingham's Colt emerged from its holster and spat flame only an instant after Parker's weapon blasted. That instant was enough, though. Whittingham's shot went wild as lead plowed into him, knocking him backward.

And suddenly there was nothing under his feet but air.

Parker raced forward as Whittingham fell into the ravine. He was ready to fire again, but a glance over the rim told him it wouldn't be necessary. Whittingham was tumbling loosely down the steep slope toward the creek. He landed in it with a splash, and red streaks appeared in the water from the blood welling from his body.

With a grin that was more a savage grimace, Parker looked down at the body of his former leader for a second, then slid his gun back in its holster and swung around to face the rest of the gang. Looking squarely at the men who had not been in on his plan, he asked, "Anybody have any problem with what just happened?"

Slowly, one by one, the outlaws shook their heads. If they were bothered by the way Parker had cut down Whittingham, now wasn't the time to show it. Anyway, loyalty wasn't their strong suit.

Parker strode over to Whittingham's horse and stripped the packsaddle full of money from it. He threw it over the back of his own horse, in front of the saddle, matching the pack behind it. The horse might not care for being loaded down like this, but hell, greenbacks didn't weigh all that much, Parker thought. And he wanted the experience of riding with all that money. . . .

"It's the goddamn cavalry!"

The cry from one of the other outlaws made Parker's head jerk around. Sure enough, as he looked across the valley he spotted the blue-coated riders heading toward them. His mouth twisted in a snarl. "We've still got a good lead on 'em!" he called to the other men. "They'll never catch us! Anyway, once we get back to the hideout, we can hold off a whole army in there if we have to!" He stepped up into the saddle and tightened the reins, taking his place in the lead.

"Come on!" he ordered, kicking his horse into a gallop. "Let's ride!"

CHAPTER
14

"I'll bet you were surprised to find out those two girls are twins," Seth said to Cody as they crouched in a cluster of boulders.

Cody replied, "I was more surprised to find out Sara was still alive. And I sure as hell never figured she was staying with Whittingham because she was in love with him."

Seth shook his head slowly. "I reckon there's just no figurin' women."

Cody grinned but didn't say anything.

Jinglebob Hanrahan wasn't so reticent, though. He cackled and said, "Now you're learnin', boy!"

The three men were hidden in the rocks overlooking the hollow where Whittingham's hideout was located. It had been a tough climb up, but now they had a good field of fire as well as good cover. When the gang arrived back here, they were going to ride right into a hornet's nest without knowing it.

The body of Amos Bower had been taken into the cabin to get it out of sight. Tug Mitchell was in there, too, tied and gagged so that he couldn't give any warning to the gang. Cody could tell that Seth felt a little sorry for Tug—and for Amos as well. He wanted to tell the young Ranger not to waste his sympathy on owlhoots, but it was really none of his business, Cody supposed. Besides, things could've happened in the past couple of weeks that Cody knew nothing about, things that had created a bond between Seth and the other two young men. And when Cody thought about it, he remembered what it was like to have friends go bad.

Barry Whittingham was a prime example of that.

Cody leaned back against the rocks, tipping his hat forward to shade more of his face from the hot sun. He wondered how Breedlove and the girls were making out. He had taken them out of the hideout through the tunnel—which was big enough for horses, but just barely—and started them on a looping path that would eventually take them back to Fort Davis without as big a risk of running into trouble. He hoped they didn't get lost. Still, they were better off out on the trail than they would have been staying here. Once the outlaws returned, things were liable to get hotter'n the hinges of hell.

Jinglebob suddenly pointed and said, "Take a look over yonder. 'Pears somebody's comin', and they ain't movin' slow."

Cody and Seth looked where the old man indicated and saw the haze of dust rising in the afternoon air, dulling the brilliant blue sky. A lot of horses were coming, Cody speculated. Had to be the gang.

A moment later the popping and crackling of gunfire reached their ears. Seth grinned and said, "Somebody's after 'em."

"Probably the cavalry," Cody said, thinking about Rufe Gresham. If the sergeant had finally gotten on the trail of the outlaws, he'd hang on like a bulldog.

"Them owlhoots prob'ly figger they can hold off anybody who's chasin' 'em once they get in here," Jinglebob said. He slapped his buckskin-clad thigh and laughed again. "They're in for a helluva surprise!"

"That's what I'm counting on," Cody said. He lifted his Winchester and jacked a shell into the chamber. Seth and Jinglebob followed suit.

A couple of minutes later they heard hoofbeats coming from the cleft that led into the hideout. Riders emerged helter-skelter from the opening and scattered. From his position in the rocks Cody saw a man he took to be Frank Parker shouting commands and trying to rally the outlaws. They were ignoring him.

There was no sign of Barry Whittingham, at least no one Cody recognized as the Englishman.

"Do you see Whittingham?" he asked Seth in a low voice.

The young Ranger shook his head. "Nope." He sounded grim. "I reckon Parker's already pulled his double cross. He's tryin' to give the orders down there."

"They ain't listenin' to him," Jinglebob put in. "I reckon he ain't as much of a boss as he figgered he was."

Somewhere nearby a cavalry bugle blew. That had to be Gresham and a patrol, Cody thought. They probably had the owlhoots outnumbered, but it'd be difficult for them to make it through that cleft. They'd be riding right into the guns of the gang.

It was time to swing the odds a little more.

"Take 'em!" Cody said sharply to Seth and Jinglebob.

He brought his own Winchester to his shoulder and settled the blade of the sight on an outlaw who was trying to bring his rearing horse under control. It was a tricky shot, but when Cody was ready, he squeezed the trigger. The roar of his shot blended with the blasts from Seth's and Jinglebob's weapons.

The outlaw Cody had targeted flew out of the saddle. Nearby, two more men fell. Before any of them hit the ground, Cody had switched his aim and fired again. The fusillade rang out, echoing back from the surrounding slopes.

The owlhoots whirled around to meet this new threat, and lead spanged off the rocks around Cody and his companions. The Rangers and the old Indian fighter ignored the flying bullets and continued to coolly pump shots into the gang. Several of the outlaws fled back into the cleft, only to run smack into their pursuers. Gunfire boomed deafeningly in the narrow confines of the passage.

With all the swirling dust and powder smoke in the air Cody had lost track of Frank Parker. As the firing from the outlaws died away, Cody lowered his rifle and searched for the man who had assumed command of the owlhoot band.

Below, the surviving outlaws were throwing down their guns and thrusting their hands in the air in surrender. Blue-uniformed riders emerged from the cleft in the rocks, their guns held ready, but all the fight had gone out of the enemy. The troopers swarmed around the outlaws.

Cody spotted Sergeant Gresham. He stood up from his crouch behind the rocks and waved his rifle in the air. "Sergeant!" he shouted.

Gresham looked up and returned Cody's wave, beckoning for the Ranger to come down. Trailed by Seth and Jinglebob, Cody half slid, half climbed down the slope. When he reached level ground, he trotted over to join Gresham, who had just dismounted.

"Should've figured I'd find you here, Cody," the sergeant said with a big grin. "So this is where Whittingham and his bunch have been hiding out."

"This is the place," Cody confirmed. "Whittingham's not here now, though."

Gresham frowned in surprise. "What? But we chased the whole bunch in here—"

"Whittingham wasn't with them. His *segundo,* a fella called Parker, planned to double-cross him on this job and take over the gang. I reckon that's just what happened. He probably killed Whittingham and left his body in a gully somewhere."

Gresham pounded a fist into his palm. "Dammit! I wanted Whittingham." Quickly, he told Cody and the others about the raid on the supply train, the theft of the payroll, and the wounding of Major Monroe as well as the men killed by the gang.

"His gang's broken up, Sergeant," Cody said. "Even if he's still alive, which I reckon is pretty doubtful, Whittingham won't ever bother anybody around here again."

"Soon as I get a chance, I'm going to do some backtracking. See if I can find his body." Gresham looked at Cody's companions, seeming to notice them for the first time. "Jinglebob? What the hell are you doing out here?"

"Helpin' these two young fellers take care o' them desperadoes," Jinglebob said proudly.

"This is Seth Williams," Cody said to Gresham. "He's a Ranger, too; been helping me out undercover."

"Williams . . ." Gresham mused. Then his eyes narrowed. "You were in on that bank robbery in town!"

Seth grinned ruefully. "Like Cody said, I've been undercover. That got me right in with Whittingham's bunch."

The sergeant gave a low whistle. "If I was you, boy, I wouldn't be looking forward to trying to explain that to Sheriff Randine."

"I'm not," Seth admitted.

"Don't worry about that," Cody assured him. "Right now, I want to find Parker. Maybe if he's still alive he'll tell us what happened to Whittingham."

The surviving outlaws had been left on their horses, but their hands were tied securely now. A quick glance at them told Cody that Parker wasn't among them. He felt a thread of worry growing inside him as he began to search among the bodies of the outlaws killed in the fighting.

A few minutes later he announced dourly to Gresham, "Parker's not here."

"But that's impossible!" the sergeant exclaimed. "There's only one way out, and we had it blocked."

Cody shook his head. "Nope. There's another way." He strode around the cabin toward the concealed tunnel. Gresham, Seth, and Jinglebob trailed him.

A quick glance told him that the brush over the mouth of the tunnel had been disturbed. Hairs from a horse's tail were caught on one of the bushes. Cody frowned in disappointment.

"He bolted, all right," the big Ranger said.

"And I'll bet he's got that damned payroll with him," Gresham added. "I haven't seen those stolen packsaddles anywhere around here."

"Dammit, Cody, we've got to go after him!" Seth exclaimed. "We can't let him get away!"

"We won't," Cody said, his face resolute. "Seth, you and Jinglebob stay here and give Sergeant Gresham a hand with the prisoners. I'll go after Parker."

Seth began, "Why don't I go with—"

Cody interrupted with a shake of his head. "Nope. I'm going to finish this up on my own. I'll see you back in town—with that payroll."

• • •

"Sara, I don't think we should be doing this!" Leigh Gilmore said urgently to her sister.

"I'm in complete agreement," Josiah Breedlove put in. "This is utter foolishness, Sara."

"The two of you can go on if you want to," Sara said over her shoulder as she put her horse into a trot back toward the hideout. "I have to know what happened to Barry."

The sounds of gunfire coming from the valley they had left behind had made Sara rein in sharply a few minutes earlier. Ever since they had ridden out, Leigh had been aware of Sara's reluctance to go. The bond between them, the ties that had always been there, enabled them to sense each other's feelings. And while Leigh might never understand how Sara could have any affection for a bloodthirsty bandit like Whittingham, she would never deny the reality of her sister's emotion.

Now, as Sara rode away, urging her horse on to greater speed, Leigh looked at Breedlove. The lawyer met her gaze and sighed. After everything they had gone through to find Sara, they couldn't let her just ride away now, and both of them knew it.

They rode after her.

The gunfire grew louder as they retraced their tracks and neared the hideout, but then it began to fade away, and a few moments later it ceased entirely. Whatever had happened back there, it was over now. Sara's face was pale and drawn with anxiety. Whittingham could have easily been killed in the fighting.

On the other hand, if Cody, Seth, and Jinglebob had lost the battle, then the three of them were riding right back into a deadly situation. That thought had Leigh looking as concerned as Sara.

Suddenly a rider appeared at the top of a rise in front of them. He was quirting his horse and racing toward them hell-bent for leather. Sara reined in and studied the oncoming rider, and a moment later announced in a startled voice, "That's Frank Parker!"

Leigh and Breedlove had brought their horses to a stop,

too. Breedlove licked dry lips and wrapped his fingers around the butt of the pistol Cody had taken from Tug Mitchell and given to him. The gun was tucked behind the attorney's belt, fully loaded except for the chamber that the hammer was resting on.

"We'd better get out of sight," he advised. "We can't trust that man—"

"No!" Sara turned sharply toward him. "Frank can tell us what happened. He can tell us about Barry!"

"Sara, please . . . !"

"It won't do any good to argue with her, Josiah," Leigh said softly. "She has to know."

Parker's frantic pace faltered for a second when he spotted them, but then he drove his mount on at even greater speed. As he came up to them, he hauled the animal to a sliding stop.

"What the hell are you three doin' out here?" he demanded. "And who was that who ambushed us back at the hideout?"

Breedlove edged his horse up a few steps, putting himself between Parker and the girls. "There were two Texas Rangers, along with Mr. Hanrahan," he said. "You can't escape, Parker, not with the Rangers on your trail. It's my considered legal advice that you go back and give yourself up."

"Well, my advice is you shut your goddamn mouth, mister!" Parker snapped.

Sara pushed up next to Breedlove. "What happened to Barry? Were you the only one who got away, Frank?"

"Yeah, the only one." The outlaw's face twisted in a sneer. "But Whittingham never got back to the hideout. He's layin' dead in a ravine on the other side of Madera Canyon!"

"No!" The anguished cry was torn from Sara's throat. "You're lying!"

"I don't care what the hell you think, lady. Now, shut up and come on, all three of you." Parker grinned. "Luck's good enough to give me three hostages, I sure ain't goin' to turn 'em down."

Breedlove jerked the pistol from his belt and pointed it

at Parker. "No, sir! Drop your gun, Parker. You're my prisoner now. We're going back to Fort Davis."

Parker didn't flinch from the threat of the lawyer's weapon. He just grinned and said, "Before you go pointin' a gun at folks, you tenderfoot bastard, you'd better learn how to cock it."

Horror flashed across Breedlove's face as he realized Parker was right—the gun wasn't cocked. Desperately he reached for the hammer with his thumb.

Parker's hand swept down and came up with his own revolver, thumbing back the hammer with practiced ease as he lifted the gun. It boomed before Breedlove could get off a shot.

Leigh screamed as Breedlove was knocked out of the saddle by Parker's slug. The lawyer fell heavily to the ground, the gun spinning out of his hand. When he landed, he rolled over and clutched his side where a bloodstain showed on his shirt. He moaned softly.

"Well, I reckon two hostages'll do as well as three," Parker said to the stunned Leigh and Sara.

Two things happened at once then. Sara flung herself out of the saddle and dove toward the gun Breedlove had dropped, and at the same instant a rifle bullet hummed over Parker's head. He jerked around in the saddle to see a rider galloping toward them, and the stranger fired another shot from the Winchester at his shoulder as he guided the horse with his knees. Once again the bullet came uncomfortably close.

Spooked by the shooting, Parker's horse began to lunge back and forth. As the outlaw cursed and hauled back on the reins, trying to bring the animal back under control, Sara scooped up the fallen pistol. But before she had the chance to fire, Parker snapped a shot at her. Leigh screamed again as Sara stumbled and fell.

"Come on!" Parker shouted as he urged his horse over beside Leigh's. He jammed his gun in its holster, and then his arm looped out and grabbed her around her waist. Jerking Leigh from the saddle, he kicked his horse into a run.

Leigh struggled and tried to twist out of Parker's grip, but the outlaw was too strong. He got her onto the horse in front of him and grated into her ear, "Settle down or I'll kill you!"

Wind whipped Leigh's hair into her face. Her heart was pounding with terror as the horse raced along the rocky ground. She stopped struggling. Even if she was able to get away from him, if she fell from the horse at this speed, the spill might kill her. She had to hold on and hope that Cody would catch up and rescue her. Even though she'd had only a quick glimpse of the man who had fired at Parker, it was enough for her to recognize the big Ranger.

Fear for her sister ate at Leigh at the same time. She had seen Sara fall when Parker fired at her. Had they all endured the ordeal only to have Sara taken from them at the last moment? And what about Breedlove? Was he dead or alive?

There were no answers to the questions. Only the thunderous pounding of the horse's hooves, echoed by the pounding of Leigh Gilmore's heart.

Cody pulled the roan to a halt as he galloped up to Sara and Breedlove. The girl was kneeling next to the attorney, using strips torn from her petticoat to bind up a wound in Breedlove's side. "Are you all right?" Cody called to the girl. He noticed a bruise on Sara's face.

"I'm fine," she said without looking up from her work. "I just tripped and fell a minute ago. That probably kept me from getting shot by Parker."

"What about Breedlove?" The lawyer was unconscious, Cody saw.

"He's just fainted. Parker shot him, but the bullet just dug a crease in his ribs. He'll be all right." Sara's face was haggard when she finally looked up at Cody. "But Parker took Leigh with him. You've got to stop him."

Cody nodded, his face grim. "Just what I intend to do."

He dug his heels into the roan's flanks and sent it leaping forward again.

He spotted Parker several hundred yards ahead of him. The lead wouldn't matter much, for the the outlaw's horse had already run a long way today whereas Cody's roan was relatively fresh. It lacked the speed of his rangy lineback dun, but it had plenty of grit. It was only a matter of time until he ran Parker down.

Up ahead the trail circled around a rocky bluff. Cody thought he saw his chance. As Parker veered his horse to skirt the bluff, Cody lifted the Winchester and fired, placing the bullet several yards to the side of the outlaw. Parker jerked away from the spurt of dust kicked up by the slug. Cody fired again, driving the outlaw off the main trail and toward the bluff, which was too steep for a horse to negotiate, almost a cliff. Being careful not to put his shots too close to Parker—and Leigh Gilmore—Cody herded the outlaw toward the dead end.

When he could go no farther, Parker reined in and dropped out of the saddle, taking a flailing Leigh with him. The girl was putting up a fight again now that they had stopped, but she wasn't strong enough to get away from Parker. The outlaw dragged her toward some rocks at the base of the cliff.

Cody flung himself out of the saddle as Parker twisted around and threw a couple of shots at him. He landed rolling and came up in a crouching run, heading for a thicket of mesquite trees that'd give him at least a little cover. Parker would be better protected behind the rocks, but he'd also be pinned down.

Cody bellied down among the scrubby mesquites as Parker dragged Leigh behind the rocks. "Might as well give it up, Parker!" the Ranger called. "You're not going anywhere!"

Parker didn't show himself, but his shouted reply carried clearly to Cody's ears. "Well, this girl's goin' to hell if you don't leave me alone, mister! Clear out and let me ride away, and maybe she'll live!"

Despite the heat of the day, Cody felt a chill go through him. He didn't doubt for an instant that Parker meant his threat. Parker had the girl—and probably that Army payroll—and he wasn't likely to give up either one without a fight.

Suddenly movement at the top of the shallow cliff behind Parker's hiding place caught Cody's eye. He looked up to see a figure rising unsteadily into view—a tall slender figure wearing a shirt that had once been white but was now crimson with blood. The man's blond hair riffled in the wind.

Barry Whittingham.

Cody recognized the Englishman immediately. He didn't know how Whittingham had managed to get there, but his presence might be enough to break this desperate standoff.

A gun was in Whittingham's hand. Wavering there on the lip of the cliff, determinedly hanging on despite what was probably a mortal wound, he lifted the weapon and pointed it at Parker below. "Sara!" he shouted, his voice strong, not betraying a tenuous grip on life. "Let her go, Parker! Let her go, you bastard!"

Whittingham had mistaken Leigh for Sara, Cody realized, but that didn't matter now. As the Ranger leapt to his feet and dashed forward, he saw Parker whirl around and snap off a shot at the same time Whittingham fired at him. Whittingham's bullet went wild, but Parker's caught the Englishman in the stomach. Whittingham went up on his toes and clutched himself with his free hand, then plummeted forward off the cliff.

In his shock at Whittingham's appearance, Parker had let go of Leigh when he spun around to fire. Now Cody saw the girl jump to safety, throwing herself down between two of the boulders. "Parker!" the Ranger yelled as he drew his Colt. "Elevate, damn you! In the name of the state of Texas!"

Snarling curses, Parker got off one shot at Cody before the big man's Colt began to roar. Ranger lead thudded into the outlaw's chest, driving him back against the base of the cliff. The impact of the bullets jolted him in a dance of death as they turned his chest into a bloody ruin. Cody shot him four times, then held his fire. For a second Parker seemed to hang there, pressed against the rock face; then he crumpled forward lifelessly.

Cody dashed over to Leigh and knelt beside her. She was all right, he saw as she rolled over, and he helped her to her feet. She was pale and trembling, shaken from the violent ordeal, but at last it was over.

"S-Sara . . ."

The hoarse whisper came from Barry Whittingham's broken body, which was sprawled on the rocky ground not far from Parker's bloody corpse. With his hand on Leigh's arm Cody hurried over to the Englishman, who was somehow still holding on to a spark of life.

Whittingham blinked his eyes and peered up at them. "Sara," he repeated, staring at Leigh. She glanced at Cody, who squeezed her arm and nodded.

Leigh dropped to her knees beside Whittingham and said in a choked voice, "I'm here, Barry. I'm here."

"Couldn't . . . let Parker hurt you. . . . He . . . he betrayed me. . . . I knew he'd come back and hurt you. . . . Had to follow him. . . ." Whittingham laughed softly, which clearly must have hurt. He closed his eyes with pain for a few seconds, then managed to lift his head again and continue. "Frank thought . . . I was dead . . . but he was wrong. . . . I found my horse . . . followed the shooting. . . . Thank God I . . . got here in time. . . ."

"You don't have to talk any more, Barry," Leigh told him. No doubt swallowing her fear and revulsion, she reached out and touched his cheek. "Just be quiet now. You'll be all right."

Moving with surprising speed, Whittingham caught her hand and pressed it tightly in his fingers. "No . . . it's too late . . . for me. . . . But I want you to know . . . I . . . always loved you . . . Sara. . . ."

His voice trailed off, and his fingers slipped away from Leigh's hand.

"He's gone," Cody said quietly.

Leigh took a deep, ragged breath. "I can't cry for him," she said. "He . . . he was a killer."

"Yes, he was," Cody replied as he took her arm again and helped her to her feet. "But he was a good man once, and I reckon he really did love your sister, as much as somebody like him could love anybody. And he helped save your life just now, even if he did it because he thought you were Sara."

"I . . . I suppose you're right."

Looking down at the Englishman, Cody's gunpowder-grimed face was solemn. "If you mourn for anybody," he said, "mourn for the man Barry Whittingham used to be."

CHAPTER
▓▓▓▓▓▓▓▓▓▓▓▓▓▓▓▓ **15** ▓▓▓▓▓▓▓▓▓▓▓▓▓▓▓▓

Cody and Seth were waiting on the front porch of the Limpia Hotel for Leigh, Sara, and Josiah Breedlove to emerge. The eastbound stagecoach was pulled up in front of the hotel to take on passengers. The three visitors from Dallas would ride in the coach to San Antonio, then catch a train there for Dallas.

Both of the Gilmore sisters looked attractive but subdued in dark traveling outfits as they stepped onto the hotel porch. Breedlove followed them, moving a bit stiffly due to the bandages wrapped around his midsection under the expensive suit and shirt. He smiled at the Rangers and said, "Good morning, gentlemen."

"Morning, sir," Cody replied. He tugged his Stetson off and nudged Seth to follow suit. "Ladies."

"Hello, Mr. Cody," Leigh said. Of the two, she was the more animated this morning. Sara had a haunted look on her face, and Cody figured it would stay there for a while, until the memories of Barry Whittingham faded away—if they ever did.

Several days had passed since the series of battles in the mountains had destroyed Whittingham's gang. The payroll had been delivered to the military post, and the loot cached in the outlaw hideout had been returned, as far as was possible, to its proper owners. That included most of the money stolen from the bank by Amos, Tug, and Seth. The return of the money had helped to mollify Sheriff Randine when he found out that Seth was actually a Ranger and had been working undercover. He still blustered around and threatened to throw the youngster in jail anyway, but

Cody had talked him out of that, pointing out that without Seth's help, Whittingham and his followers might still be ravaging the countryside.

Now Cody asked the lawyer, "How are you feeling this morning, Mr. Breedlove?"

"Oh, I've been better, but the doctor assures me that not only will I survive, but I'm also healthy enough to travel." Breedlove smiled slightly to take the sting out of the words as he went on, "If I survive the ride in that rolling torture chamber, I'll be greatly surprised."

Cody and Seth both shook hands with him, and then Breedlove stepped down to the street to make sure their baggage had been properly loaded into the coach's boot. Facing Leigh, Cody smiled and told her, "I reckon we'll miss you a mite. You were pretty unpredictable, but you kept things interesting."

Leigh laughed quietly. "My, aren't you the charmer this morning, Mr. Cody?" She came up on her toes and brushed her lips across his cheek. "Thank you. From . . . from both of us."

Cody glanced at Sara, whose eyes were downcast, and nodded. "I understand," he said.

Leigh shook hands with Seth and then impulsively kissed him, too, leaving the young Ranger with a surprised look on his face and a blush on his ears. Then Leigh led her sister over to the coach and helped her climb in. Pausing, Leigh looked over her shoulder at Cody. "I was hoping Mr. Hanrahan would be here."

"Jinglebob's been doing a lot of celebrating since we got back," Cody said with a grin. "Seems his cronies think he's some kind of hero."

"And he hasn't been discouragin' them from thinkin' that," Seth added, chuckling.

"Anyway, I imagine he's sleeping off some of that celebrating," Cody went on. "But I'll tell him you said goodbye."

"Please do that. By the way, I left an envelope for him with the clerk in the hotel. Would you see that he gets it?"

"Money?" Cody asked.

"Well . . . I thought he deserved a bonus, and Josiah agreed."

Cody nodded. "I'll see that he gets it," he promised.

Leigh climbed inside the coach, and a moment later the driver closed the door and stepped up onto the box to take the reins. Within minutes the vehicle was rolling away down the street, heading east and taking its three passengers away from Fort Davis forever.

Seth leaned on the railing at the edge of the porch and watched the dwindling stagecoach. "You reckon Miss Sara will ever get over Whittingham?" he asked.

Cody shrugged and said, "She's still mighty young. It'd be damned foolish of her if she didn't."

"I'm glad Leigh and Mr. Breedlove agreed not to tell her family about what really happened with her and Whittingham. Wouldn't do anybody back in Dallas any good to know about it."

Cody had to go along with that. He straightened and asked, "You about ready to ride? Cap'n Vickery'll probably have a new job for us, time we get back to Del Rio."

"Yeah." Seth hesitated. "I'd like to stop by the jail and say so long to Tug first, though."

"Sure. Sounds like a good idea."

The Rangers walked over to the sheriff's office. Randine glanced up from his desk when they walked in, glared for a second when he saw Seth, then forced himself to grunt "Good morning" to them.

"I'd like to see Tug for a minute, if I could," Seth said.

Randine jerked a thumb over his shoulder toward the open cellblock door. "You know where he is."

"Thanks."

Cody ambled over to the door behind Seth. The cells were all full of outlaws awaiting trial as soon as the circuit judge arrived. Most of them, Cody knew, would wind up at the end of a rope.

Including Tug Mitchell. The former cowpoke had taken part in the massacre of the men with the silver shipment, after all. He might regret it, but he was still a killer.

He didn't look much like one, though, as he got to his feet and came to the bars to greet Seth with a big grin. "Howdy,

Seth," he said. "I was hopin' you'd come by 'fore you left town."

"Sure," Seth said, swallowing hard. "Had to say so long first."

Tug chuckled. "Now, don't you worry none about me. I always wanted to be a desperado—and I reckon this is how they end up. Should'a been a Ranger like you, I guess." His expression became more solemn. "Only thing I'm really sorry about is Amos. Sure didn't like the way he turned mean there at the end. I'd rather remember him the way he used to be, when we was just a couple o' hell-raisin' cowboys. Glad I'm givin' up bein' an outlaw 'fore I wound up like that."

"Yeah," Seth managed to say. "Me, too." He stuck out his hand. "So long, Tug."

"So long, Seth." Tug took the young Ranger's hand and shook it firmly. "You take care of yourself, hear?"

Seth nodded and turned away. He walked quickly past Cody, who followed him to the door of the sheriff's office. Cody paused there and looked back at Randine long enough to say, "We'll be riding out in a few minutes, Sheriff. Thanks for your help."

"Yeah." Randine leaned back in his chair. "Maybe we'll cross trails again sometime, Cody." He paused. "But not too soon, all right?"

Cody grinned and waved as he went on out, catching up to Seth as the youngster headed toward the livery stable.

Five minutes later their horses were saddled and ready to go. They led the animals out into the street, mounted up, and headed east.

They had gone only a few yards when Cody spotted Sergeant Rufe Gresham riding toward them. They reined in as the noncom came up. "Leaving town, are you?" Gresham asked.

"That's right," Cody said. "I was planning to stop by the fort and let Major Monroe know we're riding out, but I reckon you can tell him for us and save us a little time."

"Be glad to," Gresham said, nodding.

"How's the major feeling?"

The sergeant grinned. "Ornery as ever. The post surgeon says he'll be up and around again in a week or so. I reckon everything that happened shook his faith in going by the book. He's been asking me a lot of questions about how things really get done in this man's Army." Gresham nodded. "The boy'll be all right . . . one of these days."

"Maybe so," Cody said. And as long as the Army had sergeants like Rufe Gresham, he thought, it would continue to function somehow, no matter what its officers were like.

He sketched a casual salute, which Gresham returned smartly. As he and Seth trotted off, Cody thought that once Gresham finally retired, he'd have those grandkids doing close order drill on the front porch in no time.

They had ridden another few yards when Seth chuckled and said, "Look over yonder."

Cody looked where Seth was pointing and saw Jinglebob Hanrahan sitting on a bench in front of the general store, surrounded by a mixture of kids and old men. He was spinning a yarn, waving his arms around as he embellished the details of the battle against the Whittingham gang.

"Them outlaws had me surrounded, y'see," he was saying, "an' ever' damn one of 'em had his smoke pole pointed right at me. But was I scared of 'em? Nosirreebob. Hell, I fit Injuns for years and years—lookee here; see what a Comanch' did to muh ear—so I sure wasn't scared of no bunch o' raggedy-ass owlhoots!"

Cody and Seth both waved as they rode past, but Jinglebob just gave them a curt nod, then a friendlier wink.

"Who're those fellas?" one of his elderly friends asked him.

"Them two? Why, they're just a couple o' younkers who give me a little-bitty mite of a hand when I was fightin' them desperadoes. Now where was I? Oh, yeah, them outlaws was all pointin' their six-shooters at me, and then they opened up, a-firin' to beat the band. So I commenced to dodgin' bullets as fast as I could. . . ."

The Rangers rode on, the old-timer's voice fading away as they left him behind.

Cody wasn't going to miss the Davis Mountains. Pretty country around here, all right, but he was going to be glad to get back to the Rio Grande. With any luck he'd have a few days to rest up, maybe spend some time with Marie Jermaine, before Captain Vickery had a new assignment for him.

But one thing was certain. Somewhere in the great state of Texas trouble was bound to be brewing. And it'd only be a matter of time until Cody rode out once more, carrying with him silver spurs, a homemade badge, a well-used Colt—and Lone Star law.

CODY'S LAW Book 7:

END OF THE LINE

by Matthew S. Hart

Coming off an assignment in east Texas, Ranger Sam Cody is literally plummeted into peril. The boiler of a riverboat he's riding on explodes, and Cody—along with all other passengers—is hurled into the waters of Big Cypress Creek. Numerous people die, and one woman unaccounted for is the wife of the powerful Texas state senator Calvin Brady.

Cody soon learns that two other transportation disasters occurred on the very same day—a train wreck near Terrell in north central Texas and a stagecoach robbery near Austin, during which women passengers were shot. Reassigned by headquarters to find those responsible for the train wreck, Cody goes to Terrell posing as a railroad investigator. Working with Sheriff Howard Patterson, a man grown complacent over the years and now overwhelmed by the disaster within his jurisdiction, Cody soon finds suspects—a father and son who've long held a grudge against the railroad—and the case is considered closed.

But when Cody takes a closer look at the seemingly unrelated disasters, he finds a common link: Listed as a passenger on all three conveyances is Mary Brady, Calvin Brady's wife. Determined to find out why she made three separate travel arrangements for the same destination all on the same day, Cody is again plummeted into peril—only this time the danger comes in human form.

**Read END OF THE LINE,
on sale autumn 1992 wherever Bantam Books are sold.**

As Sam Cody climbed the stairs to the second floor of the Jefferson Hotel, his right hand casually dipped into the pocket of his jacket and gripped the butt of the .38-caliber Remington nestled there. Pointing the revolver ahead of him, he lightly rested his forefinger over the trigger, ready to fire through the pocket if necessary.

The pistol, an inch sawed off its barrel, felt awkward and light in a hand accustomed to the heft of a Frontier Colt, but it snuggled tidily into the pocket of the constricting brown suit that the Texas Ranger wore. The dandyish clothing on his tall, sinewy frame and the brown derby perched atop his head were as alien to his body as the six-shooter was to his hand. Though in his early thirties, Cody could count the number of times he had worn a suit on the fingers of one hand—without using all of them up.

Pausing at the head of the stairs, he glanced to the right down an L-shaped hallway, then peered straight ahead. A black-suited gentleman with muttonchop sideburns stopped before a room at the end of the hall, unlocked the door, then disappeared inside. Cody heard the faint click of the lock returning to its niche as the man secured the door from within. The man was just another of the hotel's occupants.

Cody sighed inaudibly, then glanced over a shoulder and nodded to the man and woman waiting at the foot of the stairs, signaling that the way was clear. But the big Ranger's right hand remained around the pistol in his pocket—just in case.

He was overreacting, he chided himself. But then, playing bodyguard to one of the nation's biggest railroad moguls wasn't exactly his forte. Renegade Indians, border *banditos*, and cattle rustlers were far more suited to his tastes and abilities.

But when a man was a Ranger, that man did what his superiors ordered.

Major John B. Jones, commander of the Frontier Battalion, which included Cody's own Company C headquartered in Del Rio, had assigned Cody as one of two bodyguards to Jay Gould and his wife during their stay in Jefferson, Texas. So for the past five days Cody had been a bodyguard, along with fellow Ranger Aaron Hayden, who hailed from San Antonio.

Gould and his wife climbed within three steps of the Ranger, who then turned to his right and walked ahead of the couple as they moved down the hallway. Cody paused again when he reached a left-hand turn in the hall and glanced around the corner to see Hayden standing outside the door to the Goulds's room. Hayden nodded that all was fine.

Cody turned to the couple. "Mr. and Mrs. Gould, the way is clear. Have a restful night."

Neither the short, full-bearded Gould nor his petite wife replied as they walked past Cody toward Hayden, who unlocked their room for them.

Cody idly tugged at his thick, dark mustache while he watched the man and woman saunter down the hall. Maybe he *wasn't* overreacting. If Jay Gould evoked the same dislike in other men that he stirred in Cody, it was easy to understand somebody deciding to take a shot at him. The man seemed to compensate for his five-foot-two height with at least a rod of arrogance. If there was one thing Texans didn't tolerate, it was a man who set himself above others. And as a native son of the Lone Star State, the ways of Texans were something Cody personally knew.

Gould had come here amid the east Texas Piney Woods

to convince the Jefferson city fathers that it'd be economically advantageous for them to allow his Texas & Pacific Railroad to pass through this, Texas's largest city, as the railway sought to connect the expanding frontier with the eastern states.

Of course, having Texas's booming trade center placed on the railroad line didn't come without a price, and that was the hitch as far as Jefferson's city elders were concerned. Gould demanded free land to lay his railroad tracks on as well as land within the city itself for his enterprise.

"They're all mine for the night, Cody," Aaron Hayden said as he locked the hotel room behind the Goulds.

Cody released the Remington, slipped his right hand from his pocket, and sketched a casual salute at Hayden. "I'll check back with you before I turn in," he said. "Right now I want to find something to eat. I haven't had a bite since breakfast."

When Hayden waved him on his way, Cody retraced his steps along the hotel hallway and down the stairs into a lobby spacious even by Texas standards. Despite now being officially off duty, his gaze automatically darted around the room. But except for two women deep in conversation on a sofa to his left and a young clerk behind the desk, the lobby was empty. Cody walked to the double-doored entrance and stepped into the warm, sticky humidity of an East Texas summer night.

Walking to a saloon down the street, Cody entered and found an empty table near the bar, hailed a passing waiter, and was informed that the fare for the evening meal was fried catfish, new potatoes and green beans, and cornbread. The Ranger gave a crooked grin. "Then I guess I'll have the catfish. Oh, and bring a beer now and a fresh one with my meal."

The waiter hurried off, then quickly returned with a mug of cold beer. Sipping it with satisfaction, Cody looked around the saloon. Friday night had brought an increase in business compared to the other nights he had visited the place. At least a hundred men sat crowded about tables or stood elbow to elbow along the bar. Most had the look of farmers come to the big city to celebrate the weekend.

Now and then Cody caught a glimpse of a barmaid leading one of the patrons up a flight of wooden stairs at the back of the saloon to disappear behind one of the five doors at the top of the landing. On another night he might have been tempted to take the trip up those stairs himself to sample the pleasures to be found behind those doors, but tonight the rumbling of his stomach took precedence over the desire of another portion of his anatomy.

And speaking of his anatomy . . . Cody's right hand crept toward the stiff, starched collar of the white dress shirt biting at his neck. He willed the hand back to the table before his fingers loosened the tie, which felt like a noose around his neck, and popped open the collar studs. As long as he was in Jefferson, he wasn't Samuel Clayton Woodbine Cody, but Sam Cass, railroad agent.

Disgust curled Cody's mouth. He was something of a lone wolf and used to undercover assignments from Captain Wallace Vickery, who commanded Ranger Company C. But this assignment bordered on being ridiculous. Here he was, a badge-wearing Texas Ranger, play acting the role of another kind of lawman—or an *almost* lawman, since railroad agents weren't peace officers under the Texas Constitution.

For a second time in as many minutes he quelled the nagging urge to rip away the tie and open the collar. Or even better, return to his hotel room and change into the familiar comfort of the blue work shirt and denim pants he normally wore. Of equal pleasure would be the familiar feel of his high-topped boots and well-worn Stetson. The ugly brown shoes laced to his feet cramped his toes until they felt as though they were going to knot one on top of the other. And as for the damn derby perched on his head . . . Well, he just gave silent thanks that his fellow Rangers back in Del Rio couldn't see him now.

The only good thing Cody could think of when it came to the monkey suit he wore was that he hadn't shelled out good money to buy it. Clothes, food, weapons, horses, and tack were usually out-of-pocket expenses for a Texas Ranger. But the taxpayers of the state of Texas had footed the bill for these duds. An amused smile replaced Cody's scowl. Half of those taxpayers would no doubt agree with him that their money had been misappropriated.

The distinctive sound of shuffling cards drew his attention to a table at the middle of the room, where a man in a green-checkered suit and brown derby dealt five cards to each of his companions at the table. Cody smiled. Five-card draw. Now *there* was a gentlemanly pastime worthy of pursuing on a Friday night—and one he would attend after his meal. That was if either of the two empty chairs at the table remained vacant.

The waiter returned, bringing Cody's second beer along with a plate piled with a couple of one-pound catfish and a small mountain of new potatoes and green beans as well as rings from a fresh-cut onion. Draining the last swallow of the first beer, Cody attacked the meal.

The picked bones of one of the catfish lay to one side of the plate before he took a small breather and glanced over at the poker table. The two vacant chairs had stayed empty.

A steamboat whistle screamed in the distance, and as Cody returned to his meal, thoughts of Gould, railroads, and riverboats edged aside images of a royal flush. Gould wasn't the most reputable man Cody had ever had the pleasure to meet. The Ranger couldn't blame Jefferson's businessmen for the leery arch of their eyebrows that he had noticed more than once. Back East, Gould had inflated the price of Erie

Line stock until it was all but valueless, creating a scandal as well as court litigation when the railroad was sold for $5 million. Worse to Cody's way of thinking was Gould's scheme to corner the gold market in '69. The result was one of the worse panics in American financial history when the bottom suddenly dropped out and gold prices plummeted. Black Friday was the name the newspapers had given to that infamous day.

And now Major Jones had assigned Cody to wet nurse such a man.

The thought was more than a little disgusting to the Ranger. Worse, he had been pulled from a two-week-long chase across half of Texas, taking him from El Paso to San Antonio, that would have resulted in the arrest of the Mexican rustler Diego Alvarez. Would have, Cody thought angrily, had Major Jones not yanked him off Alvarez's trail to guard Gould during his Jefferson trip.

A week had passed since Cody had traveled deep into the Piney Woods of east Texas. Diego Alvarez and two hundred head of rustled prime beef on the hoof seemed so distant now. In truth, though, the Ranger would've taken no pleasure in bringing Alvarez in. On more than one occasion the Mexican bandit had saved his hide—risking his own in the process. Cody admitted to himself that the man was downright likable . . . except for his downright annoying habit of conducting all his business outside the law.

Alvarez would have to wait, whether Cody liked it or not. For the time being he was stuck in Jefferson, making certain no one decided to take a potshot at Jay Gould until the man's business in the port city was complete.

The crisp, alluring sound of cards being shuffled wedged its way into Cody's reflections. Protecting Jay Gould and his wife had occupied his every waking moment since arriving in Jefferson. Tonight Cody was determined to reward his sustained vigilance with a few hours of relaxation.

And perhaps even a little profit, he thought, a hint of a smile quirking his mouth.

Slipping a hand into the left pocket of his brown trousers, he withdrew a small roll of bills and counted the greenbacks. Forty dollars. More than enough for a stake in a friendly game. If the pots required greater resources, he had no business sitting down at the table.

Draining the last of his beer, Cody waved the waiter over. He ordered a third round, then requested, "Please inquire at that table if those two empty seats are reserved or open." He cocked his head toward the poker game.

The waiter glanced over at the players, then told Cody, "Doc Pruitt and Harvey Caldwell usually sit in on Sheriff Howell's Friday night game. My bet's them chairs are open to whoever's got the spirit, since Doc and Harv're down in Austin. But I'll check it out for you, if you're a-mind."

"I'm a-mind," Cody confirmed.

Rather than going to the bar for the ordered beer, the waiter first walked over to the poker table and bent to whisper into the ear of a man with his back to Cody. When the waiter straightened, the seated man shifted in his chair and glanced over his shoulder. The face that sought out Cody appeared to be a year or two younger than himself, in spite of the bushy mustache that drooped below the corners of the man's mouth. When the man's dark-eyed gaze found Cody, he nodded to the waiter, who stepped back across the room.

"The sheriff says them chairs are open to all comers," the waiter announced.

Asking that his beer be brought to the game table, Cody got up and crossed to the waiting players, taking the closest vacant chair. Sheriff Howell rose and stretched out a welcoming hand. "Name's Manly Howell, city sheriff here in Jefferson. I've seen you durin' the day with our distinguished visitor, Mr. Jay Gould. Work for Gould, do you?"

"Just while he's in town. Hired on as a bodyguard," Cody answered while he shook Howell's hand. "My name's Sam Cass."

The sheriff openly assessed Cody, as though by studying his external characteristics he could gauge his internal character. Well above average height, Cody's sinewy physique, some called him thin, was all muscle—a fact that anyone who challenged him didn't find out until sampling the lightning reflexes that guided solid fists. And while he could never be called handsome, his rugged, weathered face set many a female heart aflutter.

"Over here's Glevis Hudler"—Howell released Cody's hand and gestured to the man on his left—"town blacksmith. And this is . . ."

The introductions proceeded around the table. Besides Howell and Hudler, the remaining three players were Wade Moore, farmer; William Egger, cotton broker from New Orleans; and, in the green-checkered suit, Titus Newman, a traveling shoe salesman whom Cody had sat next to.

As Cody shook Newman's hand, Howell explained, "This is a friendly game. White chips'll cost you a nickel, red ones a dime, and blue two bits. And I'll warn you ahead of time, the cards've been kind to Newman there all evenin'. He's done taken twenty-five dollars off me."

Which was fifteen dollars more than the point when he himself would call the game a bust and turn in for the night, Cody thought. He pulled twenty dollars from his pocket and exchanged it for ten dollars in chips and two fives.

"Ante's a nickel," Newman said. He tossed a white chip to the middle of the table and began to shuffle the cards. "The game's five-card draw. No wild cards, gentlemen."

Dropping a white chip at the center of the table, Cody waited for Newman to complete the deal before picking up his hand.

Rule one of a friendly game: Set a loss limit, and when

it's reached, fold the cards and bid one's fellow players a good night. Cody broke that rule. Ten dollars had been his limit. He was twenty dollars in the hole when he reached into his pocket to buy another ten dollars' worth of chips.

Gambling fever hadn't seduced him. Of that he was certain. While he enjoyed a good poker game, he wasn't addicted to the gaming tables. But right now he was hooked. He had taken the bait, and now he was being reeled in, ready for the waiting net held out by an angler.

He wasn't the only fish at the table, either. Sheriff Howell's losses now totaled sixty dollars. The farmer was thirty in the hole and the blacksmith forty. The cotton broker fared no better than Howell, having also lost sixty dollars. When tallied together the losses didn't total a single pot of some of the games Cody had sat in. But for a friendly game that had begun as recreation, relaxation, and conversation, the money that had passed across the table had the smell of blood to it.

The man with his nostrils flared wide with that scent was the shoe salesman, Titus Newman—Newman in his outrageous green-checkered suit, looking more like a circus clown than a gambler.

Cody studied the man out of the corner of his eye as Newman shuffled and dealt five cards to those around the table. The salesman smiled when he lifted his hand and fanned it open.

Cody picked up his own hand and stared in the faces of three queens. Garbage stood beside the three ladies. His gaze shifted about the table, finally settling again on Newman.

It was Newman who had hooked Cody, and it was Newman who kept Cody betting long after he had exceeded his evening's limit. The man's luck was too uncanny to be explained by the fall of the pasteboards. His manipulation of the game went beyond the simple shuffle and dealing of the cards.

Yet Cody had watched him carefully for hours. Newman didn't deal from the bottom of the deck—or if he did, he did it so skillfully that it was undetectable. And the salesman hadn't marked the deck. On the few occasions that Cody had won the deal, his fingertips carefully explored the backs of the cards as well as their edges, searching for nicks, scratches, and creases. There was nothing.

Wade Moore began the betting with a quarter. Every man at the table saw the bet. Newman called for cards. Cody tossed in two and drew two others that did nothing to improve the power of his three queens.

Cody decided that the salesman had to be using a holdout. But where did Newman hide the device? Cody hadn't seen him going to his vest or coat. He had even brushed against the salesman's arm to see if his sleeves concealed a spring-loaded mechanism. Nothing—Cody neither saw nor felt anything. Yet . . .

If Newman employed a holdout, there was only one way to find out. Cody's thumbnail scratched two parallel lines down the bottom of the deck, marking them. He passed the cards to Howell for the cut, then dealt.

Newman's luck once again changed. He won the hand and regained control of the deal. Cody sat back and waited as the salesman won the next hand and then the next.

It was when Howell took the following hand that Cody acted. With a flick of the wrist, he sent his cards sailing across the table toward Howell. The hand, as Cody had planned, scattered in five different directions at once, two of the cards falling to the floor.

"Sorry," Cody apologized immediately. "I'll pick them up for you."

The Ranger picked up the fallen cards, and as he straightened up, his smile widened. There beneath the table, positioned directly under Newman's right hand, was the holdout. The device was a simple clip made from a watch spring and tacked beneath the table. In the parlance of gamblers it was called a "bug," and the concept was so old fashioned that it hadn't been employed since the heyday of riverboats on the Mississippi before the war. A cough, a twist in his chair, or taking a swig of beer was all Newman needed to distract watching eyes while his right fingers darted beneath the table to retrieve the waiting cards.

Of the cards held in the bug, Cody glimpsed only the face of a jack of spades before he sat upright again and passed the spilled hand to Howell. The sheriff added the cards to the deck he set aside, then opened another deck of blue-backed Riverboat Playing Cards. He shuffled and passed them for the cut before dealing.

Not one card in Cody's hand matched. It didn't matter. If he wanted to catch Newman with marked cards he had holed away, he had to make the salesman use those cards now. The only way to do that was to bait a hook of his own. When a four-bit bet came around the table, the Ranger raised it to a dollar. The remaining five players saw the raise. Howell asked for discards. Cody stood pat.

A flash in Newman's brown eyes when he glanced at Cody said that the salesman was ready to take the bait. Cody dropped four more blue chips into the pot to reopen the betting.

Newman met the dollar wager, then bumped it higher with two more blue chips. Sheriff Howell saw the bet. The rest of the players folded; a dollar fifty was far too rich for a game that was supposed to be no more than a few hands of friendly Friday-night poker.

Cody glanced back at the five mismatched cards in his hand. While the pot might be high enough to drive away the weak hands the others held, it might not be steep enough to assure that Newman employed the cards he had neatly hidden in the bug tacked beneath the table. Cody had to sweeten the bet to assure that the salesman dipped into his holdout cards. At the same time the Ranger had to be certain that when the showdown came, *he* was the one who called Newman's hand, forcing the man to lay his cards on the table.

He tossed another dollar in chips to the mounting pile.

Cody turned to the salesman. "I'll see you and raise another fifty cents."

Newman didn't hesitate. He matched the raise then added a dollar of his own.

Howell shook his head when he dropped his cards facedown on the table. "You boys are gettin' too rich for my blood. Fight it out amongst yourselves."

Which was exactly what Cody wanted. He tossed in the needed dollar, then pushed in four more blue chips.

Newman smiled. "Mr. Cass, we might as make this interesting, seeing as it's come down to you and me. I'll see that raise and up it five dollars."

The farmer gasped, and Sheriff Howell cleared his throat.

Cody kept his eyes on Newman—and saw what he wanted. The salesman bent slightly forward to edge the pile of blue chips into the pot with his left hand, and his right hand dropped below the edge of the table. Cody had no doubt that the salesman switched the cards in his hand with those in the holdout.

"You're called," Cody said, shoving five dollars to the center of the table. "Let's see what you're holding."

"Royal flush." Newman fanned his cards atop the table. "In spades."

"Interesting." Cody looked at Sheriff Howell. "Seems we have a little problem here."

The Ranger reached out and snatched up the undealt cards and spread them face up on the table. He didn't have to describe what problem he meant. The faces of the spade royalty buried in the deck was all the explanation needed.

"What is this!" Newman sputtered with just the right amount of indignation. "What are you trying to pull?"

Keeping close watch on the salesman, Cody told Howell, "Sheriff, I've suspected that things have been less than above board in this game for quite a while now. Before retiring that deck beside you, I marked the bottoms of cards with two thumbnail scratches."

"I knew you were up to something!" Newman yelped, his indignation heightened to outrage. "This man's a self-proclaimed cheat! He should be run out of town on a rail! He should be taken and—"

"I believe that if you check Newman's flush," Cody said loudly enough to the sheriff to drown out the salesman's outburst, "you'll find his cards have marks that match. I also think you'll find that he has a bug tacked beneath the table where he kept—"

Newman's right hand dropped toward the bottom of his vest. Cody didn't need to see the weapon to know that the man had gone for a belly gun. . . .

CODY'S LAW

Matthew S. Hart

❏ **GUNMETAL JUSTICE** 29030-4 $3.50/$4.50 in Canada
Texas Ranger justice is about to catch up with a ruthless land baron and his henchmen. A showdown's coming, and Cody will have to ride into hell to end the trail of tyranny.

❏ **DIE LONESOME** 29127-0 $4.50/$5.50 in Canada
Two hundred Winchester repeating rifles have been stolen from an army supply depot. Undercover and alone, Cody has the brains to set a dangerous trap, and the guts to use a beautiful saloonkeeper as bait. But someone is desperately waiting for a chance to plug this lawman full of lead.

❏ **BORDER SHOWDOWN** 29371-0 $3.50/$4.50 in Canada
A band of ruthless desperadoes is spreading a reign of bloody terror...and Cody comes up with an ingenious plan to bring these hard cases to justice. It will take every ounce of courage Cody possesses to bring the culprits to justice.

❏ **BOUNTY MAN** 29517-9 $3.50/$4.50 in Canada
All Cody wants is to get his uncle, a notoriously ruthless bounty hunter, out of Twin Creeks. But when a posse of hired killers shows up to spring his relative's prisoner, Cody and his uncle must join forces—or watch Twin Creeks drown in a sea of blood.

❏ **MANO A MANO** 29670-1 $3.50/$4.50 in Canada
Cody is drawn into a deadly contest beyond the Texas frontier when a beautiful singer is kidapped. But in the scorching heat of the Mexican desert, Cody has no authority, and the ultimate law is fixed on the blade of a bowie knife.

It all began with
WAGONS WEST
America's best-loved series by Dana Fuller Ross

❏ *Independence!* 26822-8 $4.95/$5.95 in Canada

A saga of high adventure and passionate romance on the first wagon train to Oregon territory.

❏ *Nebraska!* 26162-2 $4.95/$5.95 in Canada

Indian raids and sabotage threaten the settlers as "Whip" Holt leads the wagon train across the Great Plains.

❏ *Wyoming!* 26242-4 $4.95/$5.95 in Canada

Facing starvation, a mysterious disease, and a romantic triangle, the expedition pushes on.

❏ *Oregon!* 26072-3 $4.50/$4.95 in Canada

Three mighty nations clash on the fertile shore of the Pacific as the weary pioneers arrive.

❏ *Texas!* 26070-7 $4.99/$5.99 in Canada

Branded as invaders by the fiery Mexican army, a band of Oregon volunteers rallies to the cause of liberty.

❏ *California!* 26377-3 $4.99/$5.99 in Canada

The new settlers' lives are threatened by unruly fortune seekers who have answered the siren song of gold.

❏ *Colorado!* 26546-6 $4.95/$5.95 in Canada

The rugged Rockies hold the promise of instant wealth for the multitudes in search of a new start.

❏ *Nevada!* 26069-3 $4.99/$5.99 in Canada

The nation's treasury awaits a shipment of silver just as the country is on the brink of Civil War.

❏ *Washington!* 26163-0 $4.50/$4.95 in Canada

Ruthless profiteers await wounded Civil War hero Toby Holt's return to challenge his landholdings.

❏ *Montana!* 26073-1 $4.95/$5.95 in Canada

The lawless, untamed territory is being terrorized by a sinister gang led by a tough and heartless woman.

❏ *Dakota!* 26184-3 $4.50/$4.95 in Canada

Against the backdrop of the Badlands, fearless Indian tribes form an alliance to drive out the white man forever.

❏ *Utah!* 26521-0 $4.99/$5.99 in Canada

Chinese and Irish laborers strive to finish the transcontinental railroad before currupt landowners sabotage it.

❏ *Idaho!* 26071-5 $4.99/$5.99 in Canada

The perilous task of making a safe homeland from an untamed wilderness is hampered by blackmail and revenge.

❏ *Missouri!* 26367-6 $4.50/$4.95 in Canada

An incredible adventure on a paddle-wheel steamboat stirs romantic passions and gambling fever.

❏ *Mississippi!* 27141-5 $4.95/$5.95 in Canada

New Orleans is home to an underworld of crime, spawned by easy money and ruthless ambitions.

❏ *Louisiana!* 25247-X $4.99/$5.99 in Canada

Smuggled shipments of opium and shanghaied Chinese workers continue to invade the country.

❏ *Tennessee!* 25622-X $4.99/$5.99 in Canada

Unscrupulous politicians lead an army of outlaws and misfits to threaten America's cherished democracy.